0 0001 6527

MAIN

P9-CDM-625

NOV - - 2002

ALL ★ AMERICAN

Girl

BOOKS BY

Meg Cabot

ALL ★ AMERICAN Girl

Meg Cabot

HARPERCOLLINS*PUBLISHERS*

★

All-American Girl

Copyright © 2002 by Meggin Cabot

All rights reserved. No part of this book may be used or reproduced in any manner whatsoever without written permission except in the case of brief quotations embodied in critical articles and reviews. Printed in the United States of America. For information address HarperCollins Children's Books, a division of HarperCollins Publishers, 1350 Avenue of the Americas, NewYork, NY 10019.

www.harperteen.com

Library of Congress Cataloging-in-Publication Data
Cabot, Meg.
   All-American girl / Meg Cabot.
   p. cm.
   Summary: A sophomore girl stops a presidential assassination attempt, is appointed teen ambassador to the United Nations, and catches the eye of the very cute First Son.
   ISBN 0-06-029469-8 — ISBN 0-06-029470-1 (lib. bdg.)
   [1. Presidents—Fiction. 2. Heroes—Fiction.
3. Interpersonal relations—Fiction. 4. High schools—
Fiction. 5. Schools—Fiction. 6. Washington (D.C.)—
Fiction. 7. Humorous stories.] I. Title.
PZ7.C11165 Al 2002   2002019049
[Fic]—dc21   CIP
                                 AC

Typography by Karin Paprocki

1 2 3 4 5 6 7 8 9 10

First Edition

★

TO THE REAL AMERICAN HEROES OF
9/11/01

★

★

ACKNOWLEDGMENTS

Many thanks to Beth Ader, Jennifer Brown, Barbara Cabot, SWAT officer Matt Cabot, Josh Horwitz, Michele Jaffe, Laura Langlie, Abby McAden, Ericka Markman, Ron Markman, David Walton, and Benjamin Egnatz.

Special thanks to Tanya, Julia, and Charlotte Horwitz, who were the inspiration for this story.

★

$Okay$, here are the top ten reasons why I can't stand my sister Lucy:

10. I get all her hand-me-downs, even her bras.

9. When I refuse to wear her hand-me-downs, especially her bras, I get the big lecture about waste and the environment. Look, I am way concerned about the environment. But that does not mean I want to wear my sister's old bras. I told Mom I see no reason why I should even have to wear a bra, seeing as how it's not like I've got a lot to put in one, causing Lucy to remark that if I don't wear a bra now then if I ever do get anything up there, it will be all saggy like those tribal women we saw on the Discovery Channel.

8. This is another reason why I can't stand Lucy. Because she is always making these kind of remarks. What we should really do, if you ask me, is send Lucy's old bras to those tribal women.

7. Her conversations on the phone go like this: "No way. . . . So what did he say? . . . Then what did *she* say? . . . No way. . . . That is so totally untrue. . . . I do not. I so do not. . . . Who said that? . . . Well, it isn't true. . . . No, I do not. . . . I do *not* like him. . . . Well, okay, maybe I do. Oh, gotta go, call-waiting."

6. She is a cheerleader. All right? A *cheerleader*. Like it isn't bad enough she spends all her time waving pom-poms at a bunch of Neanderthals as they thunder up and down a football field. No, she has to do it practically every night. And since Mom and Dad are fanatical about this mealtime-is-family-time thing, guess what we are usually doing at five thirty? And who is even hungry then?

5. All of my teachers go: "You know, Samantha, when I had your sister in this class two years ago, I never had to remind her to:
    a) double space
    b) carry the one
    c) capitalize her nouns in Deutsch
    d) remember her swimsuit
    e) take off her headphones during morning announcements
    f) stop drawing on her pants."

4. She has a boyfriend. And not just any boyfriend, either, but a nonjock boyfriend, something totally unheard-of in the social hierarchy of our school: a cheerleader going with a nonjock boyfriend. And it isn't even that he's not a jock. Oh, no, Jack also happens to be an urban rebel like me, only he really goes all out, you know, in the black army surplus trench coat and the Doc Martens and the straight Ds and all. Plus he wears an earring that hangs.

   But even though he is not "book smart," Jack is very talented and creative artistically. For instance, he is always getting his paintings of disenfranchised American youths hung up in the caf. And nobody even graffitis them, the way they would if they were mine. Jack's paintings, I mean.

As if that is not cool enough, Mom and Dad completely hate him because of his not working up to his potential and getting suspended for his antiauthoritarianism and calling them Carol and Richard to their faces instead of Mr. and Mrs. Madison.

It is totally unfair that Lucy should not only have a cool boyfriend but a boyfriend our parents can't stand, something I have been praying for my entire life, practically.

Although actually at this point any kind of boyfriend would be acceptable.

3. In spite of the fact that she is dating an artistic rebel type instead of a jock, Lucy remains one of the most popular girls in school, routinely getting invited to parties and dances every weekend, so many that she could not possibly attend them all, and often says things like, "Hey, Sam, why don't you and Catherine go as, like, my emissaries?" even though if Catherine and I ever stepped into a party like that we would be vilified as sophomore poseurs and thrown out onto the street.

2. She gets along with Mom and Dad—except for the whole Jack thing—and always has. She even gets along with our little sister, Rebecca, who goes to a special school for the intellectually gifted and is practically an idiot savant.

But the number-one reason I can't stand my sister Lucy would have to be:

1. She told on me about the celebrity drawings.

★ 1 ★

She says she didn't mean to. She says she found them in my room, and they were so good she couldn't help showing them to Mom.

Of course, it never occurred to Lucy that she shouldn't have been in my room in the first place. When I accused her of completely violating my constitutionally protected right to personal privacy, she just looked at me like, *Huh?* even though she is fully taking U.S. Government this semester.

Her excuse is that she was looking for her eyelash curler.

Hello. Like I would borrow anything of hers. Especially something that had been near her big, bulbous eyeballs.

Instead of her eyelash curler, which of course I didn't have, Lucy found this week's stash of drawings, and she presented them to Mom at dinner that night.

"Well," Mom said in this very dry voice. "Now we know how you got that C-minus in German, don't we, Sam?"

This was on account of the fact that the drawings were in my German notebook.

"Is this supposed to be that guy from *The Patriot?*" my dad wanted to know. "Who is that you've drawn with him? Is that . . . is that *Catherine?*"

"German," I said, feeling that they were missing the point, "is a stupid language."

"German isn't stupid," my little sister Rebecca informed me.

4

"The Germans can trace their heritage back to ethnic groups that existed during the days of the Roman Empire. Their language is an ancient and beautiful one that was created thousands of years ago."

"Whatever," I said. "Did you know that they capitalize all of their nouns? What is up with that?"

"Hmmm," my mother said, flipping to the front of my German notebook. "What have we here?"

My dad went, "Sam, what are you doing drawing pictures of Catherine on the back of a horse with that guy from *The Patriot*?"

"I think this will explain it, Richard," my mother said, and she passed the notebook back to my dad.

In my own defense, I can only state that, for better or for worse, we live in a capitalistic society. I was merely enacting my rights of individual initiative by supplying the public—in the form of most of the female student population at John Adams Preparatory School—with a product for which I saw there was a demand. You would think that my dad, who is an international economist with the World Bank, would understand this.

But as he read aloud from my German notebook in an astonished voice, I could tell he did not understand. He did not understand at all.

"You and Josh Hartnett," my dad read, "fifteen dollars. You and Josh Hartnett on a desert island, twenty dollars. You and Justin Timberlake, ten dollars. You and Justin Timberlake under a waterfall, fifteen dollars. You and Keanu Reeves, fifteen dollars. You and—" My dad looked up. "Why are Keanu and Josh more than Justin?"

"Because," I explained, "Justin has less hair."

"Oh," my dad said. "I see." He went back to the list.

"You and Keanu Reeves white-water rafting, twenty dollars. You and James Van Der Beek, fifteen dollars. You and James Van Der

Beek hang-gliding, twenty—"

But my mom didn't let him go on for much longer.

"Clearly," she said in her courtroom voice—my mom is an environmental lawyer; one thing you do not want to do is anything that would make Mom use her courtroom voice—"Samantha is having trouble concentrating in German class. The reason why she is having trouble concentrating in German class appears to be because she is suffering from not having an outlet for all her creative energy. I believe if such an outlet were provided for her, her grades in German class would improve dramatically."

Which would explain why the next day my mom came home from work, pointed at me, and went, "Tuesdays and Thursdays, from three thirty to five thirty, you will now be taking art lessons, young lady."

Whoa. Talk about harsh.

Apparently it has not occurred to my mother that I can draw perfectly well without ever having had a lesson. Except for, you know, in school. Apparently my mother doesn't realize that art lessons, far from providing me with an outlet for my creative energy, are just going to utterly stamp out any natural ability and individual style I might have had. How will I ever be able to stay true to my own vision, like van Gogh, with someone hovering over my shoulder, telling me what to do?

"Thanks," I said to Lucy when I ran into her a little while later in the bathroom we shared. She was separating her eyelashes with a safety pin in front of the mirror, even though our housekeeper, Theresa, has told Lucy a thousand times about her cousin Rosa, who put out an eye that way.

Lucy looked past the safety pin at me. "What'd I do?"

I couldn't believe she didn't know. "You told on me," I cried, "about the whole drawing thing!"

"God, you 'tard," Lucy said, going to work on her lower lashes. "Don't even tell me you're upset about that. I so totally did you a favor."

"A *favor?*" I was shocked. "I got into big trouble because of what you did! Now I have to go to some stupid, lame art class twice a week after school, when I could be, you know . . . watching TV."

Lucy rolled her eyes. "You so don't get it, do you? You're my sister. I can't just stand by and let you become the biggest freak of the entire school. You won't participate in extracurriculars. You wear that hideous black all the time. You won't let me fix your hair. I mean, I had to do *something*. This way, who knows? Maybe you'll be a famous artist. Like Georgia O'Keeffe."

"Do you even know what Georgia O'Keeffe is famous for painting, Lucy?" I asked, and when she said no, I told her:

Vaginas. That's what Georgia O'Keeffe was famous for painting.

Or as Rebecca put it, as she came ambling past with her nose buried in the latest installment of the *Star Trek* saga, with which she is obsessed, "Actually, Ms. O'Keeffe's organic abstract images are lush representations of flowers that are strongly sexual in symbolic content."

I told Lucy to ask Jack if she didn't believe me. But Lucy said she and Jack don't discuss things like that with one another.

I was all, "You mean vaginas?" but Lucy said no, art.

I don't get this. I mean, she is going out with an artist, and yet the two of them never discuss art? I can tell you, if I ever get a boyfriend, we are going to discuss *everything* with one another. Even art. Even vaginas.

★ 2 ★

Catherine couldn't even believe it about the drawing lessons. "But you already know how to draw!" she kept saying.

I, of course, couldn't have agreed more. Still, it was good to know I wasn't the only person who thought my having to spend every Tuesday and Thursday from three thirty until five thirty at the Susan Boone Art Studio was going to be a massive waste of time.

"That is just so like Lucy," Catherine said as we walked Manet through the Bishop's Garden on Monday after school. The Bishop's Garden is part of the grounds of the National Cathedral, where they have all the funerals for any important people who die in D.C. It is only a five-minute walk from where we live, in Cleveland Park, to the National Cathedral. Which is good, because it is Manet's favorite place to chase squirrels and bust in on couples who are making out in the gazebo and stuff.

Which is another thing: who is going to walk Manet while I am at the Susan Boone Art Studio? Theresa won't do it. She hates Manet, even though he's fully stopped chewing on the electrical cords. Besides, according to Dr. Lee, the animal behaviorist, that was my fault, for naming him *Mo*net, which sounds like the word *no*. Since changing his name to Manet, he's been a lot better . . . though my dad wasn't too thrilled with the five-hundred-dollar bill Dr. Lee sent him.

Theresa says that it is bad enough that she has to clean up after all of us; over her dead body is she cleaning up after my eighty-pound Old English sheepdog.

"I can't believe Lucy did that," Catherine said. "I'm sure glad I don't have any sisters." Catherine is a middle child, like me—which is probably why we get along so well. Only unlike me, Catherine has two brothers, one older and one younger . . . and neither of whom are smarter or more attractive than she is.

Catherine is so lucky.

"But if it hadn't been Lucy, it would have been Kris," she pointed out as we trudged along the narrow, twisty path through the gardens. "Kris was totally onto you. I mean about only charging her and her friends."

Which had been, really, the beauty of the whole thing. That I'd only been charging girls like Kris and her friends, I mean. Everyone else had gotten drawings for free.

Well, and why not? When, as a joke, I drew a portrait of Catherine with her favorite celebrity of all time, Heath Ledger, word got around, and soon I had a waiting list of people who wanted pictures of themselves in the company of various hotties.

At first I didn't even think about charging. I was more than glad to provide drawings to my friends for free, since it seemed to make them happy.

And then when the non-English-speaking girls in my school got wind of it and wanted portraits, too, well, I couldn't very well charge them, either. I mean, if you just moved to this country—whether to escape oppression in your native land, or, like most of the non–English speakers at our school, because one of your parents was an ambassador or diplomat—no way should you have to pay for a celebrity drawing. You see, I know what it is like to be in a strange place where you don't speak the language: it sucks. I learned this the hard way, thanks to Dad—who is in charge of the World Bank's North African division. He moved us all to Morocco for a year when I was eight. It would have been nice if somebody there had given me some drawings of Justin Timberlake for free, instead of staring at me like I was a freak just because I didn't know the Moroccan for "May I please be excused?" when I had to go to the bathroom.

Then I got hit by a bunch of requests for celebrity portraits from the girls in Special Ed. Well, I couldn't charge people in Special Ed, either, on account of how I know what it is like to be in Special Ed. After we got back from Morocco, it was determined that my speech impediment—I said *th* instead of *s*, just like Cindy Brady—wasn't something I was going to grow out of . . . not without some professional help. So I was forced to attend special speech and hearing lessons while everybody else was in music appreciation.

As if this were not bad enough, whenever I returned to my regular classroom, I was routinely mocked for my supposed stupidity by Kris Parks—who'd been my best friend up until I'd left for Morocco. Then *whammo*, I come back and she's all, "Samantha *who*?"

It was like she didn't even remember how she used to come to my house to play Barbies every day after school. No, suddenly she was all about "going with" boys and running around at recess, trying to kiss them. The fact that I, as a fourth grader, would sooner have eaten glass than allowed a fellow fourth grader's lips to touch mine—particularly Rodd Muckinfuss, who was the class stud that year—instantly branded me as "immature" (the *th* instead of *s* probably didn't help much, either). Kris dropped me like a hot potato.

Fortunately this only fueled my desire to learn to speak properly. The day I graduated from speech and hearing, I strode right up to Kris and called her a stupid, slobbering, inconsiderate simpering sycophant.

We haven't really spoken much since.

So, figuring that people who are in Special Ed really need a break now and then—especially the ones who have to wear a helmet all the time due to being prone to seizures or whatever—I declared that, for them, my celebrity-drawing services were free, as they were for my friends and the non–English speakers at Adams Prep.

Really, I was like my own little UN, doling out aid, in the form of highly realistic renderings of Freddie Prinze Jr., to the underprivileged.

But it turned out that Kris Parks, now president of the sophomore class and still an all-around pain in my rear, had a problem with this. Well, not with the fact that I wasn't charging the non–English speakers, but with the fact that it turned out the only people I *was* charging were Kris and her friends.

But what did she think? Like I was really going to charge Catherine, who has been my best friend ever since I got back from Morocco and found out that Kris had pulled an Anakin and gone over to the Dark Side? Catherine and I totally bonded over Kris's mistreatment of us—Kris still takes great delight in making fun of Catherine's knee-length skirts, which is all Mrs. Salazar, Catherine's mom, will allow her to wear, being super Christian and all—and our mutual contempt for Rodd Muckinfuss.

Oh, yeah. I'm definitely going to give free drawings of Orlando Bloom to someone like Kris.

Not.

People like Kris—maybe because she was never forced to attend speech and hearing lessons, much less a school where no one spoke the same language she did—cannot seem to grasp the concept of being nice to anyone who is not size five, blond, and decked out in Abercrombie and Fitch from head to toe.

In other words, anyone who is not Kris Parks.

Catherine and I were talking about this on our way home from the cathedral grounds—Kris, I mean, and her insufferability—

when this car approached us and I saw my dad waving at us from behind the wheel.

"Hi, girls," my mom said, leaning over my dad to talk to us, since we were closest to the driver's side. "I don't suppose either of you is interested in going to Lucy's game."

"Mom," Lucy said from the backseat. She was in full cheerleader regalia. "Do not even try. They won't come, and even if they do, I mean, look at Sam. I'd be embarrassed to be seen with her."

"Lucy," my dad said in a warning tone. He needn't have bothered, however. I am quite used to Lucy's disparaging remarks concerning my appearance.

It is all well and good for people like Lucy, whose primary concern in life is not missing a single sale at Club Monaco. I mean, for Lucy, the fact that they started selling Paul Mitchell products in our local drugstore was cause for jubilation the likes of which had not been seen since the fall of the Berlin Wall.

I, however, am a little more concerned about world issues, such as the fact that three hundred million children a day go to bed hungry and that school art programs are invariably the first things cut whenever local boards of education find they are working at a deficit.

Which is why at the start of this school year, I dyed my entire wardrobe black to show that

    a) I was in mourning for our generation, who clearly do not care about anything except what's going to happen on *Friends* next week, and

    b) fashion trends are for phonies like my sister.

And yeah, my mom nearly blew a capillary or two when she saw what I'd done. But hey, at least she knows one of her daughters actually thinks about something other than French manicures.

My mom, unlike Lucy, wasn't about to give up on me, though. Which was why, there in the car, she put on a bright sunshiny smile, even though there was nothing to feel too sunshiny about, if you ask me. There was a pretty steady drizzle going on, and it was only about forty degrees outside. Not the kind of November day anyone—but especially someone completely lacking in school spirit, like me— would really want to spend sitting in some bleachers, watching a bunch of jocks chase a ball around, while girls in too-tight purple- and-white sweaters—like my sister—cheered them on.

"You never know," my mom said to Lucy from the front seat. "They might change their minds." To us, she said, "What do you say, Sam? Catherine? Afterwards Dad is taking us to Chinatown for dim sum." She glanced at me. "I'm sure we can find a burger or some- thing for you, Sam."

"Sorry, Mrs. Madison," Catherine said. She didn't look sorry at all. In fact, she looked downright happy to have an excuse not to go. Most school events are agony for Catherine, given the comments she regularly receives from the In Crowd about her Laura Ashley–esque wardrobe ("Where'd you park your chuck wagon?" etc.). "I have to be getting home. Sunday is the day of—"

"—rest. Yes, I know." My mom had heard this plenty of times before. Mr. Salazar, who is a diplomat at the Honduran embassy here in D.C., insists that Sundays are a day of rest and makes all his kids stay home that day every week. Catherine had only been let out for a half-hour reprieve in order to return *The Patriot* (which she has seen seventeen times) to Potomac Video. The trip to the National Cathedral had totally been on the sly. But Catherine figured since technically a visit to a church was involved, her parents wouldn't get *that* mad if they found out about it.

"Richard." Rebecca, beside Lucy in the backseat, looked up

from her laptop long enough to convey her deep displeasure with the situation. "Carol. Give it up."

"Dad," my mom said, glaring at Rebecca. "Dad, not Richard. And it's Mom, not Carol."

"Sorry," Rebecca said. "But could we get a move on? I only have two hours on this battery pack, you know, and I have three spreadsheets due tomorrow."

Rebecca, who at eleven should be in the sixth grade, goes to Horizon, a special school in Bethesda for gifted kids, where she is taking college-level courses. It is a geek school, as is amply illustrated by the fact that the son of our current president, who is a geek if there ever was one—the son, I mean; but now that I think about it, his dad's one, too, actually—is enrolled there. Horizon is so geeky, they do not even hand out grades, just term reports. Rebecca's last term report said: *"Rebecca, while reading at a college level, has yet to catch up to her peers in emotional maturity, and needs to work on her 'people skills' next semester."*

But while her intellectual age might be forty, Rebecca acts about six and a half, which is why she's lucky she doesn't go to a school for regularly intelligent people, like Lucy and me: the Kris Parkses of the eleven-year-old set would eat her alive. Especially considering her lack of people skills.

My mother sighed. She was always very popular in high school, like Lucy. She was, in fact, voted Miss School Spirit. My mom doesn't understand where she went wrong with me. I think she blames my dad. My dad didn't get voted anything in high school, because, like me, he spent most of his time while he was there fantasizing about being somewhere else.

"Fine," Mom said to me. "Stay home then. But don't—"

"—open the door to strangers," I said. "I know."

As if anyone ever even came to our door except the Bread Lady.

The Bread Lady is the wife of a French diplomat who lives down the street from us. We don't know her name. We just call her the Bread Lady, because every three weeks or so she goes mental, I guess from missing her native country so much, and bakes about a hundred loaves of French bread, which she then sells from door to door in our neighborhood for fifty cents each. I am addicted to the Bread Lady's baguettes. In fact, they are practically the only thing I will eat, besides hamburgers, as I dislike most fruits and all vegetables, as well as a wide variety of other food groups, such as fish and anything with garlic.

The only person who ever comes to our door besides the Bread Lady is Jack. But we are not allowed to let Jack into the house when my parents or Theresa aren't home. This is because of the time Jack shot out the windows of his dad's Bethesda medical practice with his BB gun as a form of protest over Dr. Ryder's prescribing medications that had been tested on animals. My parents positively refuse to see that Jack was forced to take this drastic action in order to get his father to pay attention to the fact that animals are being tortured. They seem to think he did it just for the fun of it, which is so obviously untrue. Jack never does things just for the fun of them. He is seriously trying to make this world a better place.

Personally, I think the real reason Mom and Dad don't want Jack in the house when they aren't home is that they don't want him and Lucy making out. Which is a valid concern, but they could just say so, instead of hiding behind the BB gun defense. It is highly unlikely Jack is ever going to shoot out OUR windows. My mom is fully on the side of the good guys, seeing as how she's an attorney for the Environmental Protection Agency.

"Come on, you guys," Lucy whined from the backseat. "I'm going to be late for the game."

"And no drawing celebrities," my mom called as Dad pulled

away, "until all your German homework is done!"

Catherine and I watched them go, the sedan's wheels scrunching on the dead leaves in the road.

"I thought you weren't allowed to draw celebrities anymore," Catherine said as we turned the corner.

Manet, spotting a squirrel across the street, dragged me to the curb, nearly giving me whiplash.

"I can still draw celebrities," I said, raising my voice to be heard over Manet's hoarse barking. "I just can't charge people for them."

"Oh." Catherine considered this. Then she asked, in a pleading tone, "Then would you PLEASE draw Heath for me? Just once more? I promise I'll never ask again."

"I guess," I said with a sigh, as if it were this very big pain in the neck for me.

Except of course it wasn't. Because when you love something, you want to do it all the time, even if no one is paying you for it.

At least that's how I felt about drawing.

Until I met Susan Boone.

Top ten reasons I wish I were Gwen Stefani, lead singer of the best ska band of all time, No Doubt:

10. Gwen can dye her hair whatever color she wants, even bright pink like she did for the Return of Saturn tour, and her parents don't care, because they appreciate that she is an artist and must do these things as a form of creative expression. Mr. and Mrs. Stefani probably never threatened to cut off Gwen's allowance the way my parents did that time I tried the thing with the Kool-Aid.

9. If Gwen chose to wear black every single day, people would just accept it as a sign of her great genius and no one would make ninja comments, like they do about me.

8. Gwen has her own place, and so her older siblings can't come busting into her room whenever they want to, poking through her stuff and then telling their parents on her.

7. Gwen gets to write songs about her ex-boyfriends and sing them in front of everyone. I have never even had a boyfriend, so how could I have an ex to write about?

6. Free CDs.

5. If she were getting a C-minus in German on account of using all her class time to write songs, I fully doubt Gwen's mother would make her take a songwriting workshop twice a week. More likely, she'd let Gwen drop German and write songs full time.

4. She has dozens of websites dedicated to her. When you put the words *Samantha Madison* in any search engine, nothing whatsoever about me comes up.

3. All of the people who were mean to Gwen in high school are probably totally sorry about it now and try to suck up to her. But she can just be like, "Who are you again?" like Kris Parks was about me when I got back from Morocco.

2. She can get any boy she wants. Well, maybe not ANY boy, but she could probably get the boy *I* want. Who, sadly, is my sister's boyfriend. But whatever.

And the number-one reason I wish I were Gwen Stefani:

1. She doesn't have to take art lessons with Susan Boone.

★ 3 ★

Theresa was the one who ended up driving me to the art studio after school the next day.

Theresa is used to chauffeuring us around, though. She has been with our family since we got back from Morocco. She does everything my parents are too busy working to do: drive us places, clean the house, do the laundry, cook the meals, buy the groceries.

Not, of course, that we don't have to help out. For instance, I am completely in charge of Manet and everything to do with him, since I'm the one who wanted a dog so badly. Rebecca has to set the table, I clear it and put away the leftovers, while Lucy loads the dishwasher.

It mostly works out—if Theresa is supervising. If Theresa's gone home for the night, things generally get a little messy. One of her unofficial duties is exacting discipline in our family, since Mom and Dad, in the words of Horizon, Rebecca's school, sometimes "fail to set appropriate limits" for us kids.

On the way to Susan Boone's that first day, Theresa was totally setting some limits. She was on to the fact that I had every intention of bolting the minute she drove away.

"If you think, Miss Samantha," she was saying as we crawled down Burrito Alley, which is what people are calling Dupont Circle since lately so many burrito and wrap places have popped up all along it, "that I am not going in with you, you have another think coming."

This is one of Theresa's favorite expressions. I taught it to her.

And it really is "another *think* coming," not "*thing.*" It's a Southern saying. I got it out of *To Kill a Mockingbird*. I have worked very hard to acclimatize Theresa to our culture, since when she first started working for us she had just arrived here from Ecuador and didn't know squat about anything to do with America.

Now she is so in touch with what's hot and what's not in the U.S. of A., MTV should hire her as a consultant.

Also, she only calls me Miss Samantha when she is mad at me.

"I know exactly what you are thinking, Miss Samantha," Theresa said as we sat on Connecticut Avenue in a traffic jam caused, as usual, by the president's motorcade. That is one of the problems about living in Washington, D.C. You can't go anywhere without running into a motorcade. "I turn my back on you, and you run straight into the nearest Virgin Record Store, and that is the end of that."

I sighed like this had never occurred to me, though of course I had fully been planning on doing exactly that. But I feel like I have to. If I don't attempt to thwart authority, how will I retain my integrity as an artist?

"As if, Theresa," is all I said, though.

"Don't you '*as if Theresa*' me," Theresa said. "I know you. Wearing that black all the time and playing that punk rock music—"

"Ska," I corrected her.

"Whatever." The last of the motorcade passed by, and we were free to move again. "Next thing I know, you will be dyeing that beautiful red hair of yours black."

I thought guiltily of the box of Midnight Whisper colorfast hair dye in the bathroom medicine cabinet. Had she seen it? Because in spite of what Theresa might think, having red hair is so not beautiful. Well, maybe if you have red hair like Lucy's, which is the color they call titian, after the painter who invented it. But red hair like mine, which is the color—and consistency—of the copper wire they run through telephone poles? Not so lovely, let me tell you.

"And at five thirty," Theresa went on, "when I come to pick you up, I will be going into the building to find you. None of this meeting you at the curb."

Theresa really has the mom thing down. She has four kids of her own, all mostly grown, and three grandchildren, even though she's only a year older than my mom. This is because, as she put it, her eldest son, Tito, is an idiot.

It was because of Tito's idiocy that you could not pull anything over on Theresa. She had seen it all before.

When we finally got to the Susan Boone Art Studio, which was on the corner of R and Connecticut, right across from the Founding Church of Scientology, Theresa gave me a very dirty look. Not because of the Church of Scientology, but because of the record store Susan Boone's studio was on top of. As if I'd had something to do with picking the place out!

Although I have to say, Static, one of the few record stores in town that I'd actually never been to before, looked tempting— almost as tempting as Capitol Cookies, the bakery next door to it. You could even hear the strains of one of my favorite songs thumping through the walls as we walked toward the store (we had to go around the block once and park a million miles away on Q Street; you could tell Theresa wasn't going to be insisting on walking me to the door again after this). Static was playing Garbage's "Only Happy When It Rains." Which if you think about it really sums up my whole attitude about life, since the only time parents will actually let you stay inside and draw is when it is raining out. Otherwise it's all, "Why can't you go outside and ride your bike like a normal kid?"

But Susan Boone must have had her place soundproofed, because when we finished climbing the narrow, whitewashed staircase to her second-floor studio, you couldn't hear Garbage at all. Instead all you could hear was a radio, softly playing some classical music, and another sound I could not quite identify. The smell, as we climbed, was comfortingly familiar to me. No, it didn't smell like cookies. It smelled like the art room back at school, of paint and turpentine.

It wasn't until we got to the door of the studio, and I pushed it open, that I realized what the other sound I'd been hearing was.

"Hello Joe. Hello Joe. Hello Joe," a big black crow, sitting on top of, and not inside, a large bamboo cage, squawked at us.

Theresa screamed.

"Joseph!" A small woman with the longest, whitest hair I had ever seen came out from behind an easel and yelled at the bird. "Mind your manners!"

"Mind your manners," the bird said as he hopped around the top of his cage. "Mind your manners, mind your manners, mind your manners."

"Jesu Cristo," Theresa said, sinking onto a nearby paint-spattered bench. She was already out of breath from the steep staircase. The shock of being yelled at by a bird had not helped.

"Sorry about that," the woman with the long white hair said. "Please don't mind Joseph. It takes him a while to get used to strangers." She looked at me. "So. You must be Samantha. I'm Susan."

Back in middle school, Catherine and I had gone through this stage where all we would read were fantasy books. We'd consumed them like M&Ms, by the fistful, J.R.R. Tolkien and Terry Brooks and Susan Cooper and Lloyd Alexander. Susan Boone looked, to me, like the queen of the elves (there's almost always an elf queen in fantasy books). I mean, she was shorter than me and had on a strange lineny outfit in pale blues and greens.

But it was her long white hair—down to her waist!—and

bright blue eyes, peering out of a lined and completely unmade-up face, that cinched it for me. Even the corners of her mouth curled upward, the way an elf's would, even when there was nothing to smile about.

Back in the days when Catherine and I had gone around tapping on the backs of wardrobes, hoping to get transported to a land where there were fauns and hobbits, not Lunchables and Carson Daly, meeting someone like Susan Boone would have been a thrill.

Now it was just kind of weird.

I reached out and took the hand she'd stretched toward me, and shook it. Her skin was dry and rough.

"Call me Sam," I said, impressed with Susan Boone's grip, which wasn't at all elflike: the woman could definitely have handled Manet in a pinch.

"Hi, Sam," Susan Boone said. Then she let go of my hand and turned toward Theresa. "You must be Mrs. Madison. It's nice to meet you."

Theresa had caught her breath. Now she stood up and shook her head, saying that she was Mrs. Madison's housekeeper, Theresa, and that she would be back at five thirty to pick me up.

Then Theresa left and Susan Boone took me by both shoulders and steered me toward one of the paint-spattered benches, which had no back, just a tall board along one end, against which leaned a large drawing pad.

"Everyone," Susan Boone said as she pushed me down onto the bench, "this is Sam. Sam, this is——"

Then, exactly like brownies popping out from behind giant toadstools, the rest of the art class popped their heads out from behind huge drawing pads to look at me.

"Lynn, Gertie, John, Jeffrey, and David," Susan Boone said, pointing at each person as she said his or her name.

No sooner had the heads appeared than they disappeared again, as everyone went back to scribbling on their pads. I was awarded no more than a fleeting glance of Lynn, a skinny woman in her thirties; Gertie, a plump middle-aged woman; John, a middle-aged guy with a hearing aid; Jeffrey, a young African-American man; and David, who was wearing a Save Ferris T-shirt.

Since Save Ferris is one of my favorite bands, I figured at least I'd have somebody to talk to.

But then I got a closer look at David, and I realized the chances of him even talking to me were, like, nil. I mean, he looked kind of familiar, which meant he probably went to Adams with me. And I have been one of the most hated people at Adams ever since I suggested the school donate the money we raised selling holiday wrapping paper to the school's art department.

But Lucy and Kris Parks and people like that wanted to go to Six Flags Great Adventure theme park.

Guess who won?

And the whole wearing-black-every-day-because-I-am-mourning-for-my-generation thing hasn't exactly helped boost my popularity much, either.

David looked like he was about Lucy's age. He was tall—well, at least from what I could see of him, sitting on the bench—with curly dark hair and these very green eyes and big hands and feet. He was kind of cute—though not as cute as Jack, of course—which meant that, if he did go to Adams, he probably hung out with the jocks. All the cute boys at Adams hang with the jocks. Except for Jack, of course.

So when David winked at me after I sat down, and said, "Nice boots," I was completely shocked. Thinking that he was mocking me—as most of the boys who hang out with the jocks at Adams are wont to do—I looked down and realized that he, like me, was wearing combat boots.

Only David, unlike me, wasn't making the satirical statement with his that I was making with mine, having decorated mine with daisies (of Wite-Out and yellow highlighter) one day in seventh period.

While I was busy turning bright red because this cute boy spoke to me, Susan Boone said, "We're doing a still life today." She handed me a pencil, a nice soft-leaded one. Then she pointed at a pile of fruit on a small table in the middle of the room and went, "Draw what you see."

Then she walked away.

Well, so much for her trying to stamp out my individuality and natural ability. I was relieved to see I had been wrong about that. Telling myself to forget about Cute David and his boot comment—undoubtedly he was only being nice to me on account of me being the new kid, and all—I looked at the pile of fruit on the table, nestled against a wrinkled-up piece of white silk, and began to draw.

Okay, I thought to myself. This isn't so bad. It was actually somewhat pleasant in the Susan Boone studio. Susan was interesting, with her elf queen hair and smile. A cute boy had said he liked my boots. The classical music playing softly in the background was nice. I never listen to classical music unless it's playing in the background of some movie I'm watching, or something. And the smell of turpentine was refreshing, like hot apple cider on a crisp autumn day.

Maybe, I thought as I drew, this wasn't going to be so bad. Maybe it would even be fun. I mean, there are a lot of worse ways to blow four hours a week, right?

Pears. Grapes. An apple. A pomegranate. I drew without much thinking about what I was doing. I wondered what Theresa was making for dinner. I wondered why I hadn't taken Spanish instead of German. If I'd taken Spanish, I could have gotten help on my homework from two native speakers, Theresa and Catherine. No one I knew spoke German. Why had I taken such a dumb language in the first place? I'd only done it because Lucy had, and she'd said it was easy. Easy! Ha! Maybe for Lucy. But what wasn't easy for Lucy? I mean, Lucy has everything: titian hair, a totally righteous boyfriend, the corner bedroom with the big closet . . .

I was so busy drawing and thinking about how much better Lucy's life was than mine that I didn't notice Joe the crow had hopped down off the top of his cage and wandered over to check me out until he'd yanked a few strands of my hair.

Seriously. A bird stole some of my *hair*!

I shrieked, causing Joe to take flight, scattering black feathers everywhere.

"Joseph!" Susan Boone cried when she saw what was happening. "Put down Sam's hair!"

Obediently, Joe opened his beak. Three or four copper-colored hairs floated to the ground.

"Pretty bird," Joe said, tilting his head in my direction. "Pretty bird."

"Oh, Sam," Susan Boone said, stooping down to pick up my hair. "I'm so sorry. He's always been very attracted to bright, shiny things." She came over and handed me back my hair, as if there was some way I could glue it all back onto my head.

"He's not a bad bird, really," Gertie said, like she was concerned I had gotten the wrong impression, or something, of Susan Boone's bird.

"Bad bird," Joe said. "Bad bird."

I sat there with my hair lying in my outstretched palm, thinking that Susan Boone would do well to shell out five hundred big ones to an animal behaviorist, since her pet had some major issues. Meanwhile, fluttering back to the top of his cage, Joe wouldn't take his beady black eyes off me. Off my hair, to be more exact. You could tell he really wanted to take another swipe at it, if he could. At least, that's how it looked to me. Do birds even feel things? I know dogs do.

But dogs are smart. Birds are kind of stupid.

But not, I realized later, as stupid as humans can be. Or at least this particular human. Around five fifteen—I could tell because the classical music station had started doing the news—Susan Boone said, "All right. Windowsill."

And everyone but me got up from the benches and propped his or her drawing pad, with the drawing facing into the room, on the windowsill. Windows ran around all three sides of the corner room, big, ten-foot factory-style windows, above a sill wide enough to sit on. I hurried to put my pad with the others, and then we all stood back and looked at what everyone had drawn.

Mine was clearly the best. I felt pretty bad about it. I mean, here I was on my very first day of class, already drawing better than everyone else in it, even the grown-ups. I felt sorriest for John: his drawing was just a big old mess. Gertie's was blocky and smeared. Lynn's looked as if a kindergartner had drawn it, and Jeffrey had drawn something unrecognizable as fruit.

UFOs, maybe. But not fruit.

Only David had drawn anything remotely good. But he hadn't drawn quickly enough to finish his. I had gotten in ALL the fruit, and I had even added a pineapple and some bananas, to kind of balance it all out.

I hoped Susan Boone wouldn't make too big a deal out of how much better my drawing was than everybody else's. I didn't want to make anybody feel bad.

"Well," Susan Boone said. And then she stepped forward and started discussing each person's drawing.

She was really quite diplomatic about the whole thing. I mean, my dad could probably have used her over in his offices, she was so tactful (economists are pretty good with numbers, but when it comes to human relations, they, like Rebecca, don't do so well). Susan went on about Lynn's dramatic use of line and Gertie's nice sense of placement on the page. She said John had improved a lot, and everyone seemed to agree, which made me wonder how bad John had been when he started. David got an "excellent juxtaposition," and Jeffrey a "fine detail."

When she finally got to my drawing, I felt like slinking out of the room. I mean, my drawing was so obviously the best one. I really don't mean to sound like a snob, but my drawings are *always* the best ones. Drawing is the one thing I can do well.

And I really hoped Susan Boone wasn't going to rub it in. The rest of the class had to feel badly enough already.

But it turned out I needn't have worried about how the rest of the class was going to feel as Susan Boone sang the praises of my drawing. Because when Susan Boone got to my drawing, she didn't have a single nice thing to say about it. Instead, she peered at it, then stepped up to it and looked at it even more closely. Then she took a step back and went, "Well, Sam. I see that you drew what you knew."

I thought this was a pretty weird thing to say. But then, the whole thing had been pretty weird so far. Nice—except for the hair-stealing bird, which hadn't been so nice—but weird.

"Um," I said. "I guess so."

"But I didn't tell you to draw what you know," Susan Boone said. "I told you to draw what you see."

I looked from my drawing to the pile of fruit on the table, then back again, confused.

"But I did," I said. "I did draw what I see. I mean, saw."

"Did you?" Susan Boone asked, with another of her little elf smiles. "And do you see a pineapple on that table?"

I didn't have to glance back at the table to check. I knew there was no pineapple there. "Well," I said. "No. But——"

"No. There is no pineapple there. And this pear isn't there, either." She pointed at one of the pears I had drawn.

"Wait a minute," I said, still confused but getting defensive. "There are pears there. There are four pears there on the table."

"Yes," Susan Boone said. "There are four pears on the table. But none of them is *this* pear. This is a pear from your imagination. It is what you know to be a pear—a perfect pear—but it is not any of the pears you actually saw."

I didn't have the slightest idea what she was talking about, but Gertie and Lynn and John and Jeffrey and David knew, apparently. They were all nodding.

"Don't you see, Sam?" Susan Boone picked up my drawing pad and walked over to me. She pointed at the grapes I had drawn. "You've drawn some beautiful grapes. But they aren't the grapes on the table. The grapes on the table aren't so perfectly oblong, and they aren't all the same size, either. What you've drawn here is your idea of how grapes should look, not the grapes that are actually in front of us."

I blinked down at the drawing pad. I didn't get it. I really didn't. I mean, I guess I sort of understood what she was saying, but I didn't see what the big deal was. My grapes looked a lot better than anybody else's grapes. Wasn't that a good thing?

The worst part of it was, I could feel everybody looking at me sympathetically. My face started getting hot. That is the thing about being a redhead, of course. You go around blushing something like ninety-seven percent of the time. And there is absolutely nothing you can do to hide it.

"Draw what you *see*," Susan Boone said, not in an unkind way. "Not what you know, Sam."

And then Theresa, panting from her climb up the stairs, came in, causing Joe to start shrieking "Hello Joe! Hello Joe!" all over again.

And it was time to go. I thought I would collapse with relief.

"I'll see you on Thursday," Susan Boone called cheerfully to me as I put on my coat.

I smiled back at her, but of course I was thinking, Over my dead body will you see me on Thursday.

I didn't know then, of course, how right I was. Well, in a way.

When I told Jack about it—what had happened at the Susan Boone Art Studio, I mean—he just laughed.

Laughed! Like it was funny!

I was kind of hurt by this, but I guess it *was* kind of funny. In a way.

"Sam," he said, shaking his head so that the silver ankh he wears in one ear caught the light. "You can't let the establishment win. You've got to fight against the system."

Which is easy for Jack to say. Jack is six foot four and weighs over two hundred pounds. He was assiduously courted by our school football coach after the team's best linebacker moved to Dubai.

But Jack wouldn't have any part of Coach Donnelly's scheme to dominate our school district's sectionals. Jack doesn't believe in organized sports, but not because, like me, he is resentful of their draining valuable funds away from the arts. No, Jack is convinced that sports, like the Lottery, only serve to lull the proletariat into a false sense of hope that he might one day rise above his Bud-swilling, pickup truck–driving peers.

It is very easy for a guy like Jack to fight against the system.

I, on the other hand, am only five foot two and do not know what I weigh, since Mom threw out the scale after seeing a news story on the prevalence of anorexia in today's teenage girls. Plus I have never been able to climb the rope in PE, having inherited my father's complete lack of upper body strength.

When I mentioned this, however, Jack started laughing even harder, which I thought was, you know, kind of rude. For a man who is supposed to be my soul mate, and all. Even if he maybe doesn't know it yet.

"Sam," he said. "I'm not talking about *physically* fighting the system. You've got to be more subtle than that."

He was sitting at the kitchen table, polishing off a box of Entenmann's chocolate-covered doughnuts Theresa had put out for us as an after-school snack. Entenmann's is not what we normally get as after-school snack fare. My mom only wants us to have apples and graham crackers and milk and stuff. But Theresa, unlike my parents, doesn't care about Jack's grades or the political statements he likes to make with his BB gun, so when he comes over when she's around, it's always like a big party. Sometimes she even bakes. Once she made fudge. I am telling you, Lucy's getting the one guy who will inspire Theresa to make fudge proves there is seriously no justice in the world.

"Susan Boone is stifling me creatively," I said indignantly. "She's trying to make me into some kind of art clone. . . ."

"Of course she is." Jack looked amused as he bit into another doughnut. "That's what teachers do. You tried to get a little creative, added a pineapple, and—POW!—the fist of conformity came crashing down on you."

When Jack gets excited, he chews with his mouth open. He did that now. Bits of doughnut went flying across the table and hit the back of the magazine Lucy was reading. She lowered her copy of *Cosmo*, looked at the bits of doughnut stuck to the back, looked at Jack, and said, "Dude, say it, don't spray it."

Then she went back to reading about orgasms.

See? See what I mean about her being oblivious to Jack's genius?

I took a bite of my own doughnut. Our kitchen table, at which we generally only eat breakfast and snacks, is located in this kind of glass atrium that juts out from the rest of the kitchen into the backyard. Our house is old—more than a hundred years old, like most of the houses in Cleveland Park, which are all these Victorians with a lot of stained-glass windows and widow's walks, painted bright colors. For instance, our house is turquoise, yellow, and white.

The glass atrium the kitchen table is in was added onto our house last year. The ceiling is glass, three walls are made of glass, and the kitchen table, actually, is made out of this huge piece of glass. Everywhere I looked, I could see my reflection, since it was getting dark outside. And I didn't much like what I saw:

A medium-size girl with too-pale skin and freckles, dressed all in black, with a bunch of bright red curly hair sticking straight out of the top of her head.

What I saw sitting on either side of my reflection I liked even less:

A delicately featured girl with no freckles in a purple-and-white cheerleader uniform, her own bright red hair completely under control and only curling softly where it tumbled down from a barrette.

And:

A gorgeous, big-shouldered hunk with piercing blue eyes and long brown hair in torn-up jeans and an army/navy surplus trench coat, eating doughnuts as if there were no tomorrow.

And there was me, in the middle. In between. Where I always am.

I once saw a documentary on birth order on the Health Network, and guess what it said:

First born (a.k.a. Lucy): Bossy. Always gets what she wants. Kid most likely to be CEO of a major corporation, dictator of a small country, supermodel, you name it.

Last born (a.k.a. Rebecca): Baby. Always gets what she wants. Kid most likely to end up discovering a cure for cancer, hosting her own talk show, stepping up to the alien mother ship when it lands and being all, "Hey, welcome to Earth," etc.

Middle child (a.k.a. me): Lost in the shuffle. Never gets what she wants. Kid most likely to end up a teen runaway, living on leftover Big Macs scrounged from Dumpsters behind the local McDonald's for weeks before anyone even notices she is gone.

Story of my life.

Although if you think about it, the fact that I am left-handed indicates that I was probably, at one time, a twin. According to this article I read in the dentist's office, anyway. There's this theory that most lefties actually started out as one in a pair of twins. One out of every ten pregnancies starts out as twins. One out of every ten people is left-handed.

You do the math.

For a while I thought my mom had never told me about my dead twin to spare my feelings. But then I read on the Internet that in seventy percent of pregnancies that begin as twins, one of the babies disappears. Just like that. Poof. This is called vanishing twin syndrome, and generally the mothers don't ever even realize that they were carrying two babies instead of just one because the other one gets lost so early in the pregnancy.

Not that any of this really matters. Because even if my twin had survived, I'd still be the middle child. I'd just have someone else to share the burden with. And maybe to have talked me out of taking German.

"Well," I said, dropping my gaze from my reflection and scowling instead at the place mat beneath my elbows. "What am I supposed to do now? Nobody ever said anything to me about not adding things in school when we had art. They let me add things all I wanted."

Jack snorted. "School," he said. "Yeah, right."

Jack was having an ongoing and extremely bitter feud with our school's administrative offices over some paintings he'd entered in an art show at the mall. Mr. Esposito, the principal of Adams Prep, where Jack and Lucy and I go, didn't approve of Jack's entering those paintings in Adams Prep's name—he never even saw them. So when they were accepted, he was peeved, because the subject matter of the paintings wasn't what he considered "Adams Prep" quality. The paintings were all of baseball-hatted teens slouching around outside a 7-Eleven. They were titled *Studies in Baditude, Numbers One Through Three*, though at a recent board of trustees meeting one irate parent called them *Studies in Slackitude*.

The Impressionists, I often remind Jack when he is feeling down about this, weren't appreciated in their day, either.

In any case, there is no love lost between Jack and the John Adams Preparatory School administration. In truth, were it not for the fact that Jack's parents are major contributors to the school's alumni fund, Jack probably would have been expelled a long time ago.

"You've just got to find a way to fight this Susan Boone person," Jack said. "I mean, before she drives out every creative thought in your head. You have got to draw what is in your heart, Sam. Otherwise, what is the point?"

"I thought," Lucy said in a bored voice as she flipped a page in her magazine, "that you're supposed to draw what you know."

"It's *write* what you know." Rebecca, down at the opposite end of the table from me, looked up from her laptop. "And draw what you *see*. Everyone knows that."

Jack looked at me triumphantly. "You see?" he said. "You see how insidious it is, this thing? It's even seeped into the consciousness of little eleven-year-old girls."

Rebecca shot him an aggravated look. Rebecca has always been fully on my parents' side on the whole issue of Jack.

"Hey," she said. "I am not *little*."

Jack ignored her. "Where would we be if Picasso had only drawn what he saw?" Jack wanted to know. "Or Pollock? Or Miró?" He shook his head. "You stay true to your beliefs, Sam. You draw from your heart. If your heart says put in a pineapple, then you put in a pineapple. Don't let the establishment tell you what to do. Don't let others dictate how—and what—you draw."

I don't know how he does it, but somehow, Jack always says the right thing. *Always.*

"So are you going to quit?" Catherine, calling me later that evening to discuss our bio assignment, wanted to know. Our bio assignment was to watch a documentary on the Learning Channel about people who have body dysmorphic disorder. These are people who, like Michael Jackson, think they are horribly disfigured, when in reality they are not. For instance, one man hated his nose so much he slit it open with a knife, pulled out his own nasal cartilage, and stuck a chicken bone in there.

Which just goes to show, no matter how bad you think something might be, it could always be much, much worse.

"I don't know," I said in response to Catherine's question. We had already fully discussed the whole chicken bone thing. "I want to. That class is filled with a bunch of freaks."

"Yeah," Catherine said. "But you told me there was one cute guy."

I thought about familiar-looking David, his Save Ferris T-shirt, his big hands and feet, and his liking my boots.

And the way he had seen me totally and utterly crushed, like an ant, in front of him by Susan Boone.

"He's cute," I admitted. "But not as cute as Jack."

"Who is?" Catherine asked with a sigh. "Except maybe for Heath."

So, so true.

"Will your mom let you quit?" Catherine wanted to know. "I mean, isn't this supposed to be kind of a punishment for the C-minus in German thing? Maybe you aren't supposed to like it."

"I think it's supposed to be a learning experience for me," I said. "You know, like how Debbie Kinley's parents sent her to Outward Bound after she drank all that vodka at that party at Rodd Muckinfuss's house? Art lessons are supposed to be like my Outward Bound."

"Then you can't quit," Catherine said. "So what are you going to do?"

"I'll figure something out," I said.

Actually, I already had.

Top ten reasons I would make a better girlfriend for Jack than my sister Lucy:

10. My love for and appreciation of art. Lucy doesn't know anything about art. To her, art is what they made us do with pipe cleaners that summer we both went to Girl Scout camp.

9. Having the soul of an artist, I am better equipped to understand and handle Jack's mood swings. Lucy just asks him if he is over himself yet.

8. I would never demand, as Lucy does, that Jack take me to whatever asinine teen gross-out movie is currently popular with the sixteen-to-twenty-four crowd. I would understand that a soul as sensitive as Jack's needs sustenance in the form of independent art films, or perhaps the occasional foreign movie with subtitles.

And by that I am not referring to Jackie Chan.

7. Ditto the stupid books Lucy makes Jack read. *Men Are from Mars, Women Are from Venus* is not appropriate reading material for a guy like Jack. *The Virgin and the Gypsy* by D.H. Lawrence would do far more to stimulate Jack's already brilliant mind than any of

Lucy's pathetic self-help manuals. Although I have never actually read *The Virgin and the Gypsy*. Still, it sounds like a book that Jack and I could really get into. For instance, we could take turns reading it out loud on a blanket in the park, which is something artists always do in movies. Just as soon as I am done re-reading *Fight Club,* I will give *The V. and the G.* a try to make sure it is really as intellectual as it sounds.

6. On Jack's birthday, I would not give him joke boxer shorts with Tweety Bird on them, the way Lucy did last year. I would find something highly personal and romantic to give him, such as sable paintbrushes or perhaps a leather-bound copy of *Romeo and Juliet* or one of Gwen Stefani's wristbands or something like that.

5. If Jack were ever late to pick me up for a date, I would not yell at him the way Lucy does. I would understand that artists cannot be held to pedestrian constraints like time.

4. I would never make Jack go to the mall with me. If I ever went to the mall, which I don't. Instead, Jack and I would go to museums, and I am not talking about the Aeronautical and Space Museum, which everyone goes to, or the Smithsonian to see Dorothy's stupid ruby slippers, either, but actual *art* museums, with actual *art*, such as the Hirschorn. Perhaps we could even take drawing pads with us and sit back to back on those couches and sketch our favorite paintings, and people would come up and look at what we were drawing and offer to buy the sketches, and we would say no because we would want to treasure the drawings forever as symbols of our great love for one another.

3. If Jack and I ever got married, I would not insist on a massive church wedding with a country club reception, the way I know Lucy would. Jack and I would be married barefoot in the woods near Walden Pond, where so many artistic souls have gone to receive succor.

   And for our honeymoon, instead of a Sandals in Jamaica, or wherever, we would fully go to Paris and live in a garret.

2. When Jack came over to visit me, I would never read a magazine while he sat at our kitchen table eating doughnuts. I would engage him in friendly but spirited and intellectual conversations about art and literature.

And the number-one reason I would be a better girlfriend for Jack than Lucy:

1. I would give him the loving support he so desperately needs, since I understand what it is like to be tortured by the burden of one's genius.

★5★

Fortunately, it was raining on Thursday when Theresa drove me to Susan Boone's studio. That meant that the chances of her finding a parking space, scrounging around the backseat for an umbrella, getting out of the car, and walking me all the way to the studio door were exactly nil.

Instead, she stopped in the middle of Connecticut Avenue—causing all the cars behind her to honk—and went, "If you are not out here at exactly five thirty, I will hunt you down. Do you hear me? Hunt you down like an animal."

"Fine," I said, undoing my seat belt.

"I mean it, Miss Samantha," Theresa said. "Five thirty on the dot. Or I will double-park and you will have to pay the impound fees if the station wagon gets towed."

"Whatever," I said, and stepped out into the pouring rain. "See you."

Then I ran for the door to the studio.

Only I didn't, of course, go up that narrow stairway. Well, really, how could I? I mean, I had to fight the system, right?

Besides, it wasn't like I hadn't completely *humiliated* myself in there the day before yesterday. Was I really just going to go waltzing back in like nothing had happened?

The answer, of course, was no. No, I was not.

What I did instead was, I waited about a minute inside the little foyer, with rainwater dripping off the hood of my Gore-Tex parka. While I was in there, I tried not to feel too guilty. I knew I was

41

taking a stand, and all, by boycotting Susan Boone. I mean, I was showing that I was fully on the side of art rebels everywhere.

But my parents *were* paying a lot of money for these art lessons. I had heard my father grousing that they cost almost as much per month as the animal behaviorist. Susan Boone, it turned out, was kind of famous. Just what she was famous for, I didn't know, but apparently, she charged a bundle for her art tutelage.

So even though I was fighting the system, I didn't feel too good, knowing I was wasting my parents' hard-earned money.

But if you think about it, I am actually the cheapest kid Mom and Dad have. I mean, they spend a small fortune on Lucy every month. She is always needing new clothes, new pom-poms, new orthodontia, new dermatological aids, whatever, in order to maintain her image as one of Adams Prep's beautiful people.

And Rebecca, my God, the lab fees alone at Horizon pretty much equal the gross national product of a small underdeveloped nation.

And me? How much do Mom and Dad spend on *me* every month? Well, up until I got busted for the celebrity drawing thing, nothing, besides tuition. I mean, I'm supposed to wear my sister's hand-me-down bras, right? And I didn't even need new clothes this year: I just applied black Rit to last semester's clothes, and voilà! A whole new wardrobe.

Really, as children go, I am a major bargain. I don't even eat that much, either, seeing as how I hate almost all food except hamburgers, the Bread Lady's baguettes, and dessert.

So I shouldn't have even felt guilty about ditching art class. Not really.

But as I stood there, the familiar scent of turpentine washed over me, and I could hear, way up at the top of the stairs, the faint sound of classical music, and the occasional squawk from Joe the crow. I was suddenly filled with a strange longing to climb those stairs, go to my bench, sit down, and draw.

But then I remembered the humiliation I had endured the last time I'd been in that room. And in front of that David guy, too! I mean, yeah, he wasn't as cute as Jack, or anything. But he was still a guy! A guy who liked Save Ferris! And who had said he liked my boots!

Okay, no way was I going up those stairs. I was taking a stand. A stand against the system.

Instead, I waited in the vestibule, praying nobody would come in while I was huddled there and say, "Oh, hi, Sam. Aren't you coming upstairs?"

As if anybody there would even remember my name. Except possibly Susan Boone.

But nobody came in. When two minutes were up, I cautiously opened the door and looked out at the rain-soaked street.

Theresa and the station wagon were gone. It was safe. I could come out.

The first place I went was Capitol Cookies. Well, how could I not? It looked so warm and inviting, what with the rain and all, and I happened to have a dollar sixty-eight in my pocket, exactly as much as a Congressional Chocolate Chunk. The cookie they handed me was still warm from the oven, too. I slipped it into the pocket of my black Gore-Tex coat. They don't allow food in Static, where I was going next.

They weren't playing Garbage there that afternoon. They were playing the Donnas. Not ska, but perfectly acceptable. I went over to where they had some headphones plugged into the wall so people could sample the CDs they were thinking about buying. I spent a nice half hour or so listening to the Less Than Jake CD I'd wanted but couldn't afford now that my mom had seen to it that my funding for such items was shut off.

As I listened, I snuck bits of cookie from my pocket into my mouth and told myself that what I was doing wasn't all that wrong. Fighting the system, I mean. Besides, look at Catherine: for years her parents have been forcing her to go to Sunday school while they attend mass. Since there is, like, a two-year age difference between Catherine and each of her brothers, all three of them were in different religion classes, so she never knew until this year that Marco and Javier, after their mom dropped them all off, were waving good-bye and then ducking around the corner to Beltway Billiards. She only found out when her class let out early one day, and she went to look around for her brothers, and they were nowhere to be seen.

So basically for years Catherine's been sitting there, listening to her religion teachers tell her to resist temptation, etc., while it turns out the whole time her brothers—and pretty much all the rest of the cool kids who go to her church—have been next door, getting the high score on Super Mario.

So what does Catherine do now? She waves good-bye to her mom just like Marco and Javier, and then she, too, goes to Beltway Billiards—and works on her geometry homework in the glow of Delta Force.

And does she feel bad about it? No. Why not? Because she says if the Lord really is all-forgiving, like they taught her in Sunday school, He will understand that she really does need the extra study time or she will flunk geometry and never get into a good college and make a success of herself.

So why should I feel bad about skipping my drawing lesson? I mean, it is only a *drawing lesson*. Catherine, on the other hand, is skipping out on *God*.

Surely my parents, in the unlikely event that they find out what

I've done, will understand that I was merely trying to preserve my integrity as an artist. Of *course* they will understand this. Probably. Maybe. On a good day, anyway, when there haven't been any PCBs found in some Midwestern town's water supply, or too many plunges in the North African economy.

If anybody at Static thought it was strange that this fifteen-year-old redheaded girl, dressed in black from head to toe, was hanging around for two hours, sampling CDs but not buying any, they didn't say anything about it to me. The chick behind the counter, who had the kind of spiky black hair I've always wanted but have never had the guts to get, was too busy flirting with one of the other workers, a guy in plaid pants and a Le Tigre T-shirt, to pay any attention to me.

The other customers were ignoring me, too. Most of them looked like college students wasting time between classes. Some of them might have been in high school. One of them was a kind of old guy, like in his thirties, wearing army clothes and carrying a duffel bag. For a while he was hanging out by the headphones near me, listening to Billy Joel. I was surprised that a place like Static even had any Billy Joel, but they did. This guy kept listening to "Uptown Girl" over and over. My dad is actually a Billy Joel fan—he plays it all the time in the car, which makes driving with him mad fun, let me tell you—but even he is way over "Uptown Girl."

My cookie was gone about midway through the Spitvalves' second album. I reached into my pocket and found nothing but crumbs. I thought about going over to Capitol Cookies to get another, but then I remembered I was broke. Besides, by that time it was almost five thirty. I had to go outside and wait for Theresa to pick me up.

I put my hood up and walked out into the rain. It wasn't the steady downpour it had been when I'd arrived, but I figured the hood would keep anybody coming out of the Susan Boone Art Studio from recognizing me and being all, "Hey, where were you, anyway?"

As if any of them would have missed me.

It had gotten dark outside while I'd been in the record store. All the cars going by had their headlights on. And there were a lot more of them than before, because it was rush hour and everyone was trying to get home to be with their loved ones. Or maybe just to watch *Friends*. Whatever.

I stood on the curb across from the Founding Church of Scientology, squinting into the light drizzle and headlights in the direction from which Theresa was supposed to come. As I stood there, I couldn't help feeling kind of sorry for myself. I mean, there I was, a fifteen-year-old, left-handed, redheaded, boyfriendless, misunderstood, middle child reject, broke, standing in the rain after skipping her drawing class because she couldn't take criticism. What was going to happen if I grew up and started my own celebrity portrait painting business or something? Was I just going to quit if it didn't work out right away? Was I going to go hide in Static? Maybe I could just go ahead and get a job there, to make things easier. It didn't seem like a very bad place to work, actually. I bet employees get a discount on CDs.

While I was standing there being ashamed of myself for being a quitter, the old guy who was such a big Billy Joel fan came out of Static and stood next to me, even though the crosswalk sign was green. I looked at him from the corner of my eye. He was messing around with something under his rain poncho, which was in a camouflage pattern. I wondered if he was a shoplifter. At Static I'd noticed they had a Wall of Shame, where they stuck up Polaroids of people who'd tried to swipe something. This dude looked like as prime a candidate for the Wall of Shame as I'd ever seen.

46

And when, right after this, I saw all these flashing red lights coming out of the rain and darkness, I was like, Oh, yes, here come the cops. Mr. Uptown Girl is *so* busted.

Only it turned out the sirens didn't belong to the cops at all. Instead, they were part of the president's motorcade. First came the lead car, a black SUV with a rack of flashing red lights on its roof. Then came another black SUV, and behind it, a long black limo. Behind that were some more SUVs with flashing lights.

Instead of being excited that I was going to get to see the president go by—even though you can't really see him when he's in his limo because the windows are those weird ones the people inside the car can see out of but the people outside the car can't see into—I was like, Aw, crud. Because Theresa was probably somewhere behind the motorcade, which was crawling along at a snail's pace. Not only was she going to be in a really bad mood by the time she finally picked me up, but no way was I going to miss David coming out of Susan Boone's. He would probably see me standing out here and be like, Man, she's weird, and never speak to me again. Not that I cared, because I am fully in love with my sister's boyfriend. But it had been nice of him to notice my boots. Hardly anyone else ever had.

And besides, when you live in D.C., seeing the president go by is really no big deal, since he goes by all the time.

Then the strangest thing happened. The first SUV in the motorcade pulled up right in front of me . . . and stopped. Just stopped.

And the traffic light wasn't even red.

Behind the first SUV, the second one stopped, and then the limo, and so on. Traffic was totally stopped behind them, all along Connecticut Avenue. Then these guys with these earpieces climbed out of the cars and all went toward the limo.

And then, to my utter astonishment, the president of the United

States got out of his limo and walked, with a bunch of Secret Service guys clustered around him holding up umbrellas and looking around and speaking into their walkie-talkies, into Capitol Cookies!

That's right, just walked into Capitol Cookies, like he did it every day.

I didn't know that the president liked Capitol Cookies. Capitol Cookies are good, and all, but they're not the most famous cookies around, or anything. I mean, there's just the one store.

And wouldn't you think that if you were the president you could get the owner to send you a personal supply of cookies, so you wouldn't have to go ducking out of your limo, in the rain, just to get your hands on some? I mean, if I owned a bakery and I found out that the president of the United States liked my cookies, I would fully make sure he got a steady supply of them.

On the other hand, the people who owned Capitol Cookies would probably prefer to have the president be seen ducking into the store. That is way better publicity than you could ever get by privately shipping him his own supply.

And then, as I stood there in the dark and the rain, with the red lights from the top of the SUV in front of me flashing in my face, I saw Mr. Uptown Girl throw back his rain poncho.

And it turned out what he'd been doing under there had nothing to do with him being a shoplifter. Not at all. It turned out what he'd been doing under there had to do with a great big gun, which he brought out and pointed in the direction of the door to Capitol Cookies . . . the door through which the president, his cookies having been secured with miraculous swiftness, was just exiting.

I am not what most people would call a particularly brave person. I stick up for the kids at school who get picked on only because I remember what it was like to get picked on back when I lived in Morocco, and during the whole speech and hearing thing.

But that does not mean that I am the sort of girl to throw herself into the path of danger without the slightest concern for her own personal safety. I mean, the closest thing I have been in lately that could qualify as a physical altercation would be the last time Lucy and I wrestled over possession of the remote control.

And obviously I am not much for confrontations. I mean, yeah, I was striking a blow for the creative spirit by boycotting Susan Boone's and all. But really, I was just too embarrassed to go back in there after my humiliation the last time.

But whatever. What I did next was so atypical of me that it was like someone else took over my body for a minute, or something. All I know is, one second I was standing there, watching Mr. Uptown Girl raise his gun to fire at the president as he exited Capitol Cookies . . .

. . . and the next, I had jumped him.

It turns out if you jump onto the back of a would-be assassin, and he isn't expecting you to or anything, you can really throw off his aim. So the bullet Mr. Uptown Girl had meant to send speeding into the president's head went speeding harmlessly off into the stratosphere instead.

Something else happens when you jump onto the back of a guy with a gun, though. He tends to be very surprised, and loses his balance, and falls over backward on top of you, so that you get all the wind knocked out of you and your Gore-Tex parka rides up and rainwater soaks through the seat of your pants and you get all wet.

Plus, the guy lands on your right arm, and you hear a crunching sound, and it really, really hurts, and you can't help wondering, *Was that what I think it was?*

But you don't really get a chance to mull it over for very long because you are too busy trying to keep the guy from getting off another shot, which you do by yelling, "Gun! Gun! He's got a gun!"

And even though by now everyone already knows this—that the guy has a gun, since they heard the stupid thing go off the first time—this seems to do the trick, since all of a sudden about twenty Secret Service agents crowd around you with *their* guns pulled out and pointed right into your face, all of them yelling, "Freeze!"

Believe me, I froze.

And then the next thing I knew, Mr. Uptown Girl was lifted off me—much to my relief; that dude was heavy—and then people started pulling on me, too. Somebody pulled on the arm that the guy with the gun had landed on, and I yelled "Ow!" really loud, but nobody seemed to hear me. They were all busy speaking into their walkie-talkies, saying things like "Eagle is secure. Repeat, Eagle *is* secure."

Meanwhile, sirens started to wail. People came running out from the wrap places and burrito bars to watch.

And suddenly, all these cop cars and ambulances showed up from out of nowhere, practically, brakes squealing and rainwater getting sprayed all over the place.

It was just like something out of a Bruce Willis movie, only without the sound track.

And then one of the Secret Service agents started going through my backpack, while another stooped to pat down my ankles—like I might have a bowie knife or something strapped down there—while a third was digging around the pockets of my Gore-Tex parka without even asking my permission (and ended up getting a handful of Capitol Cookie crumbs for his efforts).

He also jostled my right arm some more. I yelled "Ow" again, only even louder than before.

Then the agent who was going through my pockets went, "This one seems to be unarmed."

"Of course I'm unarmed," I yelled. "I'm only in the tenth grade!"

Which is a totally lame thing to have said, because of course there are tenth graders who have guns. They just don't happen to go to Adams Prep. Only I wasn't really thinking straight. In fact, I was almost crying. Well, you would have almost been crying, too, if

a) you were wet all over.
b) your arm was most likely broken—which actually wasn't so bad, really, because it wasn't my drawing arm or anything, and now I had a built-in excuse not to take part

51

in volleyball, which Coach Donnelly is making everyone do in PE next week—but it still really, really hurt.

c) people were yelling but you couldn't hear so well on account of Mr. Uptown Girl's gun having gone off very close to your ear, probably causing hearing damage that for all you know might be permanent.

d) you had found yourself looking down the mouths of twenty or so guns. Or even one gun, for that matter. And

e) it was starting to seem pretty likely that your parents were totally going to find out about your skipping your drawing lesson.

I mean, any one of those things would have been upsetting. But I had all *five*.

Then this older agent came up to me. He looked a little less scary than the other agents, maybe because he stooped down until his face was level with mine, which was thoughtful of him.

He went, very seriously, "You're going to have to come with us, miss. We need to ask you some questions about your friend over there."

That was when it really hit me:

They thought Mr. Uptown Girl and I were buddies! They thought we'd been trying to kill the president together!

"He's not my friend!" I wailed. I wasn't *almost* crying anymore. I was bawling my head off, and I didn't even care. It was raining, I was wet all over, my arm was killing me, my ears were ringing, and the United States Secret Service thought I was some kind of international terrorist assassin, or something.

Heck, yeah, I was crying.

"I've never even seen him before today!" I hiccupped. "He pulled out that gun, and he was going to shoot the president, and so I jumped on him, and he fell on my arm, and now it really hurts, and I just want to go ho-o-ome!"

It was really embarrassing. I was crying like a baby. Worse than a baby. I was crying the way Lucy cried the day her orthodontist told her she was going to have to keep her braces on for another six weeks.

Then a very surprising thing happened. The older Secret Service agent put his arm around me. He said something to the other Secret Service agents, then walked me away from them, toward one of the ambulances. Some paramedic types were standing there, waiting. They opened the doors to the back of the ambulance, and the Secret Service agent and I climbed in.

It was nice inside the ambulance. I got to sit on a little gurney, out of the rain and cold. You could barely hear the sirens and stuff inside there. The paramedics were very nice, too. They gave me a dry blanket to wrap around me in place of my Gore-Tex parka. They were so jokey and nice, I stopped crying.

Really, I told myself. This wasn't so bad. Everything was going to be okay.

Well, except when my parents found out about how I'd skipped drawing class. That part was not going to be okay.

But maybe they wouldn't have to find out. Maybe the Secret Service agents would check me out and realize that I am not a member of any terrorist group determined to draw attention to its cause, and let me go. Theresa was probably still stuck in all that traffic. By the time she pulled up, the whole thing might be over and I could just get into the car, and when she asked "What did you do today in class?" I could be like, "Oh, nothing." Which would not even be a lie.

The paramedics asked me where I was injured. And even though I felt dumb being such a baby about my arm, considering how serious everything was with, you know, an attempt on the life of the president and all, I showed them my wrist. I was somewhat gratified to see that it had already swelled to about twice its usual size. I was glad I hadn't been crying over nothing.

While the paramedics were examining my arm, I looked over at the Secret Service agent, who was busy filling out a report of some kind that included my name, which he had got off my school ID, which had been inside my wallet in my backpack. I didn't want to disturb him or anything, but I really needed to know how long this was all going to take. So I went, "Um, excuse me, sir?"

The Secret Service guy looked up. "Yes, sweetheart?" he asked. He obviously didn't know that no one calls me sweetheart, not even my mother. Not since Morocco, when she caught me trying to flush my dad's credit cards down the toilet (as revenge for him making us move to a foreign country where I didn't speak the language).

The sweetheart thing threw me. I didn't want to come out and just ask him how long this was all going to take, since it might seem ungracious. He was only doing his job, after all. So instead, after a few seconds during which I desperately tried to think up something else to ask, I went, "Um, is the president okay?"

The Secret Service agent smiled at me some more. "The president is just fine, honey," he said. "Thanks to you."

"Oh," I said. "Great. So, um, do you think it would be okay for me to go soon?"

The paramedics exchanged glances. They looked amused.

"Not with that arm," one of them said. "Your wrist is broken, kiddo. We'll need an X-ray to see how badly, but ten to one, you're going to have a nice big cast for all your new fans to sign."

Fans? What was he talking about?

And I couldn't get a cast! If I got a cast, my parents would want to know how I'd broken my wrist, and then I'd have to admit that I'd skipped class.

Unless . . . unless I lied and told them I tripped. Yeah, I tripped and fell down the stairs to Susan Boone's studio. Except what if they asked her?

Oh, God. I was such dead meat.

"Couldn't I—" I was really grasping at straws, but I was desperate. "Couldn't I just go to my own doctor tomorrow, or something? I mean, my arm really feels much better."

Both the paramedics and the Secret Service agent looked at me like I was insane. Okay, yeah, my arm had swollen up to the size of my thigh and was throbbing the way hearts do during open-heart surgeries on the Learning Channel. But it actually didn't hurt that much. Except when I moved.

"It's just that our housekeeper is coming to pick me up," I explained lamely. "And if you guys take me to the hospital, and I'm not where I said I'd be, she'll freak out."

The Secret Service guy said, "Why don't you give me a phone number where I can reach your parents? Because for you to receive the medical attention you need, we're going to need to contact them."

Oh, God! Then they'll know for sure I skipped class!

But, really. What choice did I have? That'd be none.

"Listen," I said, low and fast. "You don't have to tell my parents about this. I mean, of course you have to tell them about *this*, but not about how I skipped my drawing class and was hanging out in Static. I mean, you don't have to tell them that part, do you? Because I don't want to get in any more trouble than I'm already in."

The Secret Service dude blinked at me like he didn't really know what I was talking about. Which of course he didn't. How could he? Drawing class? Static?

But he apparently thought he'd better just go along with me—as if maybe I'd hit my head, too, when I'd fallen down—since he went, "Why don't we wait and see."

Well, it was better than nothing, I guess. I gave him my mom's and dad's work numbers, then closed my eyes and leaned my head back against the side of the ambulance.

Oh, well, I thought. Things could have been worse.

For instance, I could have a chicken bone where my nose should be.

Top ten pieces of incontrovertible proof that stopping a bullet from entering the skull of the president of the United States of America changes your life:

10. The ambulance you are riding in gets a police escort all the way to the hospital. George Washington University Hospital, to be exact. The same hospital they took President Reagan to when he got shot.

9. Instead of having to visit the triage nurse upon arrival at the emergency room, like everyone else, you are wheeled in right away, ahead of all the gang-bangers bleeding from knife wounds, women in labor, people with pencils wedged into their eye sockets, etc.

8. Everywhere you are sent inside George Washington University Hospital, men in black suits with ear thingies follow you.

7. When they give you a hospital gown to wear because your clothes are all wet, and you refuse to put it on because the back is all cut out, they give you another one, so you can wear one that opens in the front and one that opens in the back, thus covering all of you. No one else in the entire hospital gets two gowns but you.

6. You get your own private room with armed guards at the door, even though all that is wrong with you is your broken wrist.

5. When the doctor comes in to examine you, he goes, "So you're the girl who saved the president!"

4. When you say in abject mortification, "Well, not really," the doctor goes, "That's not what I hear. You're a national hero!"

3. When he tells you that your wrist is broken in two places and that you will have to wear a cast from the elbow down for six weeks, instead of giving you a lollipop or whatever, he asks for your autograph.

2. While you are waiting for the cast guys to come and fix your arm, you switch on your private room's TV and see that on every channel there is a Breaking News bulletin. Then Tom Brokaw comes on and says that an attempt has been made on the life of the president. Then he says that the attempt was thwarted by the heroic act of a single individual. Then they show the picture of you from your school ID.

The one where you were blinking just as the photographer took the picture. The one where your hair was looking particularly bushy and out of control. The one you have never showed to anyone for fear of being publicly mocked and ridiculed.

And the number-one way you can tell your life will never be the same:

1. You scream so loudly when you see your hideous school photo on national television that about thirty Secret Service agents burst into your room, pistols drawn, demanding to know if you're all right.

★ 7 ★

$\mathcal{I}$ $guess$, even then, it didn't really hit me.

I mean, I *knew*. You know, that I had jumped on Mr. Uptown Girl's back and kept him from firing that gun in the direction he'd meant to.

But it didn't hit me that in doing so I had actually saved the life of the leader of the free world.

At least, it didn't hit me until my parents came bursting into my hospital room a little while later, after the cast was on (and after I'd seen my face all over the major networks, as well as CNN, Headline News, and even *Entertainment Tonight*), both of them freaked beyond belief.

"Samantha!" my mom cried, falling all over me and jostling my busted arm, for which, I might add, no one had so much as offered me an aspirin. You would think that a girl who saved the life of the president would rank some painkillers, but apparently not. "Oh, my God, we were so worried!"

"Hi, Mom," I said, all faintly—you know, the way you talk when you're faking sick. Because I hadn't figured out whether the Secret Service guys had ratted me out yet about skipping my drawing class, so I wasn't sure how much trouble I was in. I figured if they thought I was in a lot of pain, they'd lay off.

But they didn't seem to have a clue about my skipping out on Susan Boone.

"Samantha," my mom kept saying, sinking down onto the edge of my bed and pushing my hair around on my forehead. "Are you all right? Is it just your arm? Does anything else hurt?"

"No," I said. "It's just my arm. I'm fine. Really."

But I still said it all faint, and stuff, just in case.

I needn't have bothered. They were both completely clueless about the whole drawing lessons thing. They were just glad I was all right. My dad was able to joke about it, a little.

"If you wanted more attention from us, Sam," he said, "all you had to do was ask. Throwing yourself in the path of a speeding bullet really wasn't necessary."

Ha ha ha.

The Secret Service guys gave us about five minutes for our tearful reunion before pouncing. It turns out there'd been a lot of stuff they'd wanted to ask me, but because I'm a minor, they'd had to wait to interview me until my parents got there. This is just a small sample of some of the things they asked me about:

SECRET SERVICE: Did you know the man who was holding the gun?

ME: No, I did not know the guy.

SECRET SERVICE: Did he say anything to you?

ME: No, he did not say a word to me.

SECRET SERVICE: Nothing? He didn't say anything as he was pulling the trigger?

ME: Like what?

SECRET SERVICE: Like "This is for Margie," or something like that.

ME: Who's Margie?

SECRET SERVICE: That was just an example. There is no Margie.

ME: He didn't say anything at all.

SECRET SERVICE: Was there anything unusual about him? Anything that caused you to pay special attention to him, out of all the people who were on the street?

ME: Yes. He had a gun.

SECRET SERVICE: Other than him having a gun.

ME: Well, he seemed to like the song "Uptown Girl" quite a bit.

And so on. It went on for hours. *Hours.* I had to describe what had happened between me and Mr. Uptown Girl like five hundred times. I talked until I was hoarse. Finally, my dad was like, "Look, gentlemen, we appreciate that you are trying to get to the bottom of this, but our daughter has been through a very traumatic event and needs to get some rest."

The Secret Service guys were very nice about it. They thanked me and left . . . but a couple of them stayed around, just outside the door to my room, and wouldn't leave. My dad told me after he came back with a Quarter Pounder for my dinner, since I absolutely could not bring myself to eat the food the hospital provided, which was some kind of stew with peas and carrots in it.

Like people in a hospital don't feel sick enough already. This is what they give them to eat?

I wasn't too happy about having to spend the night at the hospital when the only thing wrong with me was a broken wrist, but the Secret Service guys kind of insisted on it. They said it was for my own protection. I said, "I don't see why. You caught the guy, right?"

But they said Mr. Uptown Girl (only they didn't call him that; they called him The Alleged Shooter) was invoking his right to remain silent, and they weren't sure if he belonged to some terrorist organization that might choose to avenge itself against me for sabotaging its scheme to assassinate the president.

This, of course, caused my mother to flip out and call Theresa and tell her to make sure the front door was locked, but the Secret Service guy said not to worry, they had already posted agents around the house for our protection. These agents, I later found out, were also keeping the hordes of press away from our front porch. This was somewhat distressing to Lucy, with whom I spoke on the phone a little before midnight.

"Ohmigod," she gushed. "All I did was try to slip the folks from MSNBC a more flattering photo of you. I mean, they keep showing that *hideous* shot from your *school ID*. I was all, 'Dudes, she is way more attractive than *that*,' and I tried to give them that photo Grandma took at Christmas—you know, the one where you're in that Esprit dress, which used to be cute until you dyed it black, but whatever. Anyway, I open the door and go out on the porch with the photo, and all these flashbulbs start going off and all these people start yelling, 'Are you the sister? Would you care to comment on how it feels to be the sister of a national heroine?' and I was all set to say that it feels great, when these two suits practically push me back inside the house, telling me it is for my own protection. I am so sure. What I want to know is, is plastering that hideous photo of you all over the television for my protection? I mean, really, people are going to think I am related to a hideous freak—which is how you look in that photo, Sam, no offense—and believe me, that is not going to do anyone any good whatsoever."

It was good to know that however much some things might change, one thing, at least, always remained the same: my sister Lucy.

So anyway, they made me spend the night in the stupid hospital. For observation, they said. But that wasn't it. I'm sure they were still checking to make certain I didn't secretly belong to any radical antigovernment groups, and wanted to keep an eye on me in case I tried to escape and join my comrades, or whatever.

I tossed and turned quite a bit, unable to find a comfortable position to fall asleep in, because usually I sleep on my side, but it turns out the side I sleep on is the side I had the cast on, and I couldn't sleep on the cast because it was all hard and lumpy, and besides, if I put any weight on it my arm would throb. Plus I missed Manet, which is kind of funny because he is so hairy and smelly you wouldn't think I'd miss him stinking up my bed, but I totally did.

I had finally managed to doze off when my mom—who didn't seem to have any problem at all sleeping in the bed beside mine, and who woke looking fresh as a daisy—got up and threw back the curtains to my hospital room window, letting the morning light in. Then she went, in a manner that, to someone who has hardly gotten any sleep and besides which has a very sore arm, might be somewhat irritating, "Good morning, sleepyhead."

But before I had time to ask what was so good about it (the morning, I mean), Mom went, in a shocked voice as she looked out the window, "Oh . . . my . . . God."

I got out of bed and came to see what my mom was Oh-my-God-ing about, and was shocked to see that there were about three hundred people standing along the sidewalk in front of the hospital, all looking up in the direction of my room. The minute I appeared in the window, there was this roar, and all these people started pointing up at me and waving these posters and screaming.

My name. They were screaming *my* name.

My mom and I stared at each other, slack-jawed, then looked down again. There were news vans with huge satellite dishes on their roofs, and reporters standing around with microphones, and police officers everywhere, trying to hold back the huge crowd of people who had shown up, apparently just hoping to catch a glimpse of the girl who'd saved the life of the president.

Well, they caught a glimpse of me, all right. I mean, even though I was, like, three stories up, they sure didn't seem to miss me. Possibly that's because I was in two hospital gowns and had this great big wad of red bed head coming out of my scalp, but whatever. They caught a glimpse of me, all right.

"Um," my mom went as the two of us stood there, looking down at the big mess below. "I guess you should . . . I don't know. Wave?"

That sounded like a reasonable suggestion, so I lifted my good arm and waved.

More cheers and applause rose from the crowd. I waved again, just to make sure it was all because of me, but there was no doubt about it: those people were cheering. Cheering for me. *Me,* Samantha Madison, tenth grader and celebrity drawing aficionado.

It was incredible. Like being Elvis, or something.

It was after I'd waved the second time that there was a knock on my door, and a nurse came in and went, "Oh, good, you're up. We thought so when we heard the screaming." Then she added, with a sunny smile, "A few things arrived for you. I hope you don't mind if we bring them in now."

And then, without waiting for a response from us, she held the door open. A stream of candy stripers holding floral arrangements—each one bigger than the last—came pouring into my room, until every last available flat surface, including the floor, was covered with roses and daisies and sunflowers and orchids and carnations and flowers I could not identify, all overflowing from these vases and making the room smell sickly sweet.

And there weren't just flowers, either. There were balloon bouquets, too, dozens of them, red balloons, blue ones, white ones, pink ones, heart-shaped and metallic ones with "Thanks" and "Get Well Soon" written on them. Then came the teddy bears, twenty at least, of all different sizes and shapes, with bows at their throats and signs in their paws, signs that said things like JUST GRIN AND BEAR IT and THANK YOU BEARY MUCH!

Seriously. I watched them come in and pile this stuff up, and all I could think was, Wait. Wait. There's been a mistake. I don't know anyone who would send me a Thank-you-beary-much! bear. Really. Not even as a joke.

But they just kept coming, more and more of them. The nurses, you could tell, thought it was pretty funny. Even the Secret Service guys, standing in the doorway, seemed to be smirking behind the reflective lenses of their sunglasses.

Only my mom seemed as stunned as I was. She kept running to each new bouquet and tearing open the card and reading the writing on it out loud in tones of wonder:

"Thank you for your daring act of bravery. Sincerely, the U.S. Attorney General."

"We need more Americans like you. The mayor of the District of Columbia."

"For an angel on Earth, with many thanks. The people of Cleveland, Ohio."

"With much appreciation for your bravery under fire. The prime minister of Canada."

"You are an example for us all . . . the Dalai Lama."

This was way upsetting. I mean, the *Dalai Lama* thinks *I'm* an example? Um, not very likely. Not considering all the beef I have consumed in my lifetime.

"There's a lot more downstairs," one of the candy stripers informed us.

My mom looked up from a card written by the emperor of Japan. "Oh?"

"We're still irradiating most of the cards and running the fruit and candy through the X-ray machines," the Secret Service guys informed us.

"X-ray machines?" my mom echoed. "Whatever for?"

One of the agents shrugged. "Razor blades. Tacks. Whatever. Just in case."

"Can't be too careful," the other agreed. "Lot of whackos out there."

My mom looked as if she didn't feel too good after that. All her daisy freshness drained right out of her. "Oh," she said faintly.

It was right after this that my dad showed up with Lucy and Rebecca and Theresa in tow. Theresa gave me a knock on the back of the head for the scare I'd given her the day before.

"Imagine how I felt," she said, "when the policeman told me I could not get through to pick you up because there'd been a shooting. I thought you were dead!"

Rebecca was more philosophical about the whole thing. "Sam's not a member of the group with the highest risk of death from gun violence—males ages fifteen to thirty-four—so I wasn't particularly worried."

Lucy, however, was the one with the most urgent need to see me . . . and alone.

"C'mere," she said, and pulled me into the room's private bathroom, where she immediately locked the door behind her.

"Bad news," she said, speaking low but fast—the same way she spoke to her fellow squad members when she felt they hadn't been showing enough spirit during the human pyramid. "I overheard the chief hospital administrator ask Dad when you would be ready for your press conference."

"Press conference?" I sat down hard on the toilet. I really thought for a second I was going to pass out. "You're kidding me, right?"

"Of course not," Lucy said matter-of-factly. "You're a national hero. Everyone is expecting you to give a press conference. But don't worry about it. Big sister Lucy has it all under control."

With that, she slung her gym bag into the sink. Whatever was inside it—and I was pretty sure it was probably the entire contents of the medicine cabinet she and I shared—clanked ominously.

"First things first," she said. "Let's do something about that hair."

It was only because I was in such a weakened physical state, what with my sleepless night and the cast and all, that Lucy got the upper hand in that bathroom. I mean, I just didn't have the strength to fight her. I did scream once, but I guess the Secret Service guys couldn't hear me over the sound of the shower, since they didn't come busting in, guns drawn, to save me this time.

But it would have taken a troop of commandos to stop Lucy. She had been waiting for this moment since the day I hit puberty, practically. Finally she had me in a position where I was powerless to stop her. She had brought with her not only a complete set of clothes for me but a small arsenal of beauty products that she seemed intent upon squirting at me as I stood trapped in the shower stall, my broken arm, in its plaster cast, sticking out like a tree branch.

"This is awapuhi," Lucy informed me, shooting something that smelled vaguely fruity at my head. "It's a special Hawaiian ginger extract. Use it to wash your hair. And this is an apricot body scrub—"

"Lucy," I yelled as awapuhi got in my eyes, and I couldn't, having only one free hand, get it out. "What are you trying to do to me?"

"Saving you," Lucy explained. "You ought to be thanking me."

"Thanking you? For what? Permanently blinding me with Hawaiian ginger extract?"

"No, for attempting to transform you into something resembling a human being. Do you have any idea how humiliating it is for me to have people calling me—all night, they were calling me—going, 'Hey, isn't that your sister? What happened to her? Is she in some kind of cult?'"

When I opened my mouth to protest this unfair statement, Lucy just squeezed Aquafresh into it. While I choked, she went on, "Here, use this conditioner, it's the kind groomers use on their horses right before a show."

"I"—shampoo still in my eyes, I couldn't see Lucy, but I swung at her with my cast anyway— "am not a horse!"

"I realize that," Lucy said. "But you genuinely need this, Sam. Consider it an intervention . . . an emergency beauty intervention." Lucy reached into the shower and shoved me back under the spray. "Rinse and repeat, please."

By the time Lucy was done with me, I'd been scrubbed, plucked, exfoliated, and blow-dried within an inch of my life.

But I had to admit, I looked pretty good. I mean, I'd been kind of offended by the intervention comment. But under Lucy's careful supervision—and detachable defuser—my hair soon lost its copper wire stiffness, and instead of sticking straight up from the top of my head was curling loosely to my shoulders. And though she didn't quite manage to make my freckles disappear, Lucy did do something that made them not stand out so much.

I didn't mind the Hawaiian ginger extract, the apricot scrub, or the horse conditioner. I could handle the mascara and the foundation and the lip gloss.

But I fully drew the line when Lucy whipped, from her gym bag, a bright blue blouse and matching skirt.

"No way," I said, as adamantly as I could for someone who was wearing nothing but a hospital towel, and not even a very big one. "I will wear your lipstick. I will wear your eyeliner. But I am *not* wearing your clothes."

"Sam, you don't have any choice." Lucy was already holding up the blouse. "All of your clothes are black. You can't appear in front of Middle America dressed all in black. People are going to think you're a Satan worshiper. You are going to dress like a normal person for once in your life, and you are going to *like it*."

On the words *like it*, Lucy jumped me. I would just like to point out that she had an unfair advantage over me because:

a) she was two inches taller and about ten pounds heavier, and
b) she was not impaired by having one arm in a cast, and
c) she did not have to worry about clutching a towel around her, and
d) she has many, many years of reading *Glamour* magazine's Dos and Don'ts section behind her, lending her style convictions superhuman strength.

Really. Those were the only reasons I gave in. There was also the fact that Lucy had not brought any of my own clothes for me to wear, and the ones I had worn the day before had been taken away by the Secret Service for testing, since there was apparently gun powder residue on them from Mr. Uptown Girl's shooting spree.

When I finally emerged from that bathroom, I was wearing my sister's clothes, my sister's makeup, and my sister's hair products. I basically looked nothing like my usual self. Nothing at all.

But that was okay. Really, it was. Because I didn't really feel like my usual self, either, on account of the no sleep and the people with the signs down on the street and all the Thank-you-beary-much! bears, but also thanks to the awapuhi and all.

So when I came out of that bathroom, I was already pretty weirded out. In fact, I didn't think things could get much weirder than they already were.

And that was when my mom, who was standing there looking kind of nervous amid all of the flowers and the balloons, went, "Um, Samantha, there's someone here to see you," and I turned around and there was the president of the United States.

★ 8 ★

Even though I have lived in Washington, D.C., all my life—except for that year our family spent in Morocco—I have hardly ever seen the president of the United States—and there have been four of them since I was born—in person.

Oh, I have seen him driving past in motorcades, and of course I have seen him on TV. But except for the day before, at Capitol Cookies, I had never seen the president up close.

So seeing him then, standing in my hospital room with my mom and my dad and Lucy and Rebecca and Theresa and the Secret Service agents and all the flowers and the balloons and stuff . . .

Well, it was pretty strange.

Plus, standing there beside him was his wife, the first lady. I had never seen the first lady in person before, either. I had seen her on TV, and on the cover of *Good Housekeeping* magazine, touting her prizewinning brownies and all, but never in person. Up close, both the president and the first lady looked bigger than they do on TV.

Well, duh. Of course. But they also looked . . . I don't know.

Sort of older, and more real. Like, you could see wrinkles and stuff.

"So you're the little lady who saved my life." That's what he said. The president of the United States. Those were the first words the president said to me, in that deep voice I am forced to hear practically every night when my parents make me change the channel from *The Simpsons* to the news.

And how did I reply? What did I say in response to the

71

president of the United States?

I went, "Um."

Behind me, I heard Lucy heave this satisfied sigh. That was because she was relieved she'd finished her beauty makeover on time. A few minutes earlier, and I might still have had bed head.

It apparently did not matter to Lucy that I *sounded* like an idiot. All she cared about was that I did not *look* like one.

"Well, I just had to stop by and ask if it was all right for me to shake the hand," the president went on in his big voice, "of the bravest girl in the world."

Then he stuck out his big right hand.

I stared at that hand. Not because it was any different from anybody else's hand. It wasn't. Well, it was, of course, because it belonged to the president of the United States. But that wasn't why I was staring at it. I was staring at it because I was thinking about what the president had said, about how I was the bravest girl in the world.

And interestingly, even though many of the notes my mother had read off the flowers and balloons and teddy bears had mentioned something along the same line, this was the first time I actually thought about it. Me being brave, and all.

And the thing was, it simply wasn't true. I hadn't been brave. Being brave is when you have to do something because you know it is right, but at the same time you are afraid to do it, because it might hurt or whatever. But you do it anyway. Like me defending Catherine from Kris Parks when she starts in on her about her Laura Ingalls Wilder dresses or whatever, knowing that Kris is just going to start in on me next. Now, *that's* brave.

What I did—jumping onto Mr. Uptown Girl's back—hadn't been brave, because I hadn't really thought about the consequences. I had just done it. I saw the gun, I saw the president, I jumped. Just like that.

I wasn't the bravest girl in the world. I was just a girl who'd happened to have the misfortune to be standing next to a guy who meant to assassinate the president. That's all. I hadn't done anything anyone else wouldn't have done. Not at all.

I don't know how long I would have stood there and stared down at the president's hand if Lucy hadn't poked me in the back. It really hurt, too, because Lucy has these really long nails that she files into points practically every night.

But I didn't let it show that my big sister had just stabbed me in the back with one of her talons. Instead, I went, "Gee, thanks," and stuck out my own hand to shake the president's.

Except, of course, the hand I stuck out to shake was my right hand, the one in the cast. Everyone laughed like it was this hilarious joke, and then the president shook my left hand, the one not encased in plaster.

Then the first lady shook my hand, too, and said that she hoped my family and I would join her and the president for dinner at the White House sometime "when things settled down a little" so that they could really show their appreciation for what I'd done.

Dinner? At the White House? *Me?*

Thank God my mother took over then, saying that we would be delighted to join the first family for dinner sometime.

Then the first lady turned and kind of noticed someone standing in the doorway to my hospital room. And her face brightened up even more than it already was, and she went, "Oh, there's David. May we introduce our son, David?"

And into the room walked David, the president's son.

Who also happened to be David from my drawing class with Susan Boone. Save Ferris David. "Nice boots" David.

And now I knew why he'd looked so familiar.

Well, how was I supposed to know he was the son of the president of the United States?

He didn't look anything like the guy I was used to seeing on the news, the geeky one who'd trailed along after his parents on the election campaign. *That* guy had never worn a Save Ferris T-shirt, much less a pair of combat boots. *That* guy had never seemed interested in art. *That* guy had always been dressed in dweeby-looking suits, and had mostly just sat around looking interested in what his dad had to say, which was basically a lot of stuff that bored me very deeply and usually caused me to change the channel . . . although I know that as a citizen of this country and a member of this planet I should be a lot more politically aware than I actually am.

Anyway, the fact is, after David's dad became president, and David started going to school here in Washington, well, every time they showed him on the news he was in the goofy uniform all the kids who go to Horizon have to wear every day: khaki pants (skirt for girls), white shirt, navy blue blazer, red tie.

And although David certainly looked way better in his uniform than most Horizon attendees, with that dark curly hair and those green eyes and everything, he was still, you know, this huge geek. I mean, there wasn't the slightest chance that this guy was going to be on the cover of *Teen People* every other month, like Justin Timberlake. Not unless he started windsurfing shirtless in the Chesapeake Bay this summer, or something.

Even as I stood there staring at him, it was hard to believe this was the same guy who, only a few days ago, had said he liked my boots.

Then again, maybe it wasn't so hard to believe. Because, you know, seeing him like this—up close and not on TV, waving from the door of a plane, or in a still photo, looking up at his father from a seat off to the side of some dais in Kentucky—he looked much more like the cool guy in the Save Ferris T-shirt who'd liked my boots than he did the president's geeky son.

I really couldn't say which of us, between the two, was more astonished to see the other. David seemed pretty astonished, and I don't think it was because it was such a weird coincidence . . . you know, that we knew each other from drawing class. It wasn't actually all that weird: obviously the reason the president had been in the area had been to meet David after class. The whole stopping-at-Capitol-Cookies thing had just been because the commander-in-chief must have a little sweet tooth. . . .

No, David wasn't staring at me because he couldn't place me. I think he was trying to figure out what had *happened* to me. I mean, last time he'd seen me, I'd been all in black, with daisy-studded combat boots and copper wire hair and no makeup. Now here I was, in my sister's skirt and Cole Haan loafers, with nicely smooth hair and lips that were supposed to look utterly kissable . . . at least that's the result promised on the tube of gloss Lucy had smeared all over my mouth.

No wonder he was staring: I looked just like Lucy!

"Uh," David said, for which I didn't blame him one bit. "Hi."

I came right back at him with a bitingly witty reply: "Um. Yeah. Hi."

David's mom looked from him to me, and then back again. Then she went, in a curious voice, "Do you two know one another already?"

"Yeah," David said again. He was smiling now. It was a nice smile. Not as nice as Jack's, of course, but nice just the same. "Samantha is in my drawing class at Susan Boone's."

That was when it hit me.

Samantha is in my drawing class at Susan Boone's.

This guy could totally blow the one thing I'd managed, so far, to keep my parents from finding out: the whole skipping-art-class thing.

And yeah, okay, what was the big deal, right? So my parents were going to find out I skipped drawing class. So what? *I had saved the life of the president.* That had to be a get-out-of-jail-free card, if anything was.

And it probably would work on my parents. They are not exactly the sternest disciplinarians on the planet.

But it would never, ever work on Theresa, to whom I'd given my solemn word I wouldn't skip class. Much as Theresa esteems the president of this country that she has come to love so dearly, the minute she heard I'd disobeyed her, my life was going to be over with a capital O. No more Entenmann's chocolate doughnuts for me after school. It would be granola bars and graham crackers from here on out. Theresa could forgive just about anything—bad grades, missed curfews, lost homework, dirt tracked in from the park all over her newly washed kitchen floor—but lying?

No way. Even if it had been for a totally good cause, such as preserving my creative integrity.

Which was why I did what I did next, which was throw David a pleading look, hoping against hope that he would understand. I didn't see how he possibly could. I mean, he wasn't wearing his Horizon uniform, but he still had on a button-down shirt and these pants with pleats in them. He looked like a guy who had never, not once in his life, disobeyed his parents, much less his extremely strict housekeeper. How could he possibly relate?

76

Still, if there was any chance, any chance at all, that I could get him, like his dad's Secret Service agents, not to mention that I hadn't been in class last night . . .

"Oh, you have her at Susan Boone's?" the first lady asked my mother brightly. "Isn't Susan *wonderful*? David just loves her." She reached out and touched her son's shoulder in a gesture that was surprisingly momlike for a lady who was married to the most important man in the free world. "I'm just so glad David was late leaving the studio last night. Who knows what could have happened if he had walked out just as—"

She couldn't finish that sentence. I guess she meant who knows what could have happened if David had walked out just as Mr. Uptown Girl started shooting. But the fact is, nothing would have happened. Because I had been there. And I had stopped it.

Please, David. I was sending thought waves at him as hard as I could. *Please do not say anything about my not being there last night. Please just for once in your button-down shirt, son-of-a-politician life, try to open your mind and receive my plea. I know you can do it; you love Save Ferris, and so do I, so perhaps we can, on that level, communicate with one another. Don't say anything, David. Don't say anything. Don't say any—*

"I know exactly what you mean," my mom said, reaching out and touching my shoulder exactly the way the first lady had touched David's. "I don't want to think about what could have happened if the Secret Service agents hadn't disarmed him so quickly."

"I know," the first lady said. "Aren't they marvelous?"

Amazingly, the conversation appeared to be turning away from Susan Boone. Well, except for the somewhat startling revelation that John—the middle-aged guy who couldn't draw at all and who I'd thought was wearing a hearing aid—was, in actual truth, David's own personal Secret Service agent, which was a little weird.

But how weird must David have found it to walk into the hospital room of the girl who'd saved his dad from an alleged assassin, only to find *me* there?

Except that after the initial shock had worn off, David seemed pretty okay with it. In fact, he seemed to find it kind of amusing. Like he was trying not to smile, but he couldn't help it. Probably he was thinking about that pineapple. Just remembering it made my cheeks start heating up.

Oh, my God. That stupid pineapple. Why me? I told myself I'd had a perfect right to draw that pineapple. That pineapple, I thought, had come from my heart, just like Jack had said.

Only if that were true, why did I still feel so embarrassed about it?

Finally, after what seemed like twenty more minutes of awkward chitchat, the president and his wife and David left, and we were all alone again.

As soon as the door had closed behind the first family, my mom exhaled very gustily and sagged against my bed, which she'd hastily made while I'd been in the shower.

"Was that surreal," she wanted to know, "or what?"

Theresa was more in shock than anybody. "I cannot believe," she kept murmuring, "that I just met the president of the United States."

Even Rebecca had to admit it had been interesting. "I can't believe I didn't get a chance to ask the president about Area 51," she said ruefully. "I'd really like to know why the government feels it necessary to hide from us the truth about extraterrestrial visitations to this planet."

Lucy's thoughts on the matter were much less esoteric than Rebecca's.

"Dinner at the White House," she said. "Do you think it would be okay if I brought Jack?"

"NO!" both my parents said, loudly and at the same time.

Lucy sighed dramatically. "That's okay. It'll be more fun to go without him. I can flirt with that Dave guy. He's hot."

You see? You see how little Lucy deserves a guy like Jack? I sucked in my breath, filled with indignation on Jack's behalf. . . .

"Hello," I said. "Don't you have a boyfriend?"

Lucy just stared at me like I was nuts. "So?" she said. "Does that mean I can't ever look at another guy? Did you get a load of David's green eyes? And that butt—"

"That's it," my dad said. "No butts. There will be no discussions of anyone's butt while I am in the room. And preferably while I am out of it, as well."

"That goes double for me," Mom said.

I heartily concurred. Imagine, Lucy looking at another guy's butt when she already had Jack's to look at whenever she wanted!

But Lucy seemed completely oblivious to her own selfishness and disloyalty. She just shrugged and said, "Whatever," before wandering over toward the window. . . .

"Stay away from the window!" both my mom and I yelled.

But it was too late. A huge roar went up from the crowd standing outside. Lucy, startled at first, soon got over it and started waving like she thought she was the pope, or somebody.

"Hello," she called, even though there was no way they could hear her. "Hello, all you little people. Hello, Peter Jennings! Hello, Katie Couric!"

It was kind of funny that at that moment the door opened and a lady in a blouse with ruffles at the neck—who introduced herself as Mrs. Rose, the hospital's chief administrator—went to Lucy, "Miss Madison? Are you ready for your press conference?"

Lucy, her eyes wide, spun around.

"Not me," she said. "Her." And she stabbed one of her pointy nails in my direction.

Mrs. Rose looked at me.

"Oh," she said. "Fine. Are you ready, then, dear? They just want to ask you a few questions. It will only take five minutes. And then you'll be free to go home."

I looked at my mom and dad. They smiled at me encouragingly. I looked at Theresa. She did the same. I looked at Lucy. She went, "Whatever happens, don't touch your hair. I finally got it perfect. Don't mess it up."

I looked back at Mrs. Rose.

"Sure," I said. "I'm ready, I guess."

Top ten things not to do at a press conference:

10. When the reporter from *The New York Times* asks you if you were scared when Larry Wayne Rogers (a.k.a. Mr. Uptown Girl) pulled a gun out from under his rain poncho, it is probably better not to say no, that you were relieved, because you'd thought he'd been pulling out something else.

9. Just because they put water out for you doesn't mean you have to drink it. Especially if when you drink it you accidentally miss your mouth because it is so slippery with lip gloss, and all the water goes dribbling down the front of your sister's blouse.

8. When the reporter from *The Indianapolis Star* asks if you are aware that Larry Wayne Rogers attempted to shoot the president out of a desire to impress the celebrity with whom he was obsessed for many years—Billy Joel's ex-wife, the model Christie Brinkley, about whom Billy wrote the song "Uptown Girl"—it is probably better not to say, "What a loser!" Instead, you should express your concern for the very serious problem of mental illness.

7. When a CNN correspondent wants to know if you have a boyfriend, it would be cooler just to say, "Not at the current time," than to do what I did, which was choke on my own spit.

6. Staring fixedly at Barbara Walters's head, wondering if that is really her hair or some kind of space helmet? Yeah, not such a good idea.

5. When Matt Lauer stands up to ask his question, it is probably best not to squeal into the microphone, "Hey! I know you! My mom has the hugest crush on you!"

4. If a piece of your own hair becomes affixed to your lip gloss, it would probably be better to brush it away with your hand, rather than try to blow it out of the way as if you were Free Willy.

3. When a reporter from *The Los Angeles Times* asks if it is true that you just met the president and his family, and wants to know what that was like for you, you might want to come up with something more descriptive than, "Um. Fine."

2. Just as a general thing, when you have saved the life of the leader of the free world, most people really want to hear about that and, sadly, don't care to hear a long-winded description of your dog.

And the number-one thing not to do at a press conference:

1. Don't forget your sunglasses. Otherwise, because so many people will be snapping flash photos of you, all you will be able to see in front of you is a big purple blob, so when you descend from the podium, you will trip because you can't see where you are going, and you will land in local news anchorwoman Candace Wu's lap.

★ 10 ★

Here's what happens when you stop a crazy guy from killing the president of the United States:

Suddenly, everyone—everyone in the entire world—wants to be your friend.

Seriously.

And I am not just talking about get-well balloons and Thank-you-beary-much! bears (all of which we donated to the children's wing before leaving). When I got home from the hospital the day after that little incident outside Capitol Cookies, there were a hundred and sixty-seven messages on our answering machine. Only about twenty of them were from people I actually know and like, such as Grandma or Catherine or whoever. All the rest of them were from reporters or people like Kris Parks, who seemed to have forgotten all about the whole speech and hearing thing.

"Hi, Sam," she sang into the machine in her smarmy Kris Parks voice. "It's me, Kris! Just calling to see if you want to come to my party next Saturday night. My parents are going to be in Aruba, so we're going to have a blast! But it won't be any fun unless you're there."

I couldn't believe it. I mean, you would think Kris would at least *try* to be a little more subtle than that. She hadn't invited me to a party at her house since the third grade, and here she was, making out like we'd never stopped being friends. It was unreal.

Lucy didn't share my outrage, though. She just went, "Cool, party at Kris's. I'm bringing Jack."

To which both my parents replied, "Oh, no, you aren't," then added that we weren't allowed to go to parties at which there wasn't at least one parent in attendance. Especially with Jack, who got caught skinny-dipping in the Chevy Chase Country Club pool during last year's Christmas ball. (The Ryders were members, though, so the incident was hushed up. Unfortunately not enough to keep it from my parents, however. I suppose they would be happier if Lucy was going out with a guy who never questioned authority and meekly accepted what was doled out to him, like most people of our generation, instead of someone who thought for himself, like Jack.)

Lucy didn't look too upset about my parents' saying she wasn't going to be allowed to take Jack to Kris's party. Instead, she went to the window to wave some more at all the reporters who were out on our front lawn.

Kris Parks's message wasn't even the most unbelievable one, however. We also got calls from half the reporters who'd been at the press conference, wanting to know if they could arrange exclusive interviews with me. All the television news shows—like *60 Minutes, 48 Hours, Dateline, 20/20*—wanted to do a feature on me, and asked us to call them at our earliest convenience.

I am so sure. Like there is an hour's worth of stuff to even say about me. My life so far has basically been just a long series of one humiliation after another. If they want to go in depth on my lisp and how I was cured of it by my irrational desire to call Kris Parks every bad *S*-word I could think of to her face, well, then, more power to them. But somehow I suspected they were after something a little more triumph-of-the-human-spirit-y.

Then there were the calls from the soda companies. Seriously. Coke and Pepsi wanted to know if I was interested in endorsement deals. Like I was going to stand in front of a camera and go, "Drink

Coke like me. Then you, too, can throw yourself at a crazed Christie Brinkley fan and get your wrist broken in two places."

Finally, but most disturbingly of all, was the call I had most been dreading. I'd actually hoped against hope that, when we played the messages back, this one wouldn't be there. But I was wrong. So wrong.

Because message number one hundred and sixty-four contained the following, in an all-too familiar voice:

"Samantha? Hi, this is Susan Boone. You know, from the studio. Samantha, I would really appreciate it if you would call me back as soon as you get this message. There are some things we need to talk about."

Hearing this, I panicked, of course. That was it. All those pleas to the Secret Service guys had been for nothing. My cover was blown. I was dead.

I had to return Susan Boone's call in secret—so no one would overhear what I suspected was going to be a lot of groveling on my part—which meant that I had to hang around and wait while my dad called the phone company and got our number changed to a new, unlisted one. We had to do this on account of the fact that some of the one hundred and sixty-seven messages had been a little too effusive, if you know what I mean. Like some Larry Wayne Rogers types—Larry Wayne Rogers was now tucked safely away in a maximum-security prison cell, awaiting arraignment—who really, *really* wanted to meet me. Apparently, to them, my heinous school ID photo was not a turnoff at all.

The Secret Service guys recommended that we change our phone number and perhaps install an alarm system in the house. They were still hanging around outside, generally keeping people back, while some metro cops directed traffic along our street, which was suddenly getting four or five times the amount of traffic it usually got, with people who'd found out where I lived driving by very slowly, trying to catch a glimpse of me—though don't ask me *why*. I am very rarely doing anything interesting. Most of the time I am just sitting in my room eating Pop-Tarts and drawing pictures of myself with Jack, but whatever. I guess people wanted to see what a real live hero looked like.

Because that's what I am now, whether I like it or not. A hero.

Which is just another name, it turns out, for someone who was at the wrong place at the very worst possible time.

Anyway, when Dad was done dealing with the phone company, I called Susan Boone back—but not until after I'd consulted with Catherine.

"Dinner?" That was all Catherine could say. "You take a bullet for the president of the United States of America, and all you get out of it is *dinner?*"

"I didn't take a bullet for him," I reminded her. "And it's dinner at the White House. And could we please stick to the subject at hand? What am I going to say to Susan Boone?"

"Anybody can have dinner at the White House if they pay enough money." Catherine sounded truly disgusted. "I would think you'd get something better than just *dinner*. You should at least get a medal of valor, or something."

"Well," I said, "maybe I will. Maybe they'll give it to me at dinner. Now, what should I say when I call Susan Boone?"

"Samantha," Catherine said in a voice that was as close to impatient as I'd ever heard her speak. "They don't hand out medals at dinner. They have a special ceremony for that. And you saved the president's life. Your drawing teacher is not going to care that you skipped her stupid class."

"I don't know, Cath," I said. "I mean, Susan Boone is very serious about art. She might be calling to kick me out of her class, or something."

"So? I would think you'd *want* to be kicked out. I thought you hated it, right?"

I thought about that. Had I hated it? Well, not the drawing part. That had been pretty fun. And the part where David had said he liked my boots.

But the rest of it—the part where Susan Boone had tried to wipe out my right to creative expression and keep me from drawing from my heart, totally humiliating and embarrassing me in front of all those people, including, I knew now, the son of the president of the United States—that had been pretty mortifying.

On the whole, I decided, getting kicked out of Susan Boone's art class would not be a bad thing at all.

So as soon as I hung up with Catherine, I dialed Susan Boone's number, anxious to get the whole thing over with already.

"Um, hi," I said, hesitantly, when she picked up. "This is Samantha Madison."

"Oh, hello," Susan Boone said. I heard a familiar cawing in the background. So Joe the crow didn't live at the studio, but traveled to and from it with his owner. Some life for a big, ugly, hair-stealing bird. "Thank you for returning my call, Samantha."

"Um, no problem," I said. Then, after a deep breath, I took the plunge: "Listen, I'm really sorry about the other day. I don't know if you heard what happened—"

Susan Boone surprised me by chuckling. "Samantha, there isn't a human being south of the North Pole who hasn't heard what happened to you outside my studio yesterday."

"Oh," I said. Then I hurried to spill out the lie I'd made up. If I had been Jack, I'd have just told her the truth; you know, that I'd resented her attempt to subjugate my artistic integrity.

But since I am not Jack, I just blabbed the first thing that came into my head:

"The thing is, the reason I wasn't in class was because it was raining really hard, you know, and I got really wet, and I didn't want to come to class wet, you know, so I stopped into Static to dry off, you know, before class, and then I don't know what happened, but I guess I just sort of lost track of time, and before I knew it—"

"Never mind that, Samantha." Susan Boone, to my great surprise, had interrupted me. I will admit it wasn't the greatest lie, but it had been the best I could come up with. "Let's talk about your arm."

"My arm?" I looked down at my cast. I was already getting so used to it, it was like it had always been there.

"Yes. Was the arm you broke the one you draw with?"

"Um. No."

"Good. Then I'll see you in class on Tuesday?"

I had an ungenerous thought, then. I thought that Susan Boone, like Coke and Pepsi, only wanted me to stay in her art school so she could use my celebrity to promote it.

Well, and why shouldn't I have thought this? It wasn't as if she'd fallen all over herself trying to tell me what a good artist I was or anything, the one time I had shown up for class.

"Listen, Mrs. Boone," I said, wondering how on earth I was going to say what I had to say—about her stifling me creatively, and where would we be if someone had done that to Picasso—in a way that wouldn't offend her. Because, you know, she seemed like a pretty nice lady, aside from the whole not-liking-my-pineapple thing.

"Susan," she said.

"I beg your pardon?"

"Call me Susan."

"Uh. Okay. Susan. I really just don't think that I have time for drawing lessons right now." So what if there wasn't a chance this was going to work? It was worth a try. And it was better than telling her the truth. And, I mean, it was entirely possible, what with the reporters camped outside on our lawn, and the rubberneckers cruising up and down our street, and all the sickos leaving messages on our answering machine, that my parents might completely forget about the whole art lesson thing. Under the circumstances, that C-minus of mine in German might not seem so dire. . . .

"Sam," Susan Boone said in a no-nonsense voice, "you have a lot of talent, but you are never going to learn to draw really well until you stop *thinking* so much and start *seeing*. And the only way you are ever going to do that is if you take the time to learn how."

Learn how to see? Hello. Maybe Susan Boone thought it was my eyes and not my arm, that had been affected by my little altercation outside her studio.

Too late, I realized what she was trying to do. Exactly what Jack had warned me about! She was trying to make me into an art clone! To make me start drawing with my eyes, and not my heart!

But before I could say anything like "No, thank you, Mrs. Boone, I don't care to be made into another one of your art automatons," she went, "I will see you in class on Tuesday, or I am afraid I will have to tell your parents how much we all missed you yesterday."

Whoa. Now *that* was harsh. *Way* harsh. Especially for the queen of the elves.

"Um," I said. So much for fighting the system. All the fight went instantly out of me. "Okay. I guess."

Susan Boone said, "Good," and hung up. Right before I heard the click, Joe went, in the background, "Pretty bird. Pretty bird." Then, nothing.

She had me. She fully had me, and what's more, she *knew* it.

She *knew* it! Who would have thought that an elf queen could be so *devious*?

And now I was going to have to go back—go back to Susan Boone's with everyone in the whole class knowing that I'd ditched last time. And probably knowing why I'd ditched, too. You know, about the whole being publicly humiliated part during the critique session the class before.

God! It was all so unfair!

I was still sitting there, shaking my head over it, when Lucy came into my room without knocking, as was her custom.

"All right," she said.

I should have known then and there that I was in trouble, because Lucy had a clipboard and a pen with her. Plus she was wearing her most executive outfit, the green plaid mini with a white shirt and sweater vest.

"I've got you down for lunch and shopping in Georgetown tomorrow with the girls," she said, consulting the clipboard. "Then tomorrow night, you and Jack and I are going to see the new Adam Sandler. You'll have to put in an appearance both at the show and then at Luigi's afterwards for pizza. Then Sunday we've got brunch with the squad, then the game. Then Sunday night is dinner with the president. We can't get out of it; I've already tried. But maybe if there's time afterwards we can get someone to whiz us by Luigi's again, just to see what's up. Some of the gang show up there on Sunday nights to do their homework together. Then Monday— now, this is important, Sam, pay attention—Monday we are going to launch your new look. You are going to have to get up at least an hour before you usually do, too. I mean, there can't be any more of this rolling out of bed, putting on the first thing you see, then slouching into school like it's community service and nobody's going to care how you look, or something. You are really going to have to start making an effort. Besides, it's going to take at least half an hour every day to do your hair."

I blinked at her. "What," I said, speaking slowly because my tongue felt like it was dead weight all of a sudden. "Are. You. Talking. About."

Lucy looked heavenward, then flopped down onto my bed beside Manet and me.

"Your new social agenda, silly," Lucy said. "I'm handling all your public appearances from now on, okay? You don't even have to worry about it. Not that it's going to be easy. Don't get me wrong. I mean, let's face it, your stock is pretty low. And it doesn't help that you hang around with Catherine, who is nice, and all, but talk about fashion challenged. We might be able to overcome it if, you know, you just stop talking to her during school hours, or whatever. Now, the only thing I want to know is, did you dye *all* your clothes black? Are you sure you don't have any holdouts?"

"Lucy," I said. I couldn't believe this was happening. I really couldn't. "Get out of my room."

Lucy tossed around some of her long, silky hair. "Now, Sam, come on. Don't be that way. Opportunities like this don't come around all that often. You really have to grab them when they do. You know, like that brass ring, or whatever it is Dad's always talking about. Although I can tell you, some guy offers me a ring made out of brass, I will so be, like, 'See ya.'"

"LUCY!" I shrieked, picking up one of my shoes and hurling it at her. "GET OUT OF MY ROOM!"

Lucy ducked, then, looking offended, stood up to leave.

"God," she said. "Try to do a person a favor. See if I ever help you again."

Then, to my very great relief, she stomped from the room, leaving me alone in my unpopularity.

Top ten things Gwen Stefani would never be caught dead doing:

10. Gwen Stefani would never, ever allow her sister to pick out her clothes for her. Gwen Stefani has devised her own unique and identifiable style. Gwen finds charming little shirts in thrift shops and makes them look sporty and cool by tying them into a halter top, or whatever. Gwen would never, ever wear the three pairs of navy, gray, and tan slacks her sister spent three hundred and sixty-five dollars on for her at Banana Republic.

9. If Gwen's sister told her she was going to have to dump her best friend because of the bad clothes her mother made her wear, Gwen would probably just laugh dismissively, not throw a shoe at her.

8. It is quite unlikely that Gwen Stefani, in an effort to avoid the reporters staked out in her front yard when it came time for her to walk her dog, would sneak out the back of her house in a hooded sweatshirt, sunglasses, and a pair of her father's khakis with the legs rolled up. Gwen would have strolled boldly out amongst the reporters and used their tireless interest in her as a vehicle with which to promote ska.

7. I highly doubt that Gwen Stefani would turn bright red if the man she secretly loved—who happened to be her sister's boyfriend—told her that she looked nice in her dad's rolled-up khakis.

6. Also, Gwen Stefani has too much integrity ever to fall in love with her sister's boyfriend.

5. Probably, if Gwen Stefani had saved the president of the United States from being assassinated, she wouldn't hide in her house, embarrassed by the hordes of people telling her how brave she was. Gwen would write a song about it, filled with searing wit and self-deprecation. The video would probably feature Gwen's ex, Tony Kanal, as the president, and that weird naked drummer as Larry Wayne Rogers.

   But it would still never get higher than number 5 on *Total Request Live*, as ska is seriously underappreciated by Middle America.

4. If Kris Parks called Gwen Stefani, like she did me just now, and went, "Oh, hi, Gwen. So can you come? I mean, to my party next Saturday?" Gwen would probably say something witty and charming, not what I said, which was, "How did you get my new number?" forgetting, of course, that my sister Lucy had e-mailed our new number to practically everyone in the whole school for fear she might otherwise miss out on one of the many crucial social events taking place this weekend, such as pizza at Luigi's or an all-night Pauly Shore filmfest at Debbie Kinley's house.

3. I am thinking that if anybody ever tried to stifle Gwen's creative impulses, she would never agree, even with the threat of blackmail, to go along with it.

2. Gwen Stefani would definitely never spend her Sunday afternoon, instead of doing the German homework her best friend had brought over for her, composing a letter to her sister's boyfriend, outlining all the reasons why he should be with her and not her sister, then rip the letter into little pieces and flush it down the toilet instead of giving it to him.

And the number-one thing Gwen Stefani would never, ever do?

1. Wear a navy blue suit her mom had bought her from Ann Taylor to dinner at the White House.

★ 11 ★

I have been to the White House many times. I mean, if you live in the Washington, D.C., area, starting in, like, the third grade they make you tour the White House practically once a year, then write a stupid report on it. You know, *My Trip to the White House.* That kind of thing.

I have been to all the rooms they show you on the tour: the Vermeil Room, the Library, the China Room, the Map Room, the East Room, the Green Room, the Blue Room, the Red Room, yadda yadda yadda.

But Sunday night was the first time I'd ever been to the White House not as part of a tour but as an actual guest.

It was pretty weird. Everyone in the whole family was feeling the weirdness of it, except maybe for Rebecca. But since Rebecca had just gotten a new shipment of *Star Trek* books from Amazon.com, this was only to be expected.

Besides, I suspect Rebecca is secretly a robot and therefore immune to human emotion.

The rest of us, however, were totally freaked. I could tell my mom was especially nervous, because she wore her power suit and her pearls, the ones she only wears to court, and she took away my dad's cell phone *and* his Palm Pilot, so he couldn't try to use one of them during dinner. Theresa—who, as an important part of our family, was of course invited as well—was in her Sunday best, which included purple high heels with sparkle clips on them, and didn't yell at any of us once, not even when Manet came barreling in from outside and shook out his fur and sprayed rainwater all over the newly vacuumed living room rug. Even Lucy spent about two hours longer than usual on her beauty regimen, and emerged looking like someone going to guest star on *V.I.P.* and not someone about to enjoy a nice meal with a family who lived, if you thought about it, only a little way down the street from us.

"Now, whatever you do, Sam," Lucy said as we pulled out of the driveway—which was no mean feat, since there were still hordes of reporters hanging around, trying to photograph our every move. They liked to do things like dive onto the hood of the station wagon to snap a quick one of Dad on his way to the 7-Eleven for more milk. Backing out of the driveway had gotten perilous because there were always two or three of them darting out from behind the car. "Do not try to hide the food you don't like under your plate."

"Lucy!" I was nervous enough as it was. I fully did not need her making it worse. "God, I know how to act at a dinner party, okay? I am not a child."

The thing is, at home when we have stuff I don't like at dinner, I fully slip it under the table to Manet, who'll eat anything—carrots, eggplant, peas, cantaloupe, chicken sausage, you name it. The first family does not have a dog. They are cat people. Cats are nice, and everything, but they are no help to finicky eaters like me. I highly doubted the first cat was going to chow down on any cauliflower heads I slipped under the table.

. So the question was, what *was* I going to do if they served broccoli (gag me) or, worse, anything involving tomatoes or fish, two things I really cannot abide and that tend to show up at most fancy meals? I knew I couldn't hide stuff under my plate. Supposing somebody picked it up and saw all the food under it? That would be almost as embarrassing as having drawn a pineapple where there wasn't supposed to be one.

96

It was weird turning onto Pennsylvania Avenue. Normally the part in front of the White House is completely closed off to cars. The only way you can go up to the fence in front of the president's house is on foot.

But since we were special guests, we got to drive right up to the big barricade that blocks off the street. A bunch of policemen were there, and they checked our license plate and my dad's ID, and then they lowered the barricade into the ground, and we drove over it.

Then we were in front of 1600 Pennsylvania Avenue, which is the address of the White House.

But we weren't the only people there, by any means. For one thing, there were cops all over the place, on horseback and bikes, as well as on foot. They were all standing around, talking to one another. They looked at our car curiously as we drove by. Lucy waved. Most of them waved back.

Cops weren't the only ones standing around in front of the White House, though. There were guys selling FBI T-shirts and hats, and other guys with the life-size cardboard cutouts of the president that you could stand next to while you got your picture taken.

And even though it was dark out, there were plenty of tourists, whole families, all asking one another to snap photos of them in front of the big black wrought-iron fence that surrounded the president's house.

There were protestors, too. Some of them had obviously been there a long time, since they had made a little shantytown of tents and plywood shacks, with banners about their cause strung in front of them. NO MORE NUKES, one said. Another said, LIVE BY THE BOMB, DIE BY THE BOMB. I have to admit that, as far as radicals went, they did not look like a very impressive bunch.

Then again, it was pretty cold out, and raining a little. Who wants to protest in drizzle?

Lastly, there were the reporters. There were a lot of reporters. Almost as many as had been standing in front of our house when we'd left. Only the White House had set aside a special place on the lawn for the reporters crowding its front yard. They had huge lights and all these stands with microphones set up, one for each network. When they saw our station wagon as we pulled up to the Northwest Appointment Gate—where the cops back by the first barricade had directed us to go—the reporters started surging forward, the camera people shining bright lights at our car.

"There she is!" I could hear them saying, even though all of our windows were up. "It's her! Get the shot! Get the shot!"

The reporters weren't the only ones trying to get pictures of our car, and us in it. All the tourists standing around in front of the wrought-iron fence turned around when they heard the commotion, and they started snapping shots of us, too. It was kind of like pulling up in a limo in front of the Oscars, or whatever. Except that we were in a Volvo station wagon, and Joan and Melissa Rivers were nowhere to be seen.

A couple of guys in uniform came out of the little house behind the gate and looked over their shoulders at the horde of stampeding reporters. One of them stepped forward to block the path they were beating toward the car, while the other one waved us through the slowly opening gate.

While this was happening, my mom turned around in the front passenger seat and went, in a low, urgent voice: "Lucy, I would appreciate it if, just this once, you would not spend the entire meal talking about clothes. Rebecca, I know you have some questions you'd like to ask the president about the cover-up at Roswell, but I am personally requesting that you keep them to yourself. And Samantha. Please. I am begging you: do not pick at your food. If you don't like something, simply leave it on your plate. Do not sit ·

there rearranging it for half an hour."

I thought this unfair. When you rearrange your food, most people think you have eaten at least some of it.

Then we were driving through the open gates, past the reporters and the camera flashes and klieg lights, up to the front door of the White House.

When you are in front of it, even back where the iron fence is, on Pennsylvania Avenue, the house where the president lives actually looks quite small. That is because the Rotunda, which is the round thing with all the pillars that sticks out of the White House, is actually in the back of the house. The front, where the driveway is, isn't nearly so impressive. In fact, whenever I saw it, I was always kind of, How do they fit all those rooms into such a small space, anyway?

But then you see a shot of the back of the house, which is the one they always show on the news or in movies and stuff, and you go, Oh, yeah, that's how.

When we pulled up to the front of the house, a uniformed man who was standing at the front door snapped to attention, while another man came down to open my mom's door.

Then we all stepped out onto this red carpet, and the front door of the house opened, and there was the first lady, saying "Hello!" and "Welcome!" Right behind her stood the president, who shook my dad's hand and said, "How are you doing, Richard?" to which my dad replied, "Fine, thanks, Mr. President."

Then the president and his wife ushered us into the White House as casually as if we had just stopped by for a backyard barbecue, or something. Except, of course, you don't wear panty hose and a navy blue suit from Ann Taylor to a backyard barbecue. I have to admit, even though everyone was being so welcoming and all, I felt pretty uncomfortable. Not just because of my stupid cast, either, or the fact that Lucy had made me use the horse conditioner again, so my hair felt unnaturally smooth, or even because I knew, just knew, that somehow or other cauliflower was going to end up on my plate.

No, I was freaking out because no matter how casual the president and his wife acted, we were in *the White House*.

And not in the parts you get to see on the public tour, either, but in the private family parts you never see, except on TV, and even then it is some set director's idea of how he *thinks* the family's private quarters look, and not the real thing. The decor actually looked to me a lot like a bed-and-breakfast, like one we once stayed in in Vermont. But then I thought maybe that wasn't fair, since the president and his family had only been living there for a little less than a year, and maybe hadn't really had a chance to settle in.

And besides, it wasn't like this was their *real* house.

Then we were in the living room, and the first lady was saying "Sit down" and "Let me get you something to drink," and I sat down, and in walked David. . . .

And he looked exactly like he had that day in Susan Boone's studio! He had on a Reel Big Fish T-shirt instead of Save Ferris. But other than that, it was like that other David, the one with the pants with the creases in them, didn't even exist.

"Oh, David," his mom said in dismay when she saw him. "I thought I told you to change for dinner."

But David just grinned and reached for some of the mixed nuts in a bowl on the coffee table in front of me. "I *did* change for dinner," he said.

I noticed that he took only salted cashew nuts and left the Brazil nuts in the bowl. I could relate to this. Brazil nuts are gross.

Then dinner was ready. We ate in one of the formal dining rooms. I could tell Lucy was very pleased by this, since her outfit, which was royal blue, went better with the decor in the formal dining room than with that of the private one. Theresa, too, was excited, because of the place settings. They were the formal White House china, and they had real gold rims. Theresa said you can't put gold-rimmed plates in the dishwasher but have to do them by hand. The idea that someone was going to have to hand wash her plate when she was done eating made Theresa very happy.

I was probably the only unhappy person in the room. That is because as soon as we sat down, I knew I was in big trouble, since the first thing they served us was a salad with these big cherry tomatoes in it. Fortunately, the dressing was all right, it was just regular Ranch, so I ate all the lettuce around the tomatoes and hoped no one would notice that they were still sitting there.

Only unfortunately, I was seated in a place of honor right next to the president, and he totally noticed. He leaned over and went, "You know, those tomatoes were imported all the way from Guatemala. If you don't eat them, there could be an international incident."

I was pretty sure he was joking, but it wasn't very funny to me. I didn't want anyone to think I didn't fully appreciate that they were having this nice dinner for us, or whatever.

So what I did was, when no one was looking, I flicked the tomatoes off my plate and into the cloth napkin I had on my lap.

This worked surprisingly well. So well that when the next course came, and it turned out to be New England clam chowder, I ate all the chowder parts and then, again when no one was looking, I dropped all the clammy bits into my napkin.

By the time dessert was going to be served there was about a pound of food in my napkin, including one piece of flounder stuffed with crabmeat; a vegetable medley of peas, carrots, and baby onions; some scalloped potatoes; and a piece of onion foccacia.

It was very easy to hide all this food without anyone seeing me do it because the adults were having a very boisterous conversation about the economic situation in North Africa. The only thing I absolutely could not get away with not eating was a tomato cut up to look like a rose, which was served as a garnish on the dish of scalloped potatoes, and which the first lady scooped up and put on my plate.

"A rose for a rose," she said with a nice smile.

What could I do? I had to eat it. Everyone was looking at me. I choked it down as best I could in one swallow, then gulped down about half of my glass of iced tea, which was what the under-twenty-one crowd got to drink. When I put the glass down, I saw Rebecca, who had started watching me very intently the minute the first lady put the tomato on my plate, do the strangest thing: she lifted up her hands and pretended like she was applauding. Sometimes she does cute things like that, which makes me suspect she might not be a robot after all.

It was right about then I realized something horrible: my napkin was leaking. All the food in it hadn't stained my skirt yet, but it was about to. I had no recourse but to excuse myself, pretending like I was going to the ladies' room. Then I slyly took my napkin with me, just crumpled loosely in my hand, like I had forgotten it was there.

Everywhere you go in the White House, there are Secret Service agents standing around. They are actually very nice men and women. When I came out of the dining room, I asked one of them where the nearest bathroom was, and she walked me there. Once I was safely locked inside, I dumped my dinner into the toilet and flushed it away. I felt kind of bad, wasting all that food, when there are people starving, you know, in Appalachia and all.

But what else was I supposed to do? It would have been rude just to leave it there on my plate.

102

The problem with the napkin, which was soaked through with crabmeat juice, was easily solved by the fact that the bathroom, which was very fancy, had all these cloth hand towels laid out for guests to use, and a gilt basket to throw them in when you were done. I washed my hands and used a couple of the hand towels, then threw them into the basket over the napkin. Whoever emptied the basket would just think I forgot and threw a napkin in there.

I was feeling pretty good about the whole thing—except for the fact that, you know, I was practically starving, having almost nothing in my stomach except a tomato garnish—when, on my way back to the dining room, I practically ran into David, who appeared to be headed toward the same bathroom I had just vacated.

"Oh," he said when he saw me. "Hey."

"Hey," I said. Then—because it was weird, him being the president's son, and all—I tried to sidle away as quickly as possible.

Only I wasn't quick enough, since he gave me that little smile of his and went, "So. You didn't flush the napkin, too, did you?"

★ 12 ★

I couldn't believe it. Busted! I was so busted!

I felt myself blush all the way to my horse-conditioned roots.

Still, I tried. I tried to pretend like I didn't know what he was talking about.

"Napkin?" I asked, thinking that, with my red hair and scarlet face, I probably resembled a big bowl of strawberry ice cream. "What napkin?"

"The one you hid your entire meal in," David said, looking amused. His eyes seemed greener than ever. "I hope you didn't try to flush it. The pipes in this building are pretty old. You could cause a massive flood, you know."

It would be just my luck to cause a flood in the White House.

"I didn't flush the napkin," I said quickly, with a nervous glance at the Secret Service agent standing not far away. "I put it in the basket with the dirty hand towels. I just flushed the food." Then I had a panicky thought. "But there was a lot of it. Do you really think it could clog the pipes?"

"I don't know," he said, looking serious. "That was one big piece of flounder."

Something about his expression—maybe the way one of his dark eyebrows was up, while the other was down, kind of the way Manet's ears look when he's ready to play—made me realize that David was kidding around.

I didn't think it was so funny, though. I'd really been scared that I'd maybe broken the White House.

"That," I said in a whisper, so the Secret Service agent down the hall wouldn't hear me, "isn't very nice."

I didn't even think about the fact that he was, you know, the first son or anything. I mean, I was just mad. They say all this stuff about redheads being hot-tempered. If you are a redhead and you get mad, you can just bet that someone is going to say something like "Oooh, look out for the redhead. You know they've all got tempers."

Which usually just makes me madder than ever.

Of course, I *had* flushed most of the dinner David's mom had served to me down the toilet. In fact, maybe that was why I was so mad . . . because David had caught me doing something so wasteful. Yeah, I was mad, but I was pretty embarrassed, too.

But I was more mad. So I turned around and started back toward the dining room.

"Aw, come on," David said with a laugh, turning around and falling into step with me. "You have to admit, it was kind of funny. I mean, I really had you going there. You totally thought the pipes were going to explode."

"I did not," I said, even though that was exactly what I had been thinking. Also about the headlines in the paper the next day: GIRL WHO SAVED PRESIDENT'S LIFE CAUSES WHITE HOUSE PLUMBING TO BLOW BY STUFFING ENTIRE DINNER DOWN TOILET.

"Yeah, you did," David said. He was so much taller than I was, he only had to take one step for every two of mine. "But I ought to have known you can't take a joke."

I stopped dead in my tracks and whirled around to look up at him. He was pretty tall—taller than Jack, even—so I had to tilt my chin way up to look into those green eyes that Lucy admired so much. I didn't even want to look at that other part of him she'd commented on.

105

"What do you mean, I can't take a joke?" I demanded. "How would you even know whether or not I can take a joke? You barely know me!"

"I know you're the sensitive artist type," David said with that same know-it-all grin he'd given his mom ("I *did* change for dinner").

"I am not," I said hotly, even though of course I totally am. In fact, I don't even know why I bothered denying it. It was just that the way he said it made it sound like something bad.

Except of course that there's nothing wrong with being a sensitive artist. Jack Ryder is a living testament to that.

"Oh, yeah?" David said. "Then how come you didn't come back to the studio after the Pineapple Incident?"

That was exactly how he said it, too. Like it was capitalized. The Pineapple Incident.

I could feel myself turning red all over again. I couldn't believe he was bringing up what had happened my first day at Susan Boone's. I mean, talk about insensitive.

"I'm not disputing that you're a really good artist," David went on. "Just that, you know, you're kind of a hothead." He cocked his head back toward the dining room. "And a bit of a picky eater. You hungry?"

I looked at him like he was crazy. In fact, I was pretty sure he *was* crazy. I mean, his taste in music and footwear notwithstanding, it seemed to me that the first son had some screws loose.

Although he had admitted that I was a really good artist, so maybe he wasn't *that* nuts.

Before I had a chance to deny that I was feeling hungry, my stomach did my talking for me, letting out, at just that moment, the most embarrassing rumbling sound, indicating that all it had in it was some lettuce and a tomato garnish and that this was unacceptable.

David didn't even pretend, like a normal person, that he hadn't heard it. Instead, he went, "I thought so. Listen, I was going to go see if I could round up some real food. Want to come?"

Now I was *sure* he was crazy. Not just because he had gotten up and left the table in the middle of dinner to go look for alternative food, but also because he was asking me to look for alternative food with him. *Me.* The girl he'd just caught throwing away a napkinful of perfectly good dinner.

"I," I said, completely confused. "I mean, we . . . we can't just *leave*. In the middle of *dinner*. At the *White House*."

"Why not?" he asked with a shrug.

I thought about it. There were a lot of reasons why not. Because it was rude, for one thing. I mean, think how it would look. And because . . . because you just don't *do* things like that.

I mentioned this, but David looked unimpressed.

"You're hungry, aren't you?" he asked. Then, backing down the long, Persian-carpeted hallway, he went, "Come on. You know you want it."

I didn't know what to do. On the one hand, that dinner in there was for me, and as the guest of honor, I knew I couldn't just dine and ditch. Also, the first son was clearly a crazy person. Did I want to go wandering around a strange house with a crazy person?

On the other hand, I was starving. And he *had* said I was a good artist. . . .

I looked at the Secret Service agent to see what she thought. She smiled at me and made a motion like she was locking the side of her mouth and throwing away the key. Well, I decided, if *she* didn't think it was such a bad thing to do, and she was an adult and all—one responsible enough to carry a side arm—maybe it was all right. . . .

I turned around and hurried after David, who was halfway down the hall by that time.

He didn't seem very surprised to see me there beside him. Instead, he said, like he was continuing some conversation we'd been having in a parallel universe, "So what happened to the boots?"

"Boots?" I echoed. "What boots?"

"The ones you were wearing the first time I met you. With the Wite-Out daisies on them."

The boots he'd said were nice. Duh.

"My mom wouldn't let me wear those boots," I said. "She didn't think they were appropriate for dinner at the White House." I looked at him out of the corners of my eyes. "*None* of my own clothes are appropriate for dinner at the White House. I had to get all new clothes." I tugged uncomfortably at my navy blue suit. "Like this thing."

"How do you think I feel?" David asked. "I have to eat dinner at the White House every single night."

I looked sourly at his shirt. "Yeah, but they obviously don't make you dress up."

"Only for state dinners, not private ones. But I have to dress up all the rest of the time."

I knew this wasn't true, though. "You weren't dressed up in drawing class."

"Occasionally I get a reprieve," he said with another one of those grins. There was something kind of mysterious about those grins of David's. Most of the time, they seemed to be over some private joke he was having with himself. They made me kind of want to be let in on it. The joke, I mean. Whenever Jack thought of something funny, he just blurted it right out. Sometimes three or four times, just to be sure everyone had heard it.

David seemed perfectly content to keep his witticisms to himself.

Which was kind of irritating. Because how was I supposed to

know whether or not it was me he was laughing at?

Then David hit a button in a door, and an elevator slid open. I probably shouldn't have been surprised there was an elevator in the White House, but I was. I guess because for a minute I forgot where I was, and thought I was just in a regular house. Also, they never showed the elevator on the school tours.

We got into the elevator, and David hit the down button. The door closed, and we went down.

"So," he said as we rode. "Why'd you skip?"

I had no idea what he was talking about. Though of course I should have. "Skip what?"

"You know. Drawing class, after the Pineapple Incident."

I swallowed hard.

"I thought you already had that all figured out," I said. "You said it was on account of my being a sensitive artist, and all."

The elevator door slid open, and David gestured for me to get out before following me. "Yeah, but I want to hear your version of why."

Yeah, I bet he did.

But I was fully not going to give him the pleasure. He would only, I knew, make fun of me. Which would, in essence, be making fun of Jack. And that I would not stand for.

Instead I just went, lightly, "I don't think Susan Boone and I exactly see eye-to-eye on the issue of creative license."

David looked at me, one eyebrow up and one down again. Only this time, I was pretty sure he wasn't being playful.

"Really?" he said. "Are you sure? Because I think Susan's pretty cool about that kind of thing."

Yeah. Real cool. Cool enough to blackmail me into coming back to her class.

But I didn't say this out loud. It seemed impolitic to argue with someone who might momentarily be supplying me with food.

We went down another hallway, this one not carpeted or very fancy. Then David opened another door, and we were in a big kitchen.

"Hey, Carl," David said to a guy in a chef's outfit who was busy putting whipped cream on a bunch of glasses of chocolate mousse. "Got anything good to eat around here?"

Carl looked up from his creations, took one glance at me, and cried, "Samantha Madison! The girl who saved the world! How you doing?"

There were a lot of other people in the kitchen, all busily cleaning and putting things away. Theresa, I saw, had been wrong about the gold-rimmed plates. You could totally put them in the dishwasher, and in fact, the White House kitchen staff was doing so. But they all stopped when they saw me, and gathered around to thank me for keeping their boss from taking one in the head.

"What was the matter with the flounder?" Carl wanted to know, after congratulations had been issued to me from his staff. "That was real Maryland crab stuffed into it, you know. I bought it fresh this morning."

David went over to the industrial-size fridge and yanked it open. "I think it was just, too, you know." For a guy who went to Horizon, David certainly didn't talk much like a certified genius. "You got any more of those hamburgers we had for lunch?"

I brightened at the word *hamburger*. Carl saw this, and went, "You want a burger? The lady wants a burger. Samantha Madison, I will make you a burger the likes of which you have never had in your life. You sit right there. Don't move. This burger's gonna knock your socks off."

I was wearing panty hose, not socks, of course, but I didn't feel it was necessary to point this out. Instead I sat down on the stool

Carl had indicated. David sat down on the one next to it, and we watched as Carl, moving so fast he was almost a blur, threw two enormous hamburger patties onto a stovetop grill and started cooking them for us.

It was weird to be in the kitchen of the White House. It was weird to be in the kitchen of the White House with the son of the president. It would have been weird to me to be with a boy anywhere, since I am not exactly popular with boys. I mean, I am not Lucy. I do not have boys calling me every five minutes . . . or ever, for that matter.

But the fact that it was *this* boy, and *this* place, made it especially weird. I couldn't figure out why David was being so . . . well, I guess *nice* was the only word to describe it. I mean, teasing me about having potentially clogged a White House toilet hadn't been so nice. But offering me a burger when I was practically starving had been pretty decent of him.

It had to be because I had saved his dad. I mean, why else? He was grateful for what I had done. Which was fully understandable.

What wasn't so understandable to me was why he was going so out of his way.

I became even more puzzled about this when, after Carl slid two plates in front of us—each of which contained a huge burger and a big pile of golden fries—and went, "Bon appétit, ya'll," David picked up both his plate and mine, and said, "Come on."

Taking hold of two cans of soda Carl passed to me from the big industrial fridge, I followed David back down the hallway to the elevator.

"Where are we going?" I asked.

"You'll see," David said.

Ordinarily this would not have been enough of an answer for me. But I didn't say anything more about it, because I was in too much shock on account of a boy's being nice to me. The only boy who had ever been remotely nice to me in the past was Jack.

But Jack has to be nice to me, on account of my being his girlfriend's sister. Also, Jack is of course secretly yearning for me. It is even possible that the only reason he stays with Lucy is because he doesn't know that I return his ardor. If I could ever get up the guts to tell him how I feel, everything could be completely different. . . .

But David. David didn't *have* to be nice to me. So why was he doing it? It couldn't have been because he liked me, you know, as a girl. Because, um, hello, Lucy was right upstairs and down the hall. What guy in his right mind would rather be with me than with Lucy? I mean, that was like choosing Skipper instead of Barbie.

When we came out of the elevator, instead of turning back toward the dining room, where everyone else was, David turned in the other direction, toward a door at the opposite end of the hallway. Behind it, I soon saw, was a very formal living room-y type place, with big high windows that looked down the sloping lawn of the White House all the way to the Washington Monument, sticking all lit up into the night sky.

"How's this?" David asked, putting the burgers down on a little table in front of the windows, then moving two big chairs close to the table.

"Um," I said, because I was still in shock about—and plenty suspicious of—the fact that this cute—but somewhat weird—boy wanted to eat with me. *Me*, Samantha Madison. "Fine."

We sat down, bathed in the outdoor lights from the Rotunda. It would have been almost romantic if there hadn't been a Secret Service agent standing right outside the door. And oh, yeah, if David had been remotely interested in me in that way, which he definitely wasn't, on account of the fact that to him I am just the strange Goth-type girl who saved his dad's life, and who also likes to draw pineapples where there are none.

And even if he did like me, you know, in a romantic way, there was the little fact that I am completely and irrevocably in love with my sister's boyfriend.

Whatever. I was so hungry by then, I didn't even care that David was only being nice to me because he felt sorry for me, or whatever.

From the first bite, I knew: Carl had been right. He really had made one of the best burgers I'd ever eaten. I bolted down roughly half of mine before surfacing for air.

David, who'd been watching me eat with a sort of stunned expression on his face—on the rare occasions when I do find something I like to eat, I have a tendency to really go for it—went, "Better?"

I couldn't respond because I was too busy chewing. I gave him a thumbs-up with my cast hand, though.

"So, does it hurt?" he wanted to know, indicating my broken wrist.

I swallowed the huge wad of meat in my mouth. I really would like to be a vegetarian. Seriously. You would think an artist would be way more conscious of the suffering of others, even of the bovine variety. But hamburgers are just so good. I could never give them up.

"Not so much anymore," I said.

"How come nobody's signed it?" he wanted to know.

"I'm saving it," I said, looking down at the nice vast expanse of white plaster around my wrist. "For German class."

He got my meaning. No one else had, except of course for Jack. Only true artists understand the lure of a blank white canvas.

"Oh, sure," he said knowingly. "That'll be cool. So what are you going to go for? A sort of Hawaiian motif? Plenty of pineapples, I'm assuming."

I gave him a very sour look. "I think I'm going to go for a patriotic theme," I said.

"Oh," he said. "Of course. What could be more fitting? You being a Madison, and all."

"What does that have to do with it?" I wanted to know.

"James Madison," David said, his eyebrows up again. "Fourth president. He's a relation, right?"

"Oh," I said, feeling like a dork. "Him. Yeah. No, I don't think so."

"Really?" David looked surprised. "Are you sure? Because you and his wife Dolley have a lot in common."

"Me and *Dolley Madison*?" I laughed. "Like what?"

"Well, she saved a president, too."

"Oh, what," I said, still laughing. "She gave old James the Heimlich, or something?"

"No," David said. "She saved a portrait of George Washington from being burned up with the rest of the White House when the British attacked it during the War of 1812."

Wait a minute. The British had burned down the White House? When had this happened?

Obviously during a war we hadn't learned about yet over at Adams Prep. We don't have U.S. History until eleventh grade.

"Whoa. Cool," I said, meaning it. In history class they never tell you about cool stuff like first ladies running around saving paintings. Instead all you ever get to hear about are the stupid pilgrims and boring old Aaron Burr.

"You sure you aren't any relation?" David asked again.

"Pretty sure," I said regretfully. How cool would it be if I really were related to someone who had done something as brave as rescue a piece of fine art from a fire? Too cool for words, actually. *Were* we related to Dolley Madison? I mean, my mom frequently pointed out that I had to have inherited my artistic temperament from my dad's side of the family, since there were no artists on hers. The Madisons had clearly been great art lovers throughout the ages.

Only it must have skipped a few generations, since I was the only one in the family that I knew of who could draw.

All of a sudden David got up and went to the window.

"Come here and look at this," he said, moving aside the curtain.

I got up to follow him curiously, then saw that he was pointing down at the windowsill. It was painted white, like the rest of the trim in the room.

But embedded deeply in the paint were words that had been carved into the sill. Looking closely, I could make out some of them: Amy . . . Chelsea . . . David . . .

"What is this?" I wanted to know. "The memorial first kids windowsill?"

"Something like that," David said.

Then he pulled out something from the pocket of his jeans. It was one of those little Swiss Army knives. Then he started gouging something in the wood. I probably wouldn't have said anything about it if I hadn't seen that the first letter he'd carved was an S.

"Hey," I said with some alarm. I mean, I am an urban rebel and all, but vandalism that isn't for the sake of a good cause is still just that. Vandalism. "What are you doing?"

"Come on," David said, grinning up at me. "Who deserves it more than you? Not only are you possibly related to a president, but you saved the life of one, too."

I looked nervously back over my shoulder at the door, behind which I knew stood a Secret Service agent. I mean, come on. Son of the president or not, this was destruction of public property. Not just public property, but the *White House*. I'm sure you could go to jail for years for desecrating the White House.

"David," I said, lowering my voice so no one would overhear me. "This isn't necessary."

Intent upon his work—he had gotten to the letter *A* now—David did not reply.

"Really," I said. "I mean, if you want to thank me for saving your dad, the burger is enough, believe me."

But it was too late, because he was already starting on the *M*.

"I suppose you think just because your dad is the president," I said, "you can't get in trouble for this."

"Not that much trouble," David said as he carved. "I mean, I'm still a minor, after all." He leaned back to admire his handiwork. "There. What do you think of that?"

I looked down at my name, Sam, right there with Amy Carter's and Chelsea Clinton's, not to mention David's. I hoped a large family would not move into the White House next, as there would be no more room left on the windowsill for the kids to add their names.

"I think you're insane," I said, meaning it. It was a shame, too, because he was kind of cute.

"Oh," David said, folding up the Swiss Army knife and sticking it back in his pocket. "That really hurts, coming from a girl who draws pineapples where there are none, flushes crab-stuffed flounder down the toilet, and likes to throw herself at strange men with guns."

I stared at him for a minute, completely taken aback.

Then I started to laugh. I couldn't help it. It *was* pretty funny, after all.

David started to laugh, too. The two of us were standing there, laughing, when the Secret Service agent from the hallway came in and went, "David? Your father is looking for you."

I stopped laughing. Busted again! I looked guiltily down at the windowsill—not to mention the empty plates where the burgers had been.

But I didn't have time to dwell on my misdeeds, because we had to get back to the dining room in a hurry. I mean, you don't keep the president of the United States waiting.

When we got in there, though, it turned out the president hadn't been the only one waiting. Every face was turned expectantly toward the doors. When David and I walked through them, to my very great surprise, all the people in the room burst into applause.

At first I couldn't figure out why. I mean, were they clapping because David and I had finally found our way back from the bathroom (they couldn't possibly have known, could they, about the burgers, unless whoever had served the chocolate mousse had told them?).

But it turned out the reason they were clapping had nothing to do with that. I found out why they were clapping when, on my way back to my seat, my mom suddenly stopped me and leaped up to give me a big hug.

"Oh, honey, isn't it great?" she asked. "The president just named you teen ambassador to the United Nations!"

And all of a sudden that delicious burger felt like it might come right back up.

★ 13 ★

"So where'd you go, then?" Lucy asked me for, like, the nine hundredth time.

"Nowhere," I said. "Leave me alone."

"I'm only asking," Lucy said. "Can't I ask you a simple question? You don't have to get all upset about it. Unless, of course, you were doing something, you know, you weren't supposed to be doing."

I had been, of course. Only not what Lucy thought. I'd just been eating burgers with—and having my initials carved into a White House windowsill by—the son of the leader of the free world.

"It's just that you two looked, I don't know . . ." Lucy was examining her lips in the mirror of her compact. She had spent about half an hour lining them that morning—her lips, that is—conscious that today, my first day back at school after the whole saving-the-president thing, a lot of people were probably going to be taking her picture.

A lot of people did take her picture—and mine—as we walked out of our house and down to the station wagon (the Secret Service had suggested that for the next few weeks or so, it might not be such a good idea for Lucy and me to take the bus to school, so Theresa was driving us). So Lucy had been right about that, anyway.

What she wasn't right about was that there was anything going on between me and David.

"Chummy," she finished, snapping the compact shut. "Didn't you think they looked chummy, Theresa?"

Theresa, who is not the world's greatest driver, and who had been completely unnerved by all the photographers who had thrown themselves across the hood of the car in an effort to get my picture, only said a bunch of Spanish swear words as the car ahead of us cut her off.

"I think you looked chummy," Lucy said. "Definitely chummy."

"There was nothing chummy about it," I said. "We just ran into each other on the way out of the bathroom. That's all."

Rebecca, seated in the front seat, remarked, "I detected a frisson."

Lucy and I both looked at her like she was crazy. "A *what?*"

"A frisson," Rebecca said. "A tremor of intense attraction. I detected one between you and David last night."

I was flabbergasted. Because of course there'd been no such thing. I happened to be in love with Jack, not David.

Only of course I couldn't say that. Not out loud.

"There was no *frisson*. There was absolutely no *frisson*. Where would you even get an idea like that?"

"Oh," Rebecca replied mildly. "From one of Lucy's romance novels. I've been reading them in an effort to improve my people skills. And there was definitely a frisson between you and David."

No matter how many times I denied the existence of any frisson, however, both Rebecca and Lucy swore they'd seen one. Which doesn't even make sense, since I highly doubt frissons, if they even exist, are detectable to the human eye.

And while David is cute and everything, I am totally one hundred percent committed to Jack Ryder, who, okay, does not exactly seem to love me back, but he will. One of these days, Jack will come to his senses, and when he does, I will be waiting.

Besides which, David so fully doesn't like me that way. He was just being nice to me because I saved his dad. That's all. I mean, if they'd heard the way he'd been teasing me about the whole pineapple thing, they so totally would give up on this frisson business.

But whatever. Everyone, it seemed, was determined to make my life a living hell: my sisters; the reporters staked out on my lawn; the manufacturers of certain brands of popular soft drinks, who would not stop delivering samples of their products by the caseload to my home; my own family. Even the president of the United States.

"What exactly does the teen ambassador to the United Nations do?" Catherine asked me later that day. We were standing in the lunch line, where we had stood together every weekday of my life, with the exception of my pre-K days, summers, national holidays, and that year I had spent in Morocco.

But unlike all the rest of those times, today everyone standing around us was staring at me and speaking in reverently hushed tones. One particularly shy freshman girl had come up and asked if it would be all right for her to touch my cast.

Oh, yeah. Nothing like being a national hero.

I was trying to downplay the whole thing. Really, I was. For instance, in direct defiance of Lucy's orders, I had not risen an hour earlier for school in order to apply horse conditioner to my hair. I had not donned any of my new slacks from Banana Republic. I had on my normal, everyday, midnight-black clothes, and my hair was its normal, everyday, out-of-control mess.

Still, everyone was treating me differently. Even the teachers, who made jokes like, "For those of you who weren't dining at the White House last night, did you happen to see the excellent documentary on Yemen on PBS?" and "Please open your textbooks to page two hundred and sixty-five—those of you who did not break your arm saving the life of the president, that is."

Even the cafeteria workers were in on it. As I stepped up with my tray, Mrs. Krebbetts gave me a conspiratorial wink and said, "Here, honey," then slipped me an extra slice of peanut butter pie.

In the history of John Adams Preparatory School, Mrs. Krebbetts had never slipped anyone an extra slice of peanut butter pie. Everyone was scared of Mrs. Krebbetts, and with good reason: aggravate her, and she might deny you pie for a year.

And here she was, giving me extra pie. The world as I had once known it came crashing to an end.

"I mean, you must do *something*." Catherine, having recovered from the pie incident, followed me to the table we traditionally shared with a number of girls who, like Catherine and me, were on the outer fringes of popularity—like the frozen tundra of the social geography of Adams Prep. Too antiestablishment to join the student council and not athletic enough to be jocks, most of us either played instruments or were in the drama club. I was the only artist. We were all just trying to get through high school so we could hurry up and get to college, where, we'd heard, things were better.

"I mean, teen ambassador to the UN. What are you in charge of? Is there a committee, at least?" Catherine wouldn't let it go. "On world teen issues, or something?"

"I don't know, Catherine," I said as we sat down. "The president just said he was appointing me as representative from the United States. I assume there are representatives from other countries. Otherwise, what would be the point? Does anybody want an extra piece of pie?"

No one responded. That's because everyone at the table was staring, but not at the pie. Instead, they were all staring at Lucy and Jack, who had suddenly plunked their trays down at our table.

"Hey," Lucy said breezily, as if she sat at the unpopular girls' table every day of the week. "What's up?"

"How'd you get that extra piece of pie?" Jack wanted to know.

The thing of it was, Lucy and Jack weren't the only ones from, you know, the other side of the caf who sat at our table. To my astonishment, they were joined by about half the football team, and a bunch of other cheerleaders, too. I could see that Catherine was completely unnerved by this invasion. It was as if a bunch of swans had suddenly taken over the duck pond. All of us mallards weren't quite sure what to do with ourselves in the face of so much beauty.

"What are you doing?" I whispered to Lucy.

Lucy just shrugged as she sipped her diet Coke. "Since you won't come to us," she said, "we came to you."

"Hey, Sam," Jack said, whipping a pen out from the pocket of his black trench coat. "I'll sign your cast for you."

"Ooh," cried Debbie Kinley, her pom-poms twitching excitedly. "Me, too! I want to sign her cast, too."

I yanked my arm out of their reach and went, "Uh, no, thanks."

Jack looked crestfallen. "I was just going to draw a disaffected youth on it," he explained. "That's all."

A disaffected youth would have been cool, I had to admit. But if I let Jack draw on my cast, then everybody would want to, and soon all that lovely whiteness would be a big old mess. But if I said only Jack could draw on it, then everyone would know about my secret crush on my sister's boyfriend.

"Um, thanks anyway," I said. "But I'm saving my cast for my own stuff."

I felt bad about being mean to Jack. He was, after all, my soul mate.

Still, I wish he'd hurry up and realize it, and quit hanging out with Lucy and her dopey friends. Because these guys were acting like total idiots, tossing corn chips at one another and trying to catch them in their mouths. It was revolting. Also irritating, because they kept jostling the table, making it hard for those of us who had to eat one-handed to keep our food steady. I realize that football players are very large and maybe can't help shaking the table, but still, they could have showed a little restraint.

"Hey," I said when one of the corn chips landed in Catherine's applesauce. "Cut it out, you guys."

Lucy, poring over a magazine article about how to get perfect thighs—which Lucy, of course, already had—went, in a bored voice, "Geez. Just because she's getting a medal, she thinks she's all that," which is totally unfair, because what was I supposed to do, just meekly accept the whole corn-chip-in-the-applesauce thing?

Catherine stared at me, wide-eyed. "You're getting a medal, too? You're teen ambassador to the UN *and* you're getting a medal?"

Unfortunately so. A presidential medal of valor, to be exact. The ceremony was going to be held in December, when the White House was decorated all Christmasy, for optimum photogenic effect.

But I didn't have time to reply. That's because my second slice of pie suddenly disappeared and traveled down the row of football players like a Frisbee in a game of keep-away.

"MAY I PLEASE HAVE MY PIE BACK?" I yelled, because I'd been planning on giving the extra piece to Jack.

Lucy, of course, didn't know this. She just went, "God, it's just a piece of pie. Believe me, you do not need the extra calories," a typically Lucy remark to which I started to respond, until I was distracted by an all-too-familiar voice behind me.

"Hello, Samantha."

I turned to see Kris Parks—looking like the perfect class president that she was, clad in Benetton from head to toe, including a pink cashmere sweater thrown oh-so-casually across her shoulders—simpering down at me.

"Here's the invitation to my party," Kris said, handing me a piece of folded paper. "I really hope you can come. I know we've had our differences in the past, but I'd really like it if we could bury the hatchet and be friends. I've always admired you, you know, Sam.

You really, really, um, stick to your convictions. And I didn't mind paying for the drawings. Really."

I just stared up at her. I couldn't believe any of this was happening. Really, out of all of it—the caseloads of soda, the Thank-you-beary-much! bears, having dinner at the White House—the fact that Kris Parks—*Kris Parks*—was sucking up to me was the strangest thing of all. I was starting to know how Cinderella probably felt after the prince finally found her and got the shoe to fit. Her stepsisters had probably sucked up to her pretty much the same way Kris Parks was sucking up to me.

The thing was, though, like Cinderella, I totally didn't have the heart to tell Kris where to go. I should have. I know I should have.

But it was like this: Why? I mean, what was the point? So she'd been nasty to me her whole life. Like my being nasty back to her was going to teach her a lesson? Nastiness was all she knew.

Kindness. That was what Kris Parks needed. An example to follow. Someone whose gracious behavior she could emulate.

"I don't know," I said, slipping the invitation into my backpack, instead of following my instincts and tossing it into the nearest trash receptacle. "I'll have to see."

Leave it to Lucy to ruin everything by going, without taking her gaze off the magazine in her hands, "She'll be there."

Kris sucked in her breath excitedly. "You will? Great!"

"Actually," I said, shooting Lucy a glare that she missed because she was studying an article about proper cuticle maintenance, "I'm not sure I can go, Luce."

"Sure you can," Lucy said, flipping the page. "You and David and Jack and I can all go together."

"David?" I echoed. "Who said anything about—"

"I just think it is so sweet," Kris said with a sigh. "About you and the president's son, and all. When Lucy told me, I nearly *died*."

"When Lucy told you what?" I demanded.

"Well, about the two of you going out, of course," Kris said, in some surprise.

I really could have killed Lucy then. I mean, you should have seen what happened when Kris uttered these words. Catherine, who'd been gnawing on a chicken leg, watching the whole little drama unfold before her, dropped the chicken leg into her lap. All the cheerleaders stopped gossiping and turned to look at me like I was some kind of new sparkly nail polish, or something. Even Jack, who by then had gotten back my piece of pie, paused with a bite of it halfway to his lips and said, "No freakin' way."

I mean, it was a little upsetting.

"Right," I said. "Jack is absolutely right. No freakin' way. I am not going out with him. Okay? I am not going out with the president's son."

But Kris was already babbling, "Don't worry about it, Sam, I am the soul of discretion. I won't say a word to anyone. Do you think reporters will show up, though? I mean, at my party? Because if any-one wants to interview me, you know, that's all right. They can even take my picture. If you want me to sign a waiver, or whatever . . ."

All this, while Lucy just sat there, flipping through her maga-zine. I couldn't believe it. And I had thought the thing with the *drawing lessons* was bad?

"Hey," Lucy said, for once noticing by my expression that I wasn't exactly happy with her. "Don't blame me. You're the one who went all frisson on the guy, not me."

"I do not," I said, darting a look at Jack, to make sure he was listening, "like David. Okay?"

"Okay," Lucy said. "Don't get your panties in a— Ow!"

Really, if anybody deserved to be pinched, and on a daily basis, it was my sister Lucy.

Top ten ways you can tell that you have suddenly become one of the In Crowd:

10. Kris Parks invites you to one of her notorious make-out parties.

9. In PE, Coach Donnelly picks you as team captain for the first time all year, and when it comes to choose players, all the good athletes actually beg to be on your team.

8. A lot of the freshman girls reappear after lunch in new, all-black outfits fresh from the Gap.

7. The Adams Prep Red Steppers—who perform at halftime during games—ask if you know of a musical selection they might choreograph their next dance number to.

   And when you suggest "Pink Elephant," by the Cherry Poppin' Daddies, they actually take you seriously.

6. In Deutsch class, when you admit you did not finish your homework, someone hands you theirs.

5. You begin to notice that a lot of girls who used to wear their hair like your sister's are now teasing their hair into these giant

mushroom clouds that look not unlike the one that is sprouting from your own head.

4. Everyone in the hallway, instead of painfully averting their gazes as you pass by, like they used to, goes, "Hi, Sam!"

3. You notice your name (scrawled next to Katie Holmes's) across the front of a freshman boy's notebook—with hearts around it, no less.

2. The whole Mrs. Krebbetts/peanut butter pie thing.

And the number-one way you can tell you are now a member of the In Crowd:

1. At the sophomore class meeting last period, when the student advisor asks how the surplus funds in the tenth grade account ought to be spent, and you raise your hand and say, "On new paintbrushes and other supplies for the art department," your suggestion is seconded, put to the general assembly for a vote . . .

And wins.

★ 14 ★

It only took about two hours for it to get all the way around John Adams Preparatory School that I was bringing the president's son with me as my date to Kris Parks's party on Saturday night.

For some reason this was more interesting to people than the fact that I had stopped a bullet from entering the skull of our nation's leader, or that I was the country's new teen ambassador to the UN. While I could not help but be thankful that I was no longer constantly being complimented on my bravery—all the more upsetting because I truly did not believe what I had done had been all that brave—it was somewhat disconcerting that everyone was, instead, making jokes about what might or might not have gone on between the president's son and me in the Lincoln Bedroom.

"Look, you're taking this the wrong way," Lucy said when I remarked upon this at the kitchen table after school. "The fact that you and this David dude are an item—DO NOT PINCH ME AGAIN—is only going to elevate your already sky-high stock. You, Sam, are the new It Girl of Adams Prep. If you would just give up the whole black-on-black thing, you could be voted prom queen like *that*." Lucy snapped her fingers in the air, and Manet hurried over, thinking she might have dropped some of the chocolate chip cookies Theresa had made and that we were all now chowing down on.

"Well, I don't want to be prom queen," I said. "I just want things to be back to normal."

"I'm going to take a wild guess that *that*'s not going to happen real soon," Jack said. He pointed to the reporters we could see holding their cameras up over the backyard fence, hoping to snap a picture of us through the glass atrium.

"Jesu Cristo," Theresa said, and she went to the phone to call the police again.

I sunk my chin down into my hand and went, "I just don't see why you had to tell everybody that. I mean, it is so far from the truth." I said this very clearly, so that Jack would hear. I mean, I wanted to make sure he knew that, if ever he changed his mind about Lucy, I was still available.

"How was I supposed to know what the truth is?" Lucy asked primly. "You won't tell me where the two of you disappeared to last night."

I couldn't believe she would even bring any of that up in front of Jack. Although seeing as how Lucy was unaware of Jack's status as my soul mate, I guess I couldn't really blame her.

"Because it isn't any of your business!" I cried. "I mean, you don't tell me every single thing you and Jack do together."

"Ha!" Lucy stabbed a finger at me, her smile triumphant. "I *knew* it! You two *are* going out!"

"No, we aren't," I said. "I didn't say that."

"Yes, you did. You just admitted it. You said, 'You don't tell me every single thing you and Jack do together,' which must mean you and David are going out just like Jack and I are."

"No, it doesn't," I said. "It doesn't mean that at all—"

My extremely lucid argument was interrupted, however, by Theresa, who, having gotten off the phone with the police, had then gone to intercept a package that had arrived by special delivery.

"For you," she said, setting the package down in front of me. "From the White House, the man said."

We all looked down at the package.

"See," Lucy said. "It's from David. I told you that you two are going out."

"It isn't from David," I said, opening it. "And we aren't going out."

The package turned out to be a packet of information about my new role as teen ambassador.

Lucy, seeing this, turned back to her magazine, clearly disappointed. But Jack got quite excited, reading all the little pamphlets and stuff.

"Look at this," he said. "Hey. There's going to be an international art show. From My Window, it's called. The show will feature teen artists from around the world, depicting, in a variety of mediums, what they see every day from their windows."

Rebecca, who was going over her spreadsheets down at the other end of the table, went, "What about teens who don't have windows? Such as the teen aliens who are being held against their will in Area 51? I don't think they're going to be represented, are they? Is that very fair?"

As usual, everyone ignored her.

"Hey," Jack said, getting excited. Anything involving art excited Jack. "Hey, I'm going to enter this. You should, too, Sam. They're going to display each participating country's winning entry at the UN for the month of May. That's some great exposure. And it's New York. I mean, you get something displayed in New York, you've got it made."

I was reading the letter that had come along with the From My Window pamphlet.

"I can't enter," I said with some astonishment. "I'm a judge."

"A judge?" Jack was delighted to hear it. "That's great! So I'll enter, and you pick my painting, and I'll be breaking into the New York City art scene in no time."

Rebecca looked up from her spreadsheets and stared at Jack in disbelief. "Sam can't do that," she said. "That would be cheating!"

"It's not cheating," Jack said, "if my painting is the best."

"Yeah, but what if it's not?" Lucy wanted to know. She is the worst girlfriend. I never saw anyone so unsupportive of the man she supposedly loves!

"It will be," Jack said with a shrug of his big shoulders, like that settled that.

Jack was right, of course: his painting would be best. Jack's paintings were always the best. They had been good enough to get him into every single art show he'd ever applied to. There wasn't any doubt in my mind that next fall, in spite of his bad grades, lack of extracurriculars, and poor attendance record, Jack would get into one of the top art schools in the country, Rhode Island School of Design or Parsons or even Yale. He was just that good.

And my opinion had nothing to do with the fact that I happened to be madly in love with him.

I pretty much managed to forget the whole David thing until Catherine called later that evening, while I was trying to do my Deutsch homework.

"So," she said. "Are you going to Kris's party?"

"No way."

"Why not?"

"Um, because Kris Parks is the spawn of Satan," I said in some surprise. "You know that better than anybody."

There was this pause. Then Catherine said, slowly, "Yeah. I do know that. But I've always wanted to go to one of her parties."

I couldn't believe it. I actually took the phone away from my face and stared at it for a few seconds before putting it back up to my ear and going, "Cath, what are you talking about? After the way she's always treated you?"

"I know," Catherine said, sounding miserable. "But everyone always talks about Kris's parties afterwards, like about how fun they were. I don't know. She gave me an invitation, too. And I was kind of thinking of going. If you were going, that is."

"Well, I am not going," I said. "Even Larry Wayne Rogers could not force me to go there if he threatened to make me listen to 'Uptown Girl' fifty million times and break BOTH my arms."

There was a pause. Then Catherine said the most surprising thing. She went, "Well, I still kind of want to go."

I was speechless. If Catherine had said she was thinking of shaving her head and joining the Hare Krishnas, I would not have been more surprised.

"You want to go to Kris Parks's party?" I said it so loudly that Manet, who'd been sleeping on my bed with his head in my lap, woke up and looked around, startled. "Catherine, have you been using those fruit-scented markers again? Because I thought I told you that they make you all—"

"Sam, I'm serious," Catherine said. Her voice sounded very small. "We never do stuff normal kids do."

"That is so totally untrue," I said. "Just last month we went to the Drama Club's production of *The Seagull*, didn't we?"

"Sam, we were, like, the only people in the audience who weren't actually related to someone who was in the play. I just really want, for once in my life, to see what it feels like. To be, you know, part of the In Crowd. Haven't you ever wondered?"

"Cath, I already know. I live with one of them, remember? And it isn't pretty. There is a *lot* of hair gel involved."

Catherine's voice sounded small. "It's just that I may never get another chance, you know?"

"Cath," I said. "Kris Parks has been nothing but mean to you the whole time you've known her, and now you want to go to her *house?* I'm sorry, but that is just—"

"Sam," Catherine said, still in that same small voice. "I met a boy."

I nearly dropped the phone. "You what? You met a what?"

"A boy," Catherine said, really fast, like if she didn't get it all out at once, she'd never say it. "You don't know him. He doesn't go to Adams. He goes to Phillips Academy. His name is Paul. My parents know his parents from church. He's always at Beltway Billiards when my brothers and I are there. He's really nice. He has high score on Death Storm."

I guess I was in shock or something, since all I could think of to say was, "But . . . what about Heath?"

"Sam, I have to face reality about Heath," Catherine said, sounding braver than I'd ever heard her. "Even if I ever did get to meet him, no way is he going to go out with a high school girl. Besides, most of the time he lives in Australia. When am I ever going to be in Australia? My mom and dad barely even let me go to the mall by myself."

I was still in shock. "But they're going to let you go out with this Paul guy?"

"Well," Catherine said. "Paul hasn't exactly asked me out yet. I think he's shy. That's why I was thinking I'd ask him out. You know. To Kris's party."

I completely failed to see the logic behind this. "Cath, why don't you ask him to go see a movie with you or something? Why do you have to take him to Kris's party?"

"Because Paul only knows me from church," Catherine said. "And from Beltway Billiards. He doesn't know I don't hang with the In Crowd. He thinks I'm cool."

I didn't know quite how to put this next part, but I figured I had to say it. That's what best friends are for, after all. "But, Cath," I said.

"I mean, he's going to know you don't hang with the In Crowd when you walk through Kris's front door and she says one of her typically nasty things to you in front of him."

"She won't do that," Catherine said, more confident than I'd ever heard her.

"She won't?" I was very surprised to hear this. "Do you know something about Kris that I don't know? Has she undergone a religious conversion, or something?"

"She won't say anything mean to me if you're there," Catherine said. "And you bring David."

I burst out laughing. I couldn't help it.

"David?" I cried. "Cath, I am not going to Kris's party, and even if I did, I would never bring *David*. I mean, I don't even like him. You know I don't. You know who I like." I couldn't say the name out loud, though, just in case Lucy picked up the extension, which she did frequently, to complain that I'd been on too long and that she needed to make a call.

I didn't have to say his name, though. Because Catherine knew who I was referring to.

"I know, Sam," Catherine said. Her voice sounded small again. "Only . . . well, I just thought . . . I mean, if you think about it, he's kind of like your Heath, you know? Jack is. I mean, he doesn't live in Australia, but . . ."

. . . my chances of ever getting him were, like, nil. She didn't have to say it. I knew what she was thinking.

Except that Catherine was wrong. Because I was going to get Jack someday. I really was. If I was just patient, and played my cards right, he'd look around one day and realize that I was—that I always had been—the perfect girl for him.

It was just a matter of time.

Top ten signs that Jack loves me and not my sister Lucy and just hasn't realized it yet:

10. Whenever he sees me, he asks if I've read the latest issue of *Art in America*. He never asks Lucy if she's read it, because he knows all Lucy ever reads are fashion magazines and the Star Track section of *Parade* magazine's Sunday supplement.

9. He burned that CD for me. And true, all it had on it was whale music, which is what Jack likes to listen to while he paints, but the fact that he went to the trouble is indicative of his yearning for us to make an emotional connection.

8. He paid for my double cheeseburger meal that time at the mall when I forgot my wallet.

7. He let me have all the yellow ones out of his box of Jujubes when we all went to see the Harry Potter movie (even though technically Jack is opposed to the commercialization of children's book characters; he just went because the Jackie Chan movie playing at the theater next door was sold out).

6. He said he liked my pants that one time.

5. He complains that Lucy takes too long putting on her makeup. He told me he prefers a girl who wears no makeup. Um, that would be me. Well, except for concealer. And mascara. And lip gloss. But other than that, I wear no makeup at all.

4. When I told him my theory about how all left-handers were once part of a pair of twins, he said that made sense; he is left-handed, too, and has always felt a sense of aloneness in the world. Rebecca's theory—that we are all descended from a race of aliens who accidentally crash-landed on this planet and lost all their advanced technological knowledge in the ensuing fiery conflagration of the mother ship—did not impress him nearly as much. And Lucy's theory—that Mr. PiBB and Dr Pepper are the same drink, just with different packaging—impressed him not at all.

3. When the Drama Club needed volunteers to paint scenery for the production of *Hello Dolly!*, Jack and I both signed up, and later ended up painting *the same plywood street lamp* (he did the trim, I did the highlights). If that was not kismet, I don't know what is.

2. Jack is a Libra. I am an Aquarius. Libras and Aquarians are known for getting along. Lucy, who is a Pisces, should really be going out with a Taurus or Capricorn.

And the number-one sign that Jack loves me and just doesn't know it yet:

1. *Fight Club* is his favorite book, too. Right after *Catch-22* and *Zen and the Art of Motorcycle Maintenance*.

★ 15 ★

On Tuesday, when Theresa drove up to the corner of R and Connecticut, across from the Founding Church of Scientology, you couldn't even see Capitol Cookies. You couldn't see Static, either.

That's because so many reporters were standing on the corner, waiting to interview me as I made my way into Susan Boone's.

Don't even ask me how they found out what time my drawing lessons were. I guess they figured out when David's were, since they knew he and I were in the same class (that had been in the papers when they'd explained how I'd happened to be standing on the same street corner at the same time as Larry Wayne Rogers and the president).

Whatever. It didn't really matter how they'd found out. The fact was, I shouldn't have been surprised. I mean, they were everywhere, these reporters. Outside our house. Outside Adams Prep. Outside the Bishop's Garden when I made the mistake of going to walk Manet there. Outside Potomac Video, for crying out loud, where they'd practically ambushed me and Rebecca the other day when we'd been returning her favorite movie, *Close Encounters of the Third Kind*.

And while I could fully appreciate that they had a deadline or whatever and needed a story, I could not for the life of me fathom why that story had to be about me. I mean, all I did was save the president. It's not like I have anything to *say*.

"Excuse me!" Theresa yelled. She double-parked (it was unlikely the car was going to get towed with half a dozen cameramen draped over it) and, shielding me with her leopard-print raincoat, and using her elbows and purse as battering rams, ran with me to the studio door.

"Samantha," the reporters yelled as we went barreling through them. "How do you feel about the fact that Larry Wayne Rogers has been judged incompetent to stand trial due to mental illness?"

"Samantha," someone else screamed, "what political party do your parents belong to?"

"Samantha," another one called. "America wants to know: Coke or Pepsi?"

"Jesu Cristo," Theresa yelled at someone who made the mistake of tugging on her purse to keep us within microphone reach a little longer. "Hands off the bag! That's Louis Vuitton, in case you didn't notice!"

Then we burst into the bottom of the stairwell leading up to Susan Boone's . . .

. . . practically running over David and John, who had apparently come in just seconds ahead of us, though I hadn't noticed them in the crowd.

Theresa was so mad about someone having touched her purse, she couldn't say anything except Spanish swear words for a whole minute. John, David's Secret Service agent, tried to calm her down by saying that he had called for police backup and an officer was going to escort her back to her car. Also that the reporters would be held back by barricades when we came out again.

I looked at David, and noticed that he was smiling his secret little smile again. He had on a Blink 182 T-shirt under his brown suede jacket today, indicating that his musical taste was not, as I sometimes feared mine was, too restrictive. The shirt was black, which somehow seemed to bring out the green in his eyes more than ever. Either that, or it was just the lighting in the stairwell, or something.

"Hey," David said to me, the secret smile getting a little wider.

I don't know why, but something about that smile made my heart do this weird skittering thing.

But that of course was impossible. I mean, I don't even like David. I like Jack.

Then for some reason I remembered Rebecca and her stupid frisson thing. Was that it? I wondered. Was it frisson when you saw a guy smile and it made your heart act all weird?

All I could say was, I was glad David didn't go to Adams Prep, and so hadn't heard all the Lincoln Bedroom stuff that had been going around. I mean, it was bad enough I felt frisson for the guy. The last thing I needed was him knowing everyone in my entire school seemed to know it.

Just the thought that I could feel frisson for anyone but Jack put me in a really bad mood. Or maybe it had been all the reporters. In any case, instead of saying hi or whatever to David, I went, "Doesn't all that *bother* you?" I jerked my cast in the direction of the reporters. "I mean, that's just scary, and you're *smiling*."

"You think the *press* is scary?" David asked. Now he wasn't just smiling. He was laughing. "Aren't you the girl who jumped on the back of a crazy man who was holding a *gun*?"

I blinked at him. Laughing, I couldn't help noticing David looked even better than when he was smiling.

But I quickly squelched any such notion, and said in a businesslike way, "That wasn't scary. It was just what I had to do. You'd have done it, if you'd been there."

"I wonder," David said thoughtfully.

And then Theresa's police escort arrived and when she opened the door to go back out again, all chance of having a conversation in the stairwell was lost in the shouts of the reporters. John kind of herded us up the stairs, and we went in and there were the benches, exactly as they'd been the last—and only—time I'd been there. The only real difference was that the fruit that had been on the table in the middle of the circle of benches was gone. Instead there was just this white egg sitting there. I thought maybe Susan Boone had forgotten part of her lunch, or something. Either that or Joseph was really Josephine and nobody had bothered to mention it to me.

"So," David said as we settled onto our benches and got our drawing pads all ready, and stuff. "What's it going to be today? Pineapple again? Or are you going to try for something a little more seasonal . . . squash, perhaps?"

"Would you shut up already," I said, not loudly enough for anyone else to hear, "about the pineapple thing?" I couldn't believe I had actually experienced frisson with a guy who did nothing but tease me.

"Oh, sorry," David said, but he didn't look very sorry. I mean, he was still smiling. "I forgot about you being a sensitive artist and all."

"Just because I'm not willing," I muttered, glaring at Susan Boone, who was over at the slop sink rinsing out some brushes, "to have my creative impulses stamped out by some art dictator doesn't mean I am overly sensitive."

Both of David's eyebrows went up at the same time. "What are you talking about?" he asked.

"Susan Boone," I said, sending a dirty look in the elf queen's direction. "This whole draw-what-you-see thing. I mean, it's bogus."

"Bogus?" David had finally stopped smiling. Now he just looked confused. "How is it bogus?"

"Because where would the art world be," I whispered, "if Picasso only drew what he saw?"

David blinked at me. "Picasso did only draw what he saw," he said. "For years and years. It was only after he'd mastered the ability to draw whatever he was looking at with absolute precision that Picasso began experimenting with perceptions of line and space."

I stared at him. "What?" I asked intelligently. I hadn't understood a word he'd said.

David said, "Look, it's simple. Before you can start trying to change the rules, you have to learn what the rules are. That's what Susan is trying to teach us. She just wants you to learn to draw what you see first, before you move on to cubism, or pineapple-ism, or whatever-ism it is you choose eventually to espouse."

It was my turn to blink. This was all news to me. Jack had certainly never said anything about getting to know the rules before trying to break them. And Jack knew all about breaking the rules. I mean, wasn't that what he was always doing in order to show people—like his dad, and all those people at the country club, and Mr. Esposito, back at school—the error of their ways?

Then Susan Boone stepped away from the sink and clapped her hands.

"Okay, class," she said. "As I'm sure all of you know by now, there was some excitement last week after class"—this caused some laughter from Gertie and Lynn and the others— "maybe a little more excitement for some of us than others." Susan Boone smiled meaningfully at me. "But we're all here now, and thankfully unscathed . . . well, for the most part. So let's get back to work, shall we? See this egg?" Susan Boone pointed to the egg on the table in front of us. "Today I want you all to paint this egg. Those of you who are unaccustomed to paint may use colored pencils or chalk."

I looked at the egg on the table. It was sitting on a piece of white silk. I looked down at the handful of colored pencils Susan Boone had dropped onto my bench. There wasn't a single white one.

I sighed, and raised my hand.

Well, what was I supposed to do? I mean, here this woman had practically blackmailed me into coming back to her class, and then when I got there, she didn't even give me a white colored pencil . . . yet she expected me to draw what I saw? What was she thinking? I mean, I am all for learning the rules before I break them, but this didn't seem like it was even on the rules list.

"Yes, Sam," Susan said, coming over to my bench.

"Yeah," I said, putting my hand down. "I don't have a white-colored pencil."

"No, you don't," Susan Boone said. Then she just smiled down at me and started to walk away.

"Wait," I said, conscious that David, who was sitting next to me, was probably listening. He looked pretty absorbed in his own painting, which he'd started as soon as Susan Boone had stopped talking to the class, but you never knew.

"How am I supposed to draw a white egg sitting on a white sheet when I don't have a white pencil?" I didn't mean to sound whiny, or anything. I really couldn't figure out what it was Susan Boone wanted. I mean, was I supposed to work with negative space, or something? Just put in the shadows and leave the rest white? What?

Susan Boone looked at the egg. Then she said the most astonishing thing I had heard in a while, and I had heard some pretty astonishing things lately, not the least of which was that my best friend, Catherine, wanted to be part of the In Crowd.

"I don't see any white there," Susan Boone said mildly.

I looked at her like she was crazy. Why, that egg and that sheet were as white as . . . well, as white as the hair streaming down her shoulders.

"Um," I said. "Excuse me?"

Susan bent down so that she was looking at the egg on my same eye level.

"Remember what I said, Sam," she said. "Draw what you *see*, not what you know. You *know* there is a white egg on a white sheet in front of you. But do you really *see* any white there? Or do you see the pink reflected from the sun in the window? Or the blue and purple of the shadows beneath the egg? The yellow of the overhead light, where it is reflected on the top curve of the egg? The faint green where the silk meets the table? Those are the colors *I* see. No white. No white at all."

It didn't seem to me that, in any part of this speech, there was anything remotely smacking of an attempt to stamp out my natural creativity and style. You have to learn the rules, David had pointed out, before you can break them. Susan Boone was really trying, just as he had said, to get me to see.

So I looked. I looked hard. Harder, really, than I'd ever looked at anything before.

And I saw.

It sounds dumb, I know. I mean, I've always been able to see. I have twenty-twenty vision.

But suddenly, I saw.

I saw the purple shadow beneath the egg.

I saw the pink light from the sun outside the window.

I even saw the little yellow moon of light reflected on the top of the egg.

And so, moving really fast, I picked up the first pencil I could reach and started sketching.

Here is what I love about drawing:

When you are drawing, it is like the whole world around you ceases to exist. It is just you and the page and the pencil, and maybe the soft classical music in the background, or whatever, but you don't actually hear it, because you are so absorbed in what you are doing. When you are drawing, you are not aware of time passing, or what is happening around you. When a drawing is going really well, you could sit down at one o'clock and not look up again until five, and not even have any idea that so much time has gone by until someone mentions it, because you have been so caught up in what you are creating.

There is really nothing in the world, I have found, that is like it. Watching movies? Reading? Not really. Not unless the story is really, really good. And very few are. When you are drawing, you are in your own world, of your own creation.

And there is no world better than that.

Which is why, when you are that deeply engrossed in a drawing, and something happens to bring you out of that world, it is about a hundred times as annoying as when you are doing geometry or something and your sister comes barging into your room to ask if she can borrow a Scrunchie, or whatever. When you are drawing and someone does something like that, I think it would be almost justifiable to murder that person.

Of course, if the person is a big black crow, you would be even more justified.

"Squawk!" Joe the crow yelled in my ear as he yanked a half dozen hairs from the top of my head, then took off, his wings flapping noisily.

I screamed.

I couldn't help it. I had been so involved in my drawing, I had been completely unaware of the bird's approach, totally oblivious to his sneak attack. I didn't scream so much because what he'd done hurt—although it did—but because I just wasn't expecting it.

144

"Joseph," Susan Boone cried, clapping her hands. "Bad bird! Bad bird!"

Joe fled to the safety of his cage, where he dropped my hairs and let out a triumphant "Pretty bird!"

"You are *not* a pretty bird," Susan Boone corrected him, like he could actually understand her. "You are a very *bad* bird." Then she turned around and said to me, "Oh, Samantha, I am so sorry. Are you all right?"

I touched the raw place on my scalp Joe had created. As I did so, I looked around and noticed something: the light had changed. It was no longer pink. The sun had set. It was already after five, but to me, only about two minutes seemed to have passed since I'd started drawing, not nearly two hours.

"I forgot to lock his cage," Susan was saying. "I'll have to remember to do that every time you're here. I have no idea why he is so obsessed with your hair. I mean, it *is* very bright, but . . ."

It was around this time that I began to notice that the bench next to mine was shaking. I looked over there to see if David was having a seizure or something, then realized he wasn't seizing at all. He was laughing.

He noticed my gaze and said, between gasps from laughing so hard, "I'm sorry! I swear, I'm sorry! But if you could have seen your face when that bird landed on you . . ."

I can take a joke as well as the next person, but I did not happen to think this one was particularly funny. It *hurts* when someone— or something—pulls out your hair. Not as much as breaking your wrist, maybe, but still.

David, whose shoulders—not as big as Jack's, but still undeniably impressive as guys' shoulders go—were still shaking with laughter, went, "Come on. You gotta admit. That was funny."

145

Of course he was right. It *had* been funny.

But before I had a chance to confess this, Susan Boone was at my side, looking down at my drawing. Since she was looking at it, I looked at it, too. I had, of course, been looking at it all afternoon. But this was my first chance to sit back and really see what I had done.

And I couldn't believe what I saw. It was a white egg. Sitting on a piece of white silk. It looked exactly like the white egg and the white silk in front of me.

But I hadn't used a single bit of white.

"There," Susan Boone said in a satisfied voice. "You've got it. I knew you would."

Then she patted me on the head in a distracted way, right on the tender spot where her crow had stolen my hair.

But it didn't hurt. It didn't hurt at all. Because I knew Susan Boone was right: I had got it.

I had begun, finally, to see.

Top ten duties of the U.S. teen ambassador to the UN, as perceived by me, Samantha Madison:

10. Sit around in the White House press secretary's office and listen to him gloat over how high the president's public approval rating has shot in the wake of the botched assassination attempt on him.

9. Also listen to the press secretary moan about how the city is complaining about all the cops they keep having to dispatch to my house to keep away the press, and why can't I just go on *Dateline* or *60 Minutes* and get interviewed already. Then after they show it a million times, everybody will get sick of me and leave me alone.

   Yeah. Like I have anything to say that the American viewing public will find even remotely interesting. As if.

8. Make photocopies of the rules and regulations of the international From My Window art show for all of my artistic friends, of which I have one, my sister's boyfriend and my soul mate, Jack Ryder.

7. Autograph photos of myself for all the kids who are writing in asking for signed photos of me. Though why anyone would want to hang a photo of me in their room is completely beyond me.

6. Read my fan mail (after it has been irradiated and checked for razor blades and explosives). An enormous segment of the population seems to feel the need to write to me to tell me how brave it finds me. Some of these people even send me money. Unfortunately, this money is immediately put into a trust fund to send me to college, so it is not like I can buy CDs with it.

   I also supposedly get a lot of letters from pervs, but I don't even get to see those. The press secretary keeps all those in a special file and won't let me bring them to school to show Catherine.

5. In spite of the fact that the UN is in New York, no one has shown any sign of actually taking me there. To New York, I mean. Apparently, actually going to the UN isn't really part of the top ten duties of the teen ambassador to the UN.

4. Bouncing a Superball off the side of the wall of the press secretary's office, while it helps to pass the time while I am stuck in there, which I am supposed to be every Wednesday afternoon, is not technically a duty of the teen ambassador to the UN and only serves to annoy the press secretary and his staff, who confiscated the ball and told me I could have it back when my tenure as teen ambassador was over. Apparently they are unaware of the fact that you can buy Superballs on just about every street corner, and for less than a dollar.

3. Teen ambassadors to the UN are not encouraged to roam around loose in the White House hallways, however familiar with the layout they might be, as they could inadvertently, while checking to see if there happened to be a portrait of Dolley Madison hanging in the Vermeil Room, stumble across a peace summit.

2. It is strongly advised that teen ambassadors to the UN not dress all in black, as this, according to the White House press secretary, might give the public the false impression that the U.S.'s teen ambassador is a practicing witch.

And the number-one duty of the U.S. teen ambassador to the UN, so far as I can tell:

1. Sit still. Keep quiet. And let the press secretary do his work.

★ 16 ★

"He said yes!"

That was how Catherine greeted me at school Thursday morning. I had just fought through a throng of about a hundred reporters to get from the car to the front entrance of John Adams Preparatory School, so I have to admit, my ears were kind of ringing from all the yelling ("Samantha, what do you think of the situation in the Middle East?" "Coke or Pepsi, Samantha?" etc.). But I was pretty sure that was what Catherine had said.

"Who said yes?" I asked her as she fell into step with me on my way to my locker.

"Paul!" Catherine was clearly hurt that I didn't remember. "From church! Or Beltway Billiards. Anyway, it doesn't matter. The point is, I asked him out, and he said yes!"

"Whoa, Cath," I said. "Way to go."

Only I didn't mean it. Well, I did and I didn't. It wasn't very nice of me, I guess, and I would never have said so out loud, or anything. But the fact was, happy as I was that Catherine had a date, at the same time, I felt kind of weird about it. I mean, what she had done— calling a boy and asking him out—seemed way braver to me than what I'd done—stopping an assassination attempt on the president, I mean. All I'd risked was my life . . . which, if I'd lost it, would be no big deal, since, you know, I'd be dead, and wouldn't even know it.

Catherine had risked so much more than me: her pride.

The fact was, I was probably never going to get up the guts to ask out the boy of my dreams. I mean, for one thing, he was dating my

150

sister. And for another, well, what if he said no?

"Is it okay if I tell my mom that I'm spending the night at your house?" Catherine wanted to know. "I mean, I know they like Paul— my mom and dad, I mean—but you know they think fifteen is too young to date."

"Sure," I said. "After you guys go out, come on over. And if you want to borrow something to wear—I mean, you know, if your own stuff won't cut it—come over beforehand and we'll let Lucy do a makeover on you. You know she loves that stuff."

Catherine's face was shining. I had never seen her so happy. It was kind of nice. I mean, even though I was jealous and everything, I couldn't help feeling glad for her.

"Oh, Sam, really?" Catherine cried. "That would be so great!"

"It'll be fun. So what are you two going to do?" I asked her. "I mean, on the big date."

Catherine looked at me like I was a mental case.

"We're going to Kris's party, of course," she said. "Duh. What did you think I invited him to do?"

I was doing the combination to my locker at that point. But when Catherine said that—about going to Kris's party—the numbers (15, the age I am now; 21, the age I'd like to be; and 8, the age I never want to be again) went clean out of my head.

"Kris's party?" I hung on to the lock, staring at her. "You're taking him to Kris's party?"

"Yeah," Catherine said, ignoring someone who'd walked by and, seeing her long skirt, went, "Hey, where's the hoedown?"

"Of course I invited him, Sam," Catherine said. "We're going, aren't we? You and me and Paul and David?"

"*What?*" Now I didn't just forget my locker combination. I forgot my class schedule, what I'd had for breakfast, you name it. I was *shocked*. "Catherine, are you high? I never said I was going to Kris's party. In fact, I distinctly remember saying Larry Wayne Rogers could break both my arms and I still wouldn't go."

Catherine's pretty face, which a moment before had been shining like a new penny, crumpled with disappointment and—I did not think I could be mistaken about this—hurt. Yes, actual hurt.

"But, Sam," she cried. "You *have* to go! I can't go to Kris's party without you! You know Kris only invited me because she thought you were going—"

"Yeah, and Kris only invited me because she thought I'd bring along a bunch of reporters, and she could get her rat face on TV. Not to mention, she thought I'd bring David." I couldn't believe Catherine was trying to pull this on me. Catherine, my best friend since the fourth grade! "Which I'm not going to do. Because I don't like David that way. *Remember?*"

"Sam, I can't go without you," Catherine wailed. "I mean, if I show up at Kris's without you, people are going to be like, 'What are *you* doing here?'"

"Well, you should have thought about that," I said, wrenching open my locker door—I had finally managed to remember the combination—"before you asked Mr. High Score on Death Squad to go with you."

"Death Storm," Catherine corrected me, her dark eyes bright. "And I wouldn't have asked him at all, Sam, if I'd known you really weren't going."

"I *said* I wasn't going. Remember? And hello, my mom and dad totally put the kibosh on it. Lucy's not even allowed to go."

"Yes," Catherine said. "But she's going to go anyway. You know she is. She's just going to tell them she's going somewhere else."

"Duh," I said. "But that doesn't make it right. Besides, I am still on thin ice because of the whole C-minus-in-German thing. I mean, don't think they aren't still totally on my case—"

"Sam," Catherine interrupted, her voice sounding kind of funny, like it was clogged. "Don't you get it? Because of what you did— saving the president like that—everything can be different for us." She looked around to make sure no one was listening, then took a step closer to me and said in a low, urgent voice, "We don't have to be rejects anymore. We have a chance to hang out with Lucy's friends. We finally have a chance to see what it would be like to be Lucy. Don't you want that, Sam? Don't you want to know what it's like to be Lucy?"

I looked at her like she was nuts.

"Cath, I know what it's like to be Lucy," I said. "It's about doing backflips in the rain at football games and reading nothing but fashion magazines and separating your eyelashes with a safety pin." Having gotten the notebooks I needed and put away my coat, I slammed my locker door shut. "I am sorry, but I have way better things to do than that."

"Yeah," Catherine said, her dark eyes so bright, I realized at last, because they were filled with tears. "Right. That's fine for you, Sam. But what about me? I mean, Kris Parks has never taken the time to find out what the girl inside these stupid clothes is actually like." Catherine fingered her prairie skirt. "Well, now is my chance, Sam. My chance to show them all that there is a person in here. This is the one time when they actually might listen. All I'm asking is that you let me have it."

I stared at her. The bell had rung, but I didn't move. I couldn't move. "Catherine," I said, shocked more by what she'd said than by the tears that accompanied it. "Are you . . . I mean, do you really care what they think?"

She reached up to wipe her wet cheeks with a lace-trimmed sleeve. "Yes," she said. "Okay? Yes, Sam. I'm not like you. I'm not brave. I care what people say about me. All right? I care. And all I'm asking is that you give me this one chance to—"

"Okay," I said.

Catherine blinked up at me tearfully. "Wh-what?"

"Okay." I wasn't happy about it, but what could I do? She was my best friend. "Okay, I'll go. All right? If it means that much to you, I'll go."

A slow smile spread across Catherine's face. Her brown eyes were warm again.

"Really?" She gave a little hop. "Really, Sam? You mean it?"

"Yeah," I said. "Okay? I mean it."

"Oh!" Catherine flung both her arms around my neck and gave me a joyful squeeze. Then she pulled away and said, "You won't regret it! You will have a great time, I promise! I mean, *Jack* will be there!"

Then she ran down the hallway, since she was late for bio.

I should have run, too, since I was late for Deutsch class. But instead I just stood there, wondering what I had just gotten myself into.

I was still wondering, all the way up until I walked into Susan Boone's later that day, got to my drawing bench, and saw what was sitting on it.

That's because sitting on my bench was an army helmet dotted with Wite-Out daisies.

"Like it?" David wanted to know. He was grinning again. And for the second time in two days, the sight of that grin did something to me. It seemed to make my heart flip over in my chest. Frisson?

Or the burrito I'd had for lunch?

"I figured it was exactly what a girl like you needed," David said. "You know, as long as you were continually getting assaulted by crows and armed assassins."

It couldn't be heartburn. It was too much of a coincidence that my heart had done that weird flippy thing at the exact moment David had smiled at me. Something else was going on. Something I did not like at all.

Trying to ignore my staggering heart, I put the helmet on. It was way too big for me, but that was okay, as I had a lot of hair to cover.

"Thanks," I said, peering out from beneath the brim. I was touched—really touched—that he'd gone to the trouble. It was almost as cool as having my name carved into a White House windowsill. "It's perfect!"

It *was* perfect, too. Later that day, when Joe hopped onto my shoulder, interrupting my drawing—which was of a shoulder of raw beef Susan Boone had brought from the butcher's shop, telling us that, after having found color in a white egg on Tuesday, our challenge today was to draw something that had every color in the rainbow in it, but still retain its context as a whole—I didn't mind, because this time, Joe didn't hurt me. In fact, he just sat there, looking kind of puzzled, pecking occasionally at the helmet and letting out little interrogative whistles.

Everybody laughed, including David. He looked like the kind of guy who didn't let stuff bug him. He looked like the kind of guy who could put up with a hundred Kris Parkses.

Which is the only explanation I can give for how it was that I found myself leaning over to him right before we all got up to put our drawings on the windowsill for critique, and going softly—so softly I was worried he might not be able to hear me over the sudden pounding of my heart—"Hey, David. Do you want to go with me to this party on Saturday night?"

He looked surprised. For one pulse-stopping moment, I thought he might say no.

But he didn't. He smiled and said, "Sure. Why not?"

Top ten reasons I might have asked David to Kris Parks's party on Saturday night:

10. Complete and utter lunacy brought on by inhaling too much turpentine.

9. Out of a sense of solidarity with Catherine, who seems to have developed a bad case of Stockholm syndrome, as she appears to have a desire to bond with the very same people who for so many years tormented her mercilessly—so much so that she is willing to risk the wrath of her parents by sneaking out to attend a party, given by the ringleader of this group, with a boy she hardly knows.

8. His eyes.

7. How nice he had been that night at the White House, telling me about Dolley Madison. Plus getting me that burger. Oh, and carving my name on the windowsill.

6. How nice he'd *looked* that night at the White House, with his kind of messy thick hair and long eyelashes and big hands.

5. He can draw. He really can. Not as well as Jack, but almost as well as me. Maybe even better than me, only in a different style.

Plus you can tell he really *likes* to draw, that he feels the same way about it that Jack and I do, that it sucks him in the way it does us. Most people—like my sister Lucy, for instance—never get that feeling about anything.

4. The daisy helmet.

3. Because he has to go everywhere with the Secret Service; that means there will be adults in attendance, and so my parents will have to let us go.

2. Everybody already thinks we are going out anyway.

And the number-one—and most likely—reason I asked David to Kris's party:

1. To make Jack jealous, of course. Because it was entirely possible that if he saw me with another boy, he would realize that he could, if he did not act soon, lose me, and that might galvanize him into admitting his true feelings for me at last.

At least, I hope so.

★17★

I began to regret having asked David to Kris's party almost immediately. Not because I didn't think we'd have a good time together, or whatever. I mean, except when he was teasing me about being a sensitive artist, David was an okay sort of guy.

No, I regretted it because of everyone's reaction to the news when I told them.

Reaction Number One: Lucy

"Oh, my God, that is just so great! You two make the cutest couple, because he's so tall and you're so little, plus both of you have way sticky-outty hair, and you both like that stupid big band music. This is going to be so cool. What are you going to wear? I think you should wear my black leather mini and green cashmere V-neck, with black fishnets and my black knee-high boots. You can't wear your combat boots with a mini, they'll make your calves look fat. Not that you have fat calves, but calves always look fat in combat boots and minis. Fishnets might be too much for a sophomore, though. Maybe you should stick to tights. We could get you a pair of the ribbed kind, though. That would be all right. Want to meet with the rest of the squad and go shopping Saturday before the party?"

Reaction Number Two: Rebecca

"Ah, I see that the seed I planted about the frisson has germinated and produced a fragile, flowering bud."

158

Reaction Number Three: Catherine

"Oh, Sam, that is so great! Now Paul will have someone to talk to at the party, because he won't know anyone there, either, just like David. Maybe he and David can hang out while you and I work the room? Because I hear it is important at parties like this to mingle. I figure if you and I mingle, we might be able to get invitations to other parties, like maybe even senior parties, although I know this is probably asking a lot. But you know if we got invited to senior parties, we'd definitely be as popular as Kris in no time."

Reaction Number Four: Theresa

"*You* asked *him*? How many times have you heard me tell your sister, Miss Samantha, that if you chase boys, you are going to come to no good end? Look what happened to my cousin Rosa. I better not catch you calling him. You let *him* call *you*. And none of this instant messaging, either. It is best to be mysterious and aloof. If Rosa had been mysterious and aloof, she would not be where she is today. And where is this party, anyway? Are this girl's parents going to be there? Will alcohol be served? I am telling you, Miss Samantha, if I find out you or your sister have been to a party where there is alcohol, you will both be scrubbing toilets from here until you start college."

Reaction Number Five: Jack

"The president's kid? He's not a narc, is he?"

Reaction Number Six: My Parents (I saved the worst for last)

"Oh, Sam, how wonderful! He's such a nice boy! We couldn't dream up such a lovely date for you. If only Lucy showed as much prudence as you do in picking her boyfriends. What time is he coming to get you? Oh, we have to make sure we have film for the camera. Just a *few* pictures, that's all. Well, we have to memorialize the event. Our baby, going out with such a sweet boy. So well-mannered. And you know he goes to Horizon, so that means he's tested in the ninety-ninth percentile. In the country. The whole *country*. He's really going to make something of himself someday, maybe even follow in his father's footsteps and go into politics. Such a nice, nice boy. If only Lucy could find a boy that nice, instead of that awful Jack."

It was completely humiliating. I mean, trust me to get stuck going out on my first date with the kind of boy parents love. Not only does David not have any tattoos (at least, so far as I know) or drive a Harley (again, I'm only guessing here, but it seems unlikely), he is the son of the PRESIDENT OF THE UNITED STATES.

Okay? Could there BE anything geekier? I know we can't help who our parents are, but come on. Instead of the single welfare mom or convicted felon who would really have driven my parents around the bend, I end up going out with a guy whose parents are not only still married but are also, like, the most influential couple in the country.

Life is so unfair.

I tried my best to enrage them (my parents, I mean) by dropping little hints about how David was coming to pick me up in his CAR (not really, of course; John would be driving, since David, at seventeen, was not old enough for a license in the District of Columbia). Then I pointed out how we were going to go eat somewhere ALONE before the party (again, not strictly true, since the Secret Service would be there), as David had suggested, as we were leaving Susan Boone's, that we grab something before the party.

But neither Mom nor Dad bit. It's like just because the guy is the first son, or whatever, they completely trust him! In a million years they would never let Lucy go to a party with Jack—not without a huge fight beforehand. The only reason they capitulated this time and let her go was because they knew I would be there, too . . . well, with David and the Secret Service. But still. *Me!* Her *little sister!* I am supposedly the good one! In spite of everything I have done to try to convince them of the contrary—like dress entirely in black for a year, or my whole under-the-counter celebrity-drawing enterprise—they persist in thinking of me as the responsible one!

And my saving the president from being assassinated and being named teen ambassador to the UN certainly didn't help things, let me tell you.

I was seriously considering flunking German, just to get back at them.

The way they'd been acting lately, though, they'd probably just be all, "Sam got an F in German, isn't that the most adorable thing you ever heard?"

Anyway, the night of the party, Mom and Dad followed through with their threat and were standing there in the living room with the camera when David rang the bell at seven sharp. Catherine had already come and gone, having been transformed by Lucy into a *Seventeen* magazine fashionplate. She was meeting Paul at Beltway Billiards, and then the two of them would meet us at Kris's house in time for the party.

"Please," I whispered urgently to David as I opened the door, "forgive them, for they know not what they do."

David, who was in jeans and a black sweater, looked a little alarmed, but after he came all the way in and saw my parents, he relaxed.

"Oh," he said, like the parents of the girls he goes out with come at him with an Olympus every day—and maybe they do. "Hey, Mr. and Mrs. Madison."

As if my mom and dad weren't bad enough, prancing around with the zoom lens, Manet, excited at the prospect of meeting someone new, came barreling in from the kitchen—all eighty pounds of him—and immediately buried his nose in David's crotch. I tried to pull the dog away, apologizing for his bad behavior.

"That's okay," David said, giving Manet a pat on his shaggy head. "I like dogs."

Then Lucy had to get in on the act, floating down the stairs in her party outfit like she thought she was Susan Lucci or somebody, and then going, "Oh, David, it's you. I thought it might be my boyfriend, Jack. You'll meet Jack, of course, at the party. I think you two will really get along. Jack is an artist, too."

Then Rebecca wandered in, looked up at David and me, and went, "Oh, yes. Definite frisson," before heading upstairs to her room, most likely in order to attempt to contact the mother ship.

If my family had tried on purpose to embarrass me as fully as possible, I do not think they could have done a better job.

Once we'd successfully escaped to the safety of the porch, David looked at me and asked, "What's frisson?"

"Oh, ha, ha, ha." I laughed like a dork. "I don't know. It must be something she picked up at school."

David frowned a little. "I go to the same school she does, and I never heard of it before."

To distract him, in case he was thinking of going home after the party tonight and looking the word up, I squealed over his car. Although I had not taken Lucy's advice on my ensemble—I was wearing my own clothes, a black skirt that went all the way down to my daisy-dotted boots, coupled with a sweater that, though

V-neck, was also black—I did remember a few of her pointers, one of which had been: "Make a big deal out of his car. Guys totally have this thing about their cars."

Except I am not sure it applies to all guys, because after I'd squealed about how much I liked his black four-door sedan, David looked at it kind of dubiously.

"Um. It's not mine," he said. "It belongs to the Secret Service."

"Oh," I said. Then I noticed that John from our art class was standing next to it. Also that an almost identical car was parked behind it, with two other Secret Service agents in it.

I said, feeling like some sort of explanation was necessary, "My sister told me guys like it when you get excited about their car."

"Really?" David didn't sound very surprised. "Well, she looks like someone who would know."

It was at that moment that a reporter neither of us had noticed before jumped out from behind the bushes and went, "Samantha! David! Over here!" and snapped a few thousand photos.

I couldn't really see what happened next, since all the flashes blinded me for a few seconds, but I heard a firm voice go "I'll take that," and then a grunt and a smashing sound and the flashes were gone.

When I could see again, I realized that the firm voice belonged to a Secret Service agent—not John, another one—who was climbing back into the car parked behind David's. The reporter was standing a few feet away on the sidewalk, looking chagrined, his camera in several different pieces in his hands. He was muttering something about freedom of the press . . . but not loudly enough for the Secret Service agent to overhear.

John opened one of the back doors to the first sedan and said, looking apologetic, "Sorry about that."

I climbed into the backseat without saying anything, because what was there, really, to say?

David got in on the other side and shut the door. The inside of the Secret Service's car was very clean. It smelled new. I hate new car smell. I thought about rolling down the window, but it was pretty cold out.

Then John slid behind the wheel and said, "We all set?"

David said, "I'm all set." He looked at me. "You all set?"

"Um," I said. "Yes."

"We're all set," David said, to which John replied, "All right, then," and we started to move. I kept my face averted from the window, since I noticed that my parents had come out onto the front porch and were standing there, waving to us. A reporter who hadn't gotten his camera smashed took a picture of that, since taking pictures of David and me was so obviously *verboten*. I hoped my mom and dad would enjoy seeing a big color photograph of themselves in tomorrow morning's *USA Today*, or whatever.

Inside the car, it was very quiet. Too quiet. "There are only three things it's okay to talk to guys about," Lucy had instructed me, earlier in the day, though I had not, actually, consulted her about this. "Those things are:

"One: him.

"Two: you and him.

"Three: yourself.

"Start by talking about him. Then slowly introduce the topic of you and him. Then swing the conversation around to yourself. And keep it there."

But for some reason I couldn't bring myself to say any of the things Lucy had advised me to say. I mean, the first thing, about complimenting his car, hadn't really gone over all that well. I realized that, in going out with the president's son, I was crossing into uncharted territory, the kind even Lucy had never before encountered. I was on my own here. It was a little scary, but I figured I could handle it.

I mean, it wasn't as if he were *Jack*.

"Um," I said as John pulled onto Thirty-Fourth Street. "Sorry about my parents."

"Oh," David said with a laugh. "No problem. So where to? What do you feel like eating?"

Since I only ever feel like eating one thing—hamburgers—I was not certain how to answer this question. Fortunately, David went on, "I made reservations at a couple of places. There's Vidalia. It's supposed to be pretty nice. And the Four Seasons. I didn't know if you'd ever been there. Or there's Kinkead's, though I know how you feel about fish."

I listened to this in growing panic. Reservations? He'd made *reservations*? I hardly ever found anything I liked to eat in restaurants that required reservations.

I don't know if David was able to read the trepidation in my face, or if it was my silence that was more telling. In any case, he went, "Or we could blow the reservations off and get a pizza, or something. There's some place I hear a lot of people go to, Luigi's, or something?"

Luigi's was where Lucy and her crowd would be going before Kris's party. While I knew we were going to see all of them in a few hours anyway, I didn't think I could handle sitting at a table in front of all of them with David, knowing the whole time that we were all anyone in the restaurant was talking about. I doubted I'd be able to keep anything down. Besides, Jack would be there. How would I be able to pay attention to a thing David was saying when Jack was anywhere in the nearby vicinity?

"Or," David said, with another glance at my face, "we could just

165

grab a burger somewhere—"

"That sounds good," I said, hoping I sounded appropriately non-chalant.

He gave one of those little secretive smiles. "Burgers it is, then," he said. "John, make it Jake's. And could we have a little music, please?"

John said, "Sure thing," and hit a button in the dashboard.

And then Gwen Stefani's voice filled the car.

No Doubt. David was a No Doubt fan.

I should have known, of course. I mean, anybody who likes Reel Big Fish has to like No Doubt. It's, like, a law.

Still, it freaked me out when I realized David had Gwen in the car stereo. Because you know if I had a car, that's who would be in my stereo, too. Gwen, I mean.

And the weirdest part was, my heart did that thing again. Really. That flippy thing, as soon as I heard Gwen's voice. Only not because, you know, of Gwen. No, it was because I realized then that *David* liked Gwen. Was that what Rebecca had been talking about? Was that frisson?

But how could I feel frisson for one person when my heart belonged to someone else? It didn't make any sense. The only reason I had asked David out in the first place was to make Catherine happy. And maybe to make Jack jealous. I mean, I was completely and irrevocably in love with my sister's boyfriend, who would one day realize that I, and not Lucy, am the girl for him.

So what was with the frisson already?

Figuring if I ignored it, maybe it would go away, I commenced to doing so. And you know what? For a while, I thought it did. I mean, not that we didn't have a good time, or anything. Jake's, the place we went to for dinner, was totally my kind of joint . . . a dive in Foggy Bottom, with sticky tabletops and dim lighting. Nobody there paid the slightest bit of attention to the fact that I was the girl who saved the president and that David was his son. In fact, I don't think anybody looked at us at all, except the waitress, and of course John and the other Secret Service agents, who sat at a table a little way from ours.

And even though I'd been worried about what to talk about, it turned out I didn't have to fall back on Lucy's rules at all. David started telling me these funny stories about the crazy things that people who come to tour the White House have left behind—like retainers, and one time a pair of corduroy pants—and after that, the conversation just flowed.

And when the burgers came, they were a little burned on the outside, just the way I like them, and no one had put fresh vegetables, like tomatoes or onions or lettuce, on or anywhere near them. The fries were the skinny crispy kind, too, not the fat soggy kind, which taste all gross and potato-y.

Then David told me this story about how when he was a little kid, and his mom and dad would ask him to set the table, as a joke he would set one place with the giant oversized fork and spoon that were supposed to be used to serve salad.

And every single time, he said, his parents would laugh, even though he did it practically every night.

Inspired by this, I told him about the time in Morocco I tried to flush my dad's credit cards down the toilet. Which is actually something I've never told anybody before, except for Catherine. It wasn't as cute as the giant serving spoon and fork story, but it was all I had.

Then David told me about how much he resented having to leave his old friends and move to D.C., and how much he hated Horizon, where everyone was supercompetitive and all the emphasis was on science and not the arts, and people who liked to draw, like him, were looked down on. I so knew where he was coming from with that one, only of course at Adams Prep it's all about athletics.

So then I told him how I had to go to speech and hearing, and how everyone thought I was in Special Ed. And then for some reason, I told him about the celebrity drawings, too, and how because of them I'd ended up with a C-minus in German and a mandatory trip to Susan Boone's.

It was at some point during this part of the conversation that David's knees accidentally touched mine underneath the table. He apologized and moved them out of the way. Then, about five minutes later, it happened again.

Only this time, he didn't move them. Or apologize. I didn't know what to do. Lucy had not mentioned this on her list of things that could possibly happen.

But I noticed the frisson starting to come back. Like, all of a sudden, I was conscious of the fact that David was a boy. I mean, of course I'd always known he was a boy, and a good-looking one, too. But somehow when his knees touched mine like that beneath the table—and stayed there—I became really, really aware that David was a boy.

And suddenly I felt shy and couldn't think of anything to say—which was weird because like, two minutes before I'd been having no trouble in that department. I couldn't meet his eyes, either. I don't know why, but it was like they were too green, or something. Plus all of a sudden I felt hot, even though it was perfectly comfortable inside the restaurant.

I couldn't figure out what was happening to me. But I knew none of it had been going on before his knees touched mine. So I moved around a little in my seat, thinking maybe if I broke, you know, the contact, things would be better.

And they sort of were, but I guess not really, since David looked at me—no secret smile on his face at all now—and went, "Are you okay?"

"Sure," I said, in a voice that was way more high-pitched than my usual one. "Why?"

"I don't know," he said, those two green eyes searching my face in a manner I found infinitely alarming. "You look kind of . . . flushed."

That's when I had the brilliant idea of looking at my mermaid Swatch and going, "Oh, my God, would you look at the time? We better go if we want to get to the party."

I kind of got the feeling that David would have been happy to skip the party entirely. But not me. I wanted to get there, and get there fast. Because at the party I'd be safe from frisson.

Because at the party would be Jack.

★ 18 ★

"Oh my God, you came!"

That's what Kris Parks said when she opened the door and saw David and me standing there on her front porch. She actually didn't say it. She screamed it.

I should have known, of course. I should have known this was going to be how she—and everyone—would react.

In the car on the way over, David had been all, "Now, whose party is this?" and I had tried to explain, but I guess I didn't do a very good job—most likely on account of the frisson, which was not, unfortunately, going away—since he went, "Let me see if I can get this straight. This is a party being given by a person you don't like, at which will be a lot of people you don't know, and we're going . . . why?"

But when I explained that we had to go on account of how I'd promised my best friend, Catherine, he just shrugged and went, "Okay."

And even though he showed not the slightest sign of being aware that every single person in Kris's house fell silent when we walked in, then started whispering like crazy, he knew. I knew he knew. And not because of the frisson, either. No, I knew it because that little grin of his came creeping back . . . like he was trying not to laugh. I think he was trying not to laugh at all the morons from Adams Prep who couldn't seem to stop staring at him.

At least he could laugh about it. The only thing I seemed capable of doing was just blushing more and more deeply. What I couldn't figure out was why. I mean, it wasn't as if I *liked* him, or anything. As more than just a friend.

"Hi, I'm Kris," Kris said, thrusting her hand out at David. Kris was wearing a denim minidress. Like it wasn't thirty degrees outside.

"Hi," David said, shaking the hand of the girl who daily made life for me and so many others a living hell. "I'm David."

"Hi, David," Kris said. "I can't thank you enough for coming. It really is an honor to meet you. Your dad is doing such a good job of running this country. I was too young to vote, you know, in the election, but I want you to know that I totally handed out flyers for him."

"Thanks," David said, still smiling, only beginning to look like he might want his hand back. "That was nice of you."

"Sam and I are just the best of friends," Kris said, still pumping his fingers up and down. "Did she tell you? Since kindergarten, practically."

I could not believe this bald-faced lie. I would have said something, only I didn't get a chance to, since right then Catherine came rushing up to us.

"Omigosh, am I glad to see you," she whispered to me after introductions had been made. "You have no idea. Paul and I have just been standing here. No one will talk to us. No one at all! I am so embarrassed! He must think I am a complete social leper!"

I glanced at Paul. He didn't appear to be thinking any such thing. He was gazing adoringly at Catherine, who looked totally cute in the black jeans and silk top she'd borrowed from Lucy.

I turned back to David—who'd finally pried his hand loose from Kris's—and asked, "Want a Coke, or something?"

"What?" he asked, unable to hear me over the music, which was not, needless to say, ska.

"Coke?" I asked.

"Sure," he yelled back. "I'll get it."

"No," I said. "I invited you. I'll get it." I looked over his shoulder, at John, who was leaning against a wall and trying to blend in. "I'll get one for John, too. You stay here, or we'll lose each other."

Then I started to fight my way through the crowd in the direction that I suspected the beverages were located, as that was where the throng was thickest. I had to admit, I was relieved to be escaping David's presence. I mean, it was just so weird, this thing that was going on between us. I didn't know what it was, exactly, but I knew one thing:

I didn't like it.

As I waded through the laughing, gyrating crowd, I thought to myself, This is what I've been missing by being part of the unpopular set? Houses bursting at the seams with loud, obnoxious people and head-pounding music you can't even understand the lyrics of? Frankly, I'd have preferred to be home watching Nick at Nite and eating spumoni.

But I guess that was just me.

When I got to where I thought the drinks were, all I found was a keg. A keg! Smooth move, Kris. I mean, she had known perfectly well David was coming and that he'd be bringing Secret Service with him. Hmm, she wasn't going to get too busted or anything.

And you know what? Couldn't say I felt too sorry for her, either.

The soda, someone informed me, was in a cooler in a room off the kitchen. So I plunged back into the hordes, until I emerged into the room off the kitchen.

And wouldn't you know it? My sister and Jack were in there, making out.

Lucy let out a squeal, "You came!" she cried. "How's it going? Where's David?"

"Out there, somewhere," I said. "I'm getting us sodas."

"Idiot," Lucy said. "*He's* supposed to get *you* the sodas. God. Stay here a minute. I want to get the girls."

By girls, of course, she meant the rest of the cheerleading squad.

"Luce," I said. "Come on. Not tonight."

"Oh, don't be such a spoilsport," Lucy said. "Stay here with Jack, I'll be right back. There are some people who are dying to meet the real live son of an actual president. . . ."

And before I could say another word, she'd taken off, leaving me alone with Jack.

Who regarded me thoughtfully over the plastic cup he'd just drained.

"So," he said. "How's it going?"

"Good," I said. "Surprisingly good. Thursday, Susan Boone, she made us draw this huge chunk of meat, and it was really cool because I'd never really looked at meat before, you know? I mean, there is a lot going on in meat—"

"That's great," Jack said, apparently not realizing he was interrupting me, even though the music wasn't nearly as loud in the laundry room. "Did you get my painting?"

I looked up at him, uncomprehending. "What painting?"

"My entry," he said. "In the From My Window contest."

"Oh," I said. "No. I mean, I don't know. I'm sure they got it. I just haven't seen it yet. I haven't seen any of the paintings yet."

"Well, you're going to love it," Jack said. "It took me three days. It's the best thing I've ever done."

Then Jack started describing the painting to me in great detail. He was still going on about it a few minutes later when David showed up in the doorway.

I brightened when I saw him. I couldn't help it. Even though the object of my affections was standing right there beside me, I was glad to see David. I told myself it was only because that story about the salad serving utensils had been so cute. It had nothing to do with the whole frisson thing. Nothing at all.

"Hey," David said with the grin I now realized was practically his trademark. "I wondered where'd you'd disappeared to."

"David," I said, "this is my sister Lucy's boyfriend, Jack. Jack, this is David."

David and Jack shook hands. I saw that, actually, standing together, they looked a lot alike. I mean, they were both over six feet tall, and both dark-haired. There I guess the resemblance sort of ended, though, since Jack's hair was shoulder-length, while David's only just hit his collar. And Jack, of course, had the ankh earring, while both of David's lobes were unpierced. And, of course, Jack had on his party clothes, army fatigues with a long black duster, while David was dressed pretty conservatively.

I guess they didn't look that much alike after all.

"David's in my art class," I said to break the awkward silence that immediately followed their handshake.

Jack crumpled up his plastic cup and said, "Oh, you mean your conformity class?"

David looked confused. And no wonder. Jack is a very intense person who needs some getting used to.

I said hurriedly, "No, Jack, it turns out it's not like that. I was totally wrong about Susan Boone. She just wants me to learn to draw what I see before I go off, you know, and do my own thing. You have to learn what the rules are, you see, before you can go around breaking them."

Jack, staring at me, went, *"What?"*

"No, really," I said, sensing he wasn't getting what I was saying. "I mean, you know Picasso? David told me that Picasso spent years learning to draw, you know, whatever he saw. It wasn't until he'd totally mastered that that he started experimenting with color and form."

Only Jack, instead of finding this particular fact endlessly interesting, as I had, looked scornful.

"Sam," he said, "I can't believe you, of all people, would fall for that pedagogic bull."

"Excuse me?" David sounded kind of mad.

Jack raised both his eyebrows. "Uh, I don't think I was talking to you, First Boy."

"Jack," I said, a little shocked. I mean, Jack is an amazingly artistic person, and having that kind of, you know, creative energy bouncing around inside can be exhausting (as I well know). But that's no reason to call anybody names. "What is wrong with you?"

"What is wrong with *me*?" Jack laughed, but not like he actually thought anything was very funny. "That's not the question. The question is, what is wrong with *you*? I mean, you used to think for yourself, Sam. But now all of a sudden you're falling for all this 'draw what you see' crap like it's been handed down from the gods on a freaking stone tablet. What happened to questioning authority? What happened to making up your own mind about the creative process and how it functions?"

"Jack," I said. I couldn't believe what I was hearing. I mean, Jack had always said it was imperative for artists to be open to all new things, so that they could soak in knowledge like a sponge. Only, Jack certainly wasn't acting very spongelike. "I did make up my own mind. I—"

"Hey, you guys." Lucy suddenly reappeared, a posse of cheerleaders, each one wearing more body glitter and Lycra than the last, trailing along behind her. "Oh, hey, David, I've got some friends who want to meet—"

But I was still trying to make Jack understand.

"I looked it up, Jack," I said. "David's right. Picasso was a technical virtuoso before he began experimenting with line and—"

"David," Jack said, rolling his eyes. "Oh, yes, I am sure *David* knows all about art. Because I'm sure he's had paintings publicly exhibited before."

Lucy looked from Jack to David to me, as if trying to figure out what was going on. When she spoke, it was to Jack. "Like you have?" she asked, with one raised eyebrow.

Lucy really is the most unsupportive girlfriend I have ever seen.

"Yes," Jack said. "As a matter of fact, I have had my paintings exhibited—"

"In the *mall*," Lucy pointed out.

Jack didn't even look at Lucy, though. He was looking at me. I could feel his pale blue eyes boring into me.

"If I didn't know better, Sam," he said, "I'd think it wasn't your arm you broke that day you saved this guy's dad, but your brain."

"Okay," David said. There was no trace of that secretive little smile on his face now. "Look, dude, I don't know what your problem is, but—"

"*My* problem?" Jack jabbed a finger at himself. "*I'm* not the one with the problem, *dude*. You're the one who seems so perfectly willing to let your individuality be sapped by a—"

"Okay," Lucy said in a bored voice, slipping between Jack and David and laying both hands on the front of Jack's long black coat. "That's it. Outside, Jack."

Jack looked down at her as if noticing her for the first time. "But . . ." he said. "Luce, this guy started it."

"Right," Lucy said, pushing Jack backward, toward a door that seemed to lead into the backyard. "Sure he did. Let's just step outside and get some air. How many beers have you had, anyway?"

Then they were gone, leaving David and me alone. With Lucy's cheerleading squad.

David looked down at me and went, "What's with that guy, anyway?"

Still looking after Jack—whom I could see through the screen door, gesturing wildly to Lucy as he explained his side of the story—I murmured, "He's not so bad. He just, you know, has the soul of an artist."

"Yeah," David said. "And the brains of an orangutan."

I glanced back at him sharply. I mean, that was my soul mate he was talking about.

"Jack Ryder," I said, "happens to be very, very talented. Not only that, but he is a rebel. A radical. Jack's paintings don't just reflect the plight of the urban youth of today. They make a powerful statement about our generation's apathy and lack of moral rectitude."

The look David gave me was a strange one. It seemed equal parts disbelief and confusion.

"What?" he said. "Do you *like* that guy, or something, Sam?"

Lucy's friends, who were listening—and watching—closely, tittered. I could feel color rush into my cheeks. I was hotter now than I'd been back in the restaurant.

But it was weird. I couldn't tell whether I was blushing because of David's question or because of the way he was looking at me. Really. Not for the first time that night, I was having trouble meeting those green eyes of his. Something about them . . . I don't know . . . was making me feel really uncomfortable.

I couldn't tell him the truth, of course. Not with the entire Adams Prep varsity cheerleading team standing there, staring at us. I mean, the last thing I needed was the whole school knowing that I was in love with my sister's boyfriend.

So I went, "Duh. He's Lucy's boyfriend, not mine."

"I didn't ask you whose boyfriend he was," David said, and I realized with a sinking heart he wasn't going to let me off as easy as all that. "I asked if you like him."

I didn't want to, but it was like I couldn't help it. Something made me lift my gaze to meet his.

And for a minute, it was like I was looking at a guy I had never met before. I mean, not like he was the president's son, but like he was a really cute, funny guy who happened to be in my art class and was into the same kind of music I was and happened to like my boots. It was kind of like I was seeing David—the real David—for the very first time.

I had opened my mouth to say something—I have no idea what; something lame, I'm sure; I was pretty freaked by the whole thing, most especially by how sweaty my palms had gotten all of a sudden, and how hard my heart was beating—but I never got a chance to. That's because somebody behind the cheerleaders called out, "*There you are!*" and Kris Parks came bearing down on us with, like, sixty people in tow, all of whom, she claimed, were just dying to meet the son of the president of the United States.

And David, exactly the way a politician's son should, went to shake their hands, without another single glance at me.

★ **19** ★

"*It's not* your fault," Catherine, across the room in my daybed, said. "I mean, you can't help that you're in love with Jack."

I was curled up in my own bed, Manet snoring softly at my side.

"You met Jack first," Catherine said through the darkness all around us. "What does David think, anyway? You were just supposed to wait around and not fall in love with anybody else until he rode up on his big white horse? I mean, it's not like you're Cinderella, or something."

"I think," I said to the ceiling, "that David kind of thought if I was asking him to some party that there was a possibility I might like him, and not some other guy."

"Well, that was very old-fashioned of him," Catherine said firmly. Now that Catherine had been on her first date, and it had turned out to be a successful one—Paul had kissed her good-night on my very front porch; on the lips, she'd informed me proudly afterward—she seemed to think she was some kind of expert on love. In between worrying that her parents were going to find out. Not so much about Paul, I think, as about the black jeans and the party.

"I mean, you are an attractive and vital girl," Catherine went on. "You can't be expected to just stick with one man. You have to play the field. It's absurd that at the age of fifteen you should settle down with just one guy."

"Yeah," I said with a short laugh. "Especially one who is in love with my sister."

"Jack only thinks he is in love with Lucy," Catherine said firmly.

"We both know that. What happened tonight was just evidence that he is finally becoming aware of his deep and abiding affection for you. I mean, why else would he have been so mean to David if it wasn't for the fact that the sight of you with another man drove him into a jealous rage?"

I said, "I think he just had one too many beers."

"Not true," Catherine said. "I mean, that might have been part of it, but he was definitely threatened. Threatened by what he perceived as your happiness with another."

I rolled over—disturbing Manet, who went on snoring, not at all—and stared at Catherine's dim form in the darkness of my bedroom.

"Have you been reading Lucy's *Cosmo* again?" I asked.

Catherine sounded guilty. "Well. Yes. She left one in the bathroom."

I rolled back over to stare at the ceiling. It was kind of hard to tell what I should be thinking about everything that had happened that night when the only person with whom I could safely discuss it was spouting advice she'd garnered from the Bedside Astrologer.

"So did he kiss you good-night?" Catherine asked shyly. "David, I mean?"

I snorted. Yeah, David had really felt like kissing me after that whole thing with Jack and the Adams Prep cheerleading squad. In fact, he had barely spoken to me for the rest of the night. Instead, he'd gone around making the acquaintance of half the student population of my school. Evidently not by nature a shy sort of person, David hadn't seemed to mind a bit being the center of attention. In fact, he'd looked like he was having a pretty good time as Kris Parks and her cronies hung on his every word, laughing like hyenas every time he made a joke.

It wasn't until around eleven thirty—Theresa, who was baby-sitting while my parents were at a dinner party they hadn't left for until after David picked me up, had given us a twelve o'clock curfew—that he finally looked around for me. I was sitting by myself in a corner, flipping through Kris's mom's copies of *Good Housekeeping* (who said I don't know how to have a good time?) and trying to ignore the people who kept coming up to me and asking if they could have my autograph (or, conversely, if they could sign my cast).

"Ready?" David asked. I said I was. I went and told Catherine that we were leaving, then found Kris—I noticed I didn't have to look very far; she was practically tracking David's every move—and said thanks and good-bye. Then David and John and I headed back out to the car.

Cleveland Park isn't really all that far from Chevy Chase, where Kris lives, but I swear, that ride home was one of the longest in my life. Nobody said anything. Anything! Thank God for Gwen, singing her heart out over the stereo.

Still, I noticed that for the first time ever, the sound of Gwen Stefani's voice didn't exactly make me feel better. The worst part was, I didn't even know what I had to feel so badly about. I mean, okay, so David knew I liked Jack. Big deal. I mean, is there some kind of federal law that prohibits girls from liking their sisters' boyfriends? I don't think so.

By the time we pulled up to my house, however, the silence in the car (aside from Gwen) was oppressive. I turned to David—God knew I didn't expect him to walk me to the door or anything—and went, "Well, thanks for coming with me."

To my very great surprise, he opened his car door and went, "I'll walk you up."

Which I can't say exactly thrilled me, or anything. Because I had a feeling he was going to let me have it.

And, halfway up the stairs to the porch, he did.

"You know," he said, "you really had me fooled, Sam."

I glanced at him, wondering what was coming next, and knowing I probably wasn't going to like it. "I did? How?"

"I thought you were different," he said. "You know, with the boots and the black and all of that. I thought you were really . . . I don't know. The genuine article. I didn't know you were doing it all to get a guy."

I stopped in the middle of the steps and stared up at him, which was kind of hard, since the porch light was on, and it was burning in my eyes. "What do you mean?"

"Well, isn't that it?" David asked. "I mean, wasn't that why you asked me to the party, too? It had nothing to do with wanting to help your friend feel like she fit in. You were using me to try to make that Jack guy jealous."

"I was not!" I cried, hoping he, too, was being blinded by the porch light. That way he wouldn't be able to see that my cheeks were on fire, I was blushing so hard. "David, that's . . . I mean, that's just ridiculous."

"Is it? I don't think so."

We'd reached my front door. David stood looking down at me, his expression unreadable . . . and not because I was being blinded by the porch light anymore, but because he really had no expression—no expression at all on his face.

"It's too bad," he said. "I really thought you weren't like any of the other girls I know."

And with a polite good-night—that's it, just "Good night"—he turned around and went back down to the car. He didn't even look back. Not once.

Not that I could blame him, I guess. Despite Catherine's assertion that boys ought to know girls our age are "playing the field" (which sounds pretty funny coming from her, Miss I-Just-Went-

Out-with-a-Boy-for-the-First-Time-Ever-Tonight), I imagine it might kind of suck to find out the person who'd asked you out really liked someone else—would rather have been out with that person, instead.

I don't know. I guess I could see why David was kind of peeved with me.

But come on. I'd asked him to a party, not to marry me, or anything. It was just a *party*. What was the big deal?

And what was all that junk about being wrong about my being different from all the other girls he knew? How many other girls did he know who'd saved his dad's life lately? Uh, not that many, I was willing to bet.

Still, the evening wasn't a total washout. Some of my celebrity must have rubbed off on Catherine, because other people at the party finally started talking to her. She stood there beaming, Paul at her side, and had all of her popular girl fantasies realized. Someone even invited her to another party, the following weekend.

"You know," Catherine, the new It Girl of Adams Prep, said from the daybed, "I really think Jack was jealous."

I blinked up at the ceiling at this piece of information. "Really?"

"Oh, yes. I heard him tell Lucy that he thinks David is pompous and that you could do better."

Pompous? David was the least pompous person I had ever met. What was Jack *talking* about?

When I mentioned this out loud, though, all Catherine said was, "But, Sam, I thought that was what you wanted. To make Jack realize that you are a vital, attractive woman, desired by many."

I admitted that this was true. At the same time, however, I didn't like the idea of anybody—even my soul mate—calling David names. Because David was a very nice person.

Only I didn't want to think about that. You know, about David being so nice, and my treating him the way I had. I mean, that kind of behavior is all very well for readers of *Cosmo*, but I'm really more of an *Art in America* kind of girl.

Knowing that sleep was a long way off, but aware that Catherine, by the sound of her steady breathing, was no longer available, I got out my flashlight and opened the book the White House press secretary had given me, on the lives of the first ladies.

$\mathcal{T}op$ ten little-known facts about Dolley Payne Todd Madison, wife of the fourth president of the United States of America:

10. She spelled her name Dolley, not Dolly.

9. Born in 1768, she was raised as a Quaker, eschewing colorful bonnets and clothes, as Quaker tradition dictated.

8. She was married once before to a Quaker lawyer who died in a yellow fever epidemic.

7. After marrying James Madison in 1794, Dolley acted as "unofficial first lady" during the presidency of Thomas Jefferson, who was a widower.

6. It was apparently around this time that Dolley decided God didn't care if she wore bright colors, because she is described as having worn a gold turban with an ostrich feather tucked into it at her husband's inaugural ball.

5. The fact that Dolley abandoned her Quaker ways is further illustrated by the fact that during her husband's presidency, she became the belle of Washington society. She was best known for her Wednesday evening receptions, where politicians, diplomats, and the general public gathered. These gatherings

helped to soothe some of the tensions between Federalists, who were like today's Republicans, and Republicans, who were like today's Democrats, in a time of intense party rivalries.

4. During the War of 1812, Dolley saved not only George Washington's portrait but also tons of important government documents by pressing them against the sides of trunks. The day before the British attacked, she filled a wagon with silver and other valuables and sent them off to the Bank of Maryland for safekeeping, which just goes to show she was not only brave but also proactive.

3. But the majority of U.S. citizens in 1814, when this all happened, were not very appreciative of Dolley's actions, since they all hated her husband for starting the war in the first place. In fact, as the White House was burning down, Dolley went to the neighbors and knocked on the door, looking for sanctuary, and they told her to get lost. She didn't find a place to stay until she lied about who she was.

2. As if this was not enough, one of her sons turned out to be a profligate, which means loser, whose out-of-control spending nearly bankrupted the family.

And the number-one little-known fact about Dolley Madison:

1. She wasn't really very attractive.

★ 20 ★

$\mathcal{T}he$ $next$ week was Thanksgiving. Susan Boone had class on Tuesday, but it was cancelled on Thursday, on account of the holiday.

I figured that, when I saw David in the studio on Tuesday, I would say I was sorry for what had happened at Kris's. I mean, even though Catherine insisted I hadn't done anything wrong, and part of me felt like she was right, another part of me—a bigger part of me—disagreed. I figured at the very least I owed David an apology. I was going to ask him if he wanted to go bowling with me and Catherine and Paul the following Friday. I knew Lucy had a game that night, so there wouldn't be a chance of our running into Jack. That way David would know I'd asked him out for him, and not to make Jack jealous.

I didn't know why it was so important to me that I make David understand he was wrong . . . that I wasn't like the other girls he knew, that I wasn't trying to impress anyone, especially a guy. Especially my sister's boyfriend. That I liked to wear black. That the daisies on my boots had been my idea.

I just really wanted to make everything between us okay again.

Except that David didn't come to class on Tuesday.

David didn't come to class, and it wasn't like there was anybody there that I could ask why. You know, like if he was sick. I mean, Gertie and Lynn weren't friends with David. I was. And I didn't know why he wasn't there. Was he sick? Had he left early for Camp David, where he and the rest of his family were going to spend

Thanksgiving, according to the news and the folks in the press office? I didn't know.

All I knew was, as I sat there drawing the gourds Susan Boone had arranged on the table in front of us, my daisy helmet on my head to guard against aerial crow assaults, I felt pretty stupid.

Stupid because of how disappointed I was that David hadn't showed. Stupid because I'd actually thought it would be that simple—I'd just apologize, and that would be the end of it.

But most of all, I felt stupid that I even cared. I mean, I didn't even *like* David. Oh, sure, as a friend I liked him all right.

And yeah, there was that freaky frisson thing that happened every once in a while when I was around him.

But it wasn't like just because of that I was going to forget all about Jack. Okay, yeah, Jack had acted like a jerk at Kris's party. But that didn't mean I'd fallen out of love with him, or anything. I mean, when you have loved someone as much and for as long as I have loved Jack, you totally see beyond jerky behavior and that kind of thing. The way I felt about Jack was *deeper* than that. Just like, I knew, the way he felt about me was deeper than the way he felt about Lucy.

He just didn't know it yet.

Anyway, if David thought just by blowing off Susan Boone's on Tuesday he'd be rid of me, he had, as Theresa would say, another think coming. Because, as teen ambassador to the UN, I went to the White House every Wednesday. So what I figured I'd do was, if David hadn't left for the holidays yet, I'd just go, you know, *find* him. Sometime the Wednesday before Thanksgiving when Mr. White, the press secretary, wasn't paying attention.

Only that didn't work out too well, either, because Mr. White was totally paying attention that day. That was on account of the fact that entries for the From My Window contest at the UN were pouring in. We were getting paintings from as far away as Hawaii and as close as Chevy Chase (Jack's entry). Mr. White was doing a lot of complaining because there were so many paintings, we had nowhere to put them all. We could only pick one to send on to the U.S. Ambassador to the UN in New York.

Some of the paintings were very bad. Some of them were very good. All of them were very interesting.

The one that interested me most had been painted by a girl named Maria Sanchez, who lived in San Diego. Maria's painting depicted a backyard with freshly laundered sheets hanging from a washline. Between the hanging sheets, which were fluttering in an unseen breeze, you could catch glimpses of this barbed-wire fence a pretty far ways away . . . but not far enough away that you couldn't see that there were people sneaking through this hole they had cut in the wire. Some people had already got through the hole, and they were running away from men in brown uniforms, who had guns and sticks, and were chasing them. Maria called her painting *Land of the Free?* With a question mark.

Mr. White, the press secretary, hated this painting. He kept going, "This contest is not about making political statements."

But I felt kind of differently about it.

"The contest is about what you see from your window," I said. "This is what Maria Sanchez of San Diego sees from her window. She is not making a political statement. She is painting what she sees." Mr. White ground his teeth. He liked this painting that had come from Angie Tucker of Little Deer Isle, Maine. Angie's painting was of a lighthouse and the sea. It was a nice painting. But somehow, I didn't believe it. That that was what Angie saw every day from her window. I mean, a lighthouse? Come on. Who was she, anyway, Anne of Green Gables?

For that reason, I didn't think Angie's painting was as good as Maria's.

Neither, surprisingly, was Jack's.

Oh, Jack's was good. Don't get me wrong. Like all his paintings, Jack's entry to the From My Window contest was brilliant. It depicted three disillusioned-looking young guys standing around in the parking lot outside of the local 7-Eleven, stamped-out cigarettes at their feet and broken beer bottles lying around, the shards of glass sparkling like emeralds. It spoke eloquently of the plight of urban youth, of the hopelessness of our generation.

It was a good painting. A great painting, actually.

Except that guess what?

It was so not what Jack sees out of his window.

I know this for a fact. That's because the closest 7-Eleven to Jack's house is all the way out in Bethesda. And no way could you see it from his window. Jack lives in a great big house with lots of tall leafy trees around it and a long circular driveway out front. And while I admit, the real view out of Jack's window might be a bit on the boring side, in no way could I reward him for basically lying. Much as I loved him, I couldn't, you know, let that affect my judgment. I had to be fair.

And that meant that Jack's entry was effectively out of the running.

Mr. White and I had reached an impasse. I could tell he was bored of the argument and just wanted to get out of there. It was the Wednesday before Thanksgiving, and all. I thought I'd give him a break and went, "Well, Mr. White, listen. What do you say we cut our little visit short this week? I was thinking of stopping by the family quarters and just saying hi to David, you know, before he leaves for the holiday. . . ."

Mr. White shot me a look.

"You aren't stopping anywhere," he said. "We still have a ton of work to do. There's the International Festival of the Child coming

190

up this Saturday. The president particularly wants you there. . . ."

I perked up upon hearing this. "Really? Will David be there?"

Mr. White looked at me tiredly. Sometimes I got the feeling that Mr. White cursed the day I'd stopped Larry Wayne Rogers from killing his boss. Not that Mr. White wanted the president dead. Not at all. Mr. White worshiped the ground the guy walked on. It was me I think he would have been happy to be rid of.

"Samantha," he said with a sigh. "I don't know. There will, however, be representatives from over eighty countries in attendance, including the president, and it would really help if you would, just this once, dress up a little. Try to look like a young lady and not a video jockey."

I looked down at my boots, black tights, the kilt that had once been red plaid that I had dyed black, and my favorite black turtleneck.

"You think I look like a veejay?" I asked, touched by this unexpected compliment.

Mr. White rolled his eyes and asked if there was anything I could do about my cast. It was looking a little worse for wear. As I'd told David I would, I'd decorated it in a patriotic motif, with eagles and the Liberty Bell and even a tiny celebrity portrait—of Dolley Madison. Fourteen girls had already asked me if they could have the cast when it came off. Theresa had suggested I auction it off on the Internet.

"Because," she said, "you could probably get thousands of dollars for it. They auctioned off chunks of the Berlin Wall after it fell. Why not the cast of the girl who made the world safe for democracy?"

I didn't know what I was going to do with my cast when it came off, but I figured I had time to figure it out. It wasn't due to come off for another week.

I could see Mr. White's point, though. The cast had gotten kind of dirty, and parts of it were sort of crumbling off where I'd gotten it wet (it was very hard to wash my hair one-handed).

"Maybe your mother could rig something up," he said, looking kind of pained. "A nice sling to, um, hide it."

If I hadn't already known from his attitude about the whole painting contest, I would have known it from the way he was eyeing my cast: Mr. White had no appreciation for art.

By the time he was done yammering on about all the people who would be at the International Festival of the Child, it was five o'clock, and time to go home. No way I was going to be able to sneak off to find David now. I'd missed him once again.

This didn't exactly put me in a real festive holiday mood, know what I mean? I didn't even care that we had four whole days off from school. Ordinarily four days of being Deutsch free would have delighted me. But for some reason this year it wasn't so exciting. I mean, technically, it meant that, if David didn't show at the International Festival of the Child, it would be five whole days until I saw him again. I could have called him, I guess, but that wasn't the same. And I didn't have his e-mail address.

Even the fact that Theresa was in the kitchen baking when I got home didn't cheer me up. It was just pumpkin pies (blech) for tomorrow. And they weren't even for us. They were for Theresa's own kids, and grandkids, too. What with being with us all week, the only chance Theresa had to get ready for Thanksgiving was when she was at our house. My mom didn't mind. We always had Thanksgiving at my grandma's in Baltimore, anyway, so it wasn't like she needed the oven, or anything.

"What's the matter with you?" Theresa wanted to know when I came into the kitchen, dropped my coat and backpack, and started right in on the graham crackers without even complaining about how come we only got the good stuff when Jack came over.

"Nothing," I said. I sat down at the kitchen table and stared at the back of the novel Rebecca was reading. She'd apparently abandoned romance for sci-fi once again, since she held the latest installment in the Jedi Academy saga. I felt, all things considered, that she had made a wise decision.

"Then stop with the sighing already." Theresa was tense. Theresa was always tense before the holidays. She said it was because she never knew which one of his ex-wives Tito was going to show up with . . . or if he'd show up with an entirely new wife. Theresa said it was more than any mother should be forced to bear.

I sighed again, and Rebecca looked up from her book.

"If you're upset because Jack's not here," she said in a bored voice, "don't be. He and Lucy'll probably be rolling back in a few minutes. They just walked down to the video store to get a copy of *Die Hard*. You know that's Dad's favorite holiday movie."

I sniffed. "Why would I be upset about Jack not being here?" I demanded. When Rebecca just rolled her eyes, I went, in maybe a louder voice than I ought to have, "I don't like Jack, you know, Rebecca. In that way, I mean."

"Sure, you don't," Rebecca said—but not like she believed it—and went back to her book.

"I don't," I said. "God. As if. I mean, he's Lucy's boyfriend."

"So?" Rebecca turned a page.

"So I don't like him like that, okay?" God, was I going to have to spend the rest of my life denying my true feelings to everyone I knew? I mean, at school everyone was all, Sam and David, Sam and David. Even the press, since our big "date," had been all, Sam and David, Sam and David. There'd been something about it on the news. The *national* news. Not, like, the lead story, or anything, but one of those little human interest things five minutes before the news hour was up. It was totally humiliating. The reporters were all, "And Christmas isn't the only thing in the air here in the capital. No, young love seems to be in the air, as well."

It was totally revolting. I mean, it was no wonder David hadn't shown up at Susan Boone's. The place had been crawling with reporters, a bunch of whom had yelled, as I'd darted past them, "Did you and David have a nice time at the party, Sam?"

Which reminded me of something. I looked at Rebecca and went, in the snottiest voice I could, "Besides, if I supposedly like Jack so much, what's with this frisson thing you said you sensed between me and David? Huh? How can I have frisson with one guy if I'm supposedly in love with someone else?"

Rebecca just looked at me and went, "Because you are completely blind to what's right in front of you," then went back to her book.

Blind? What was she talking about, blind? Thanks to Susan Boone, I had never seen better in my life, thank you very much. Wasn't I drawing the best eggs in the studio? And what about those gourds I'd done yesterday? My gourds had been better than anyone's. My gourds had blown everyone else's gourds out of the water. Even Susan Boone had been impressed. During critique at the end of class, she'd even said, "Sam, you are making enormous strides."

Enormous strides. How could a blind person be making enormous strides in ART class?

I mentioned this to Rebecca, but she just went, "Yeah? Well, maybe you can see eggs and gourds, but you sure can't see anything else."

I then said the only thing that an older sister can say to a younger one who is acting like she thinks she is all that. Lord knows, Lucy has said it to me often enough.

After I said it, Theresa sent me to my room.

But I didn't care. I liked it better in my room anyway. In fact, if I had my way, I'd never come out of my room again, except maybe for meals and of course for *Buffy the Vampire Slayer*. But that's it. Because every time I leave my room, it seems like, I just get into trouble. I'm either saving people from getting assassinated or getting into arguments about Picasso or being told I'm blind.

Well, that's it. I'm staying in my room forever. And nobody can stop me.

★ 21 ★

They made me come out of my room to go to Grandma's for Thanksgiving dinner.

I tried to lock myself in there again the minute we got back, but unfortunately there was a message on the machine from Mr. White, reminding my parents about the International Festival of the Child, at which my attendance was required. Apparently, if I wasn't there some crisis of world proportions would break out, so my mom said I had to go.

But that didn't mean I had to like it.

I mean, let's face it, this teen ambassador thing was getting old. It was worse than German, practically. Every time Jack saw me he was all, "So where's my ticket to New York?" which was, of course, what the winner of the From My Window contest got, an all-expenses paid trip to New York. Plus, you know, international fame and celebrity.

And I had to pretend to be all, "Ha ha ha! A winner has yet to be announced, Jack." To which Jack would reply, "Yeah, but it's me, right?"

And then I would be all, "We'll see."

We will see. Even though I knew good and well the winner wouldn't be him. But what could I say? I mean, I didn't want to be the one to break the news to him. I knew how much the contest meant to him.

So I just said nothing. I smiled and said nothing. While inside, I wept.

Well, okay, not wept, but you know what I mean. I was bummed.

Anyway, Saturday night I showed up at the stupid International Festival of the Child, which was at the White House, and which as far as I could tell was just some bogus concert and a dinner. There weren't even any kids there, that I could see. I was the only one!

And the music, no surprise, wasn't that exciting. The Beaux Arts Trio. That's who they booked. I guess Alien Ant Farm wasn't available.

The Beaux Arts Trio wasn't that bad, though. They only played classical music, like the kind we listened to on the radio in Susan Boone's studio. And while it wasn't exactly No Doubt, it was still nice, in its own way.

Nothing else about the evening was, though. Nice, I mean. For one thing, I fully had to get dressed up. Mr. White had expressly asked my mother to make sure I didn't wear any of my own clothes. Instead, I had to wear this new dress Mom picked out for me at Nordstrom's.

On the plus side, it was black. On the minus side, it was made out of velvet and was very scratchy, and looked stupid with my now-raggedy old cast. My mom tried to make a sling for me out of this big lace shawl of hers, but it kept coming untied, so finally I just left it on my chair.

Plus I had to wear panty hose. Black panty hose, but still.

You would think there'd be something a little exciting about attending a private concert at the White House, in the Vermeil Room, which is all gold, with the president and the first lady, the prime minister of France and his wife, and some other important foreign supporters of the rights of children. You would think so, but you would be wrong. It was all extremely boring. The White House wait staff were walking around, serving glasses of champagne— 7-Up for those of us who weren't yet twenty-one, of which I appeared to be the only one—and these gross hors d'oeuvres.

I joked that the 7-Up was a particularly fine vintage, but nobody got it, everybody there being pretty much humorless . . .

Except for David, of course. But I didn't notice he was there until after I'd told my little joke. And when I did, of course—notice David, I mean—I practically spat a mouthful of 7-Up at the ambassador to Sri Lanka.

He—the ambassador—looked at me like I was crazy. But that was better than how David was looking at me, which was like I was something furry that had crawled across his salad plate. His mom, I saw, had made him dress up, too. But since he had no stupid cast on one of his arms, David actually looked good. Really good. In fact, in his dark suit and tie, he looked hot.

When I realized I was thinking this, however, I almost started choking again. *David? Hot?* Since when had I started thinking of *David* that way? I mean, sure, I'd always thought of him as cute. But hot?

And then all of a sudden *I* felt hot—though whether it was because I'd realized I thought of David as hot or whether I was merely experiencing the consummate embarrassment a girl feels when she bumps into a guy she'd used to try to make another guy jealous, I couldn't say. All I know is, my face turned about as red as my hair. I know because I caught a glimpse of myself in one of the gilt-framed mirrors on the wall.

Was this, I wondered, part of the whole frisson package? Because if it was, I wanted nothing more to do with it. Rebecca could have her stupid frisson back. It sucked as much as the hors d'oeuvres.

David, of course, was too mature, and too much of a gentleman, to snub me. He came up and said, with another one of those smiles that was just polite, nothing else, "Hi, Sam. How are you doing?"

I had to choke back what I wanted to say—which was "Terrible, thanks. And you?"—and just give him the standard "Fine, thanks," since I didn't think it would be too cool to get into the whole thing—you know, my apology—in front of all the celebrants for the International Festival of the Child.

"How about you?" I asked. "We missed you on Tuesday at Susan's."

David's green eyes were cool. "Yeah," he said. "Couldn't be there. Prior commitment."

"Oh," I said. Which wasn't what I wanted to say at all. What I wanted to say was, *David, I'm sorry! I'm sorry, all right? I mean, I know what I did was horrible. I know I'm a terrible person. But could you please, please, please forgive me?*

Only I couldn't say that. For one thing, it would smack—just slightly—of groveling. For another, David's dad went up to the front of the room and asked us all to take our places, as the concert was about to begin.

So we all filed into the room where the concert was and sat down. I ended up sitting behind and sort of off to the side of David. So I had a pretty solid view of him through the whole thing. Well, of his left ear, mostly, but still.

And I swear, I didn't hear a note those famous musicians played. All I could think, as I stared at the back of David's left ear, was: *How am I going to make this right?* It kind of surprised me how much I wanted to. Make it right, I mean. But I did.

After the concert, everyone went up and shook hands with the Beaux Arts Trio. The president introduced me to them as the girl who had saved his life and as the U.S. teen ambassador to the UN. The cellist raised my hand to his lips and kissed it. It was the first time any guy outside of my immediate family had ever kissed any part of my body. It felt weird. But that was probably only because he was so old.

"And what," the pianist wanted to know, "does the teen ambassador to the UN do?"

The president told him about the From My Window contest. Then he added, with a laugh, "And she's been giving Andy a run for his money."

Andy was the first name of Mr. White, the press secretary. And I had not been giving him a run for his money, that I knew of. In fact, I had surrendered all of my Superballs to him, and had even stopped begging to look at the perv letters.

"Apparently," the president said in a jokey voice, "there's some disagreement over which entry to the art contest best represents American interests."

This surprised me. I had not been aware before that David's dad knew what was going on in the press office.

"There's no disagreement," I said, even though the president hadn't exactly been talking to me, and also, there most certainly was a disagreement. "Maria Sanchez's painting is the best one. It's my pick for winner."

I wasn't, you know, trying to start an international incident or anything. I didn't even really think about what I was doing. You know, arguing with the president of the United States. It—the thing about Maria Sanchez—just sort of came out before I stopped to think about it.

The president said, "If Maria Sanchez is the artist of that painting with the illegal aliens, it is not the one going to New York."

Then he turned and said something in French to the prime minister, who laughed.

And I forgot all about David looking like such a hottie in his suit. I forgot all about how I wanted to apologize to him, and how rotten I felt over the way I'd treated him. I forgot all about my uncomfortable dress and panty hose. All I could think about was the fact that the president had given me this one thing to do—this teen ambassador thing—supposedly as a reward or something for saving his life . . .

And I was happy to do it, even though, you know, I kind of was beginning to feel like I was being underutilized. I mean, there were a lot more important issues out there for teens that I could have been bringing international attention to than what kids see out their windows. I mean, instead of sitting in the White House press office for three hours after school every Wednesday, or attending International Celebration of the Child concerts, I could have been out there alerting the public to the fact that in some countries, it is still perfectly legal for men to take teen brides—even multiple teen brides! What was *that* all about?

And what about places like Sierra Leone, where teens and even younger kids routinely get their limbs chopped off as "warnings" against messing with the warring gangs that run groups of diamond traffickers? And hello, what about all those kids in countries with unexploded land mines buried in the fields where they'd like to play soccer, but can't because it's too dangerous?

And how about a problem a little closer to home? How about all the teenagers right here in America who are taking guns to school and blowing people away? Where are they getting these guns, and how come they think shooting people is a viable solution to their problems? And why isn't anybody doing anything to alleviate some of the pressures that might lead someone to think bringing a gun to school is a good thing? How come nobody is teaching people like Kris Parks to be more tolerant of others, to stop torturing kids whose mothers make them wear long skirts to school?

These are important problems that I, as U.S. teen ambassador to the UN, should have been addressing. But what did they have me doing instead? Yeah, that'd be counting paintings.

And you know, it was starting to occur to me that the whole teen ambassador thing had just been made up, a way for the president—who, I was starting to think, cared more about his image than he did about the teens of this country—to look good. You know, giving a high-profile job to the girl who'd saved his life, and all.

But I didn't say all that. I should have. I totally should have.

But I was conscious of all these people—the Beaux Arts Trio, the French prime minister, and the ambassador to Sri Lanka, not to mention David—standing there, listening. I couldn't make a speech like that in front of all those people. I mean, I couldn't even talk to the reporters who hounded me every day, and all they wanted to know was which I liked better, Coke or Pepsi.

I had a lot of views about stuff—that was certainly true. What I did not have was a lot of confidence about expressing them to anyone but my family and friends.

But there was one thing I knew I had to do. I had to get Maria's painting into the From My Window show in New York. I *had* to.

And so I put my hand on the president's arm and said, "Excuse me, but that painting has to go to New York. It is the best painting. Maybe it doesn't show America at its best, but it is the best painting. The most honest painting. It has to be entered in the show."

There was a kind of silence after I said this. I don't think *every* single person in the room was looking at me. But it sure felt like it.

The president said, looking very surprised, "Samantha, I'm sorry, but that isn't going to happen. You're going to have to pick another painting. How about the one with the lighthouse? That's a good representation of what this country's all about."

Then he started talking to the prime minister some more.

I couldn't believe it. I had just been dismissed. Just like that!

Well, you know what they say about redheads. What happened next, I couldn't stop. I heard myself saying the words, but it was like some other girl was saying them. Maybe Gwen Stefani was saying them. Because I sure wasn't.

"If you didn't want the job done right," I said to the president, loudly enough so that it seemed to me that a lot of the wait staff and most of the other guests, including the Beaux Arts Trio, turned to look at me, "then you shouldn't have given it to me. Because I am not going to pick another painting. All the rest of the paintings are of what people know. That painting—Maria's painting—is of what one person sees, every day, from her window. You may not like what Maria sees, but keeping everyone else from seeing it isn't going to make it any less real, or make the problem go away."

The president looked down at me like I was mentally deranged. Maybe I was. I don't know. All I know is, I was so mad, I was shaking. And I imagine my face was a very attractive shade of umber.

"Are you personally acquainted with the artist, or something?" he asked.

"No, I don't know her," I said. "But I know her painting is the best."

"In your opinion," the president said.

"Yes, in my opinion."

"Well, you're just going to have to change your opinion. Because that painting is not going to represent this country in any international art show."

Then David's dad turned his back on me and started talking to his other guests.

I didn't say anything more. What could I say that I hadn't said already? Besides, I had been dismissed.

David, who had come up behind me without my noticing, went, "Sam."

I looked up at him. I had forgotten all about David.

"Come on," he said.

I guess if I hadn't already been so shocked about what had happened—between me and the president, I mean—I might have been more shocked that David was actually speaking to me. Speaking to me, and apparently trying, at least, to make me feel better about what had just happened. At least that's what I had to conclude when he led me out of the Vermeil Room and back into the room where we'd sat that very first night I'd come to dinner, where he'd carved my name into the windowsill.

"Sam," he said. "It's not that big a deal. I mean, I know it is to you. But it's not, you know, life and death."

Right. It wasn't Sierra Leone or Utah. Nobody was getting their hands chopped off or being forced to marry, at the age of fourteen, a guy who already had three wives.

"I realize that," I said. "But it's still wrong."

"Probably," David said. "But you have to understand. There's a lot of stuff we don't necessarily know about that they have to consider."

"Like what?" I wanted to know. "My choosing that painting is going to compromise national security? I don't think so."

David was taking off his tie like it had been bothering him.

"Maybe they just want a happy painting," he said. "You know, one that shows the United States in a positive light."

"That's not what the contest is about," I said. "It's supposed to show what a representative of each country sees from his or her window. The rules don't say anything about what the person sees having to reflect positively on his or her country. I mean, I could see someone in China or something not being allowed to show a negative aspect of that nation, but this is America, for crying out loud. I thought we were guaranteed freedom of speech."

David sat down on the arm of my chair. He said, "We are."

"Right," I said very sarcastically. "All except the teen ambassador to the UN."

"You have freedom of speech," David said. He said it with a funny sort of emphasis, but at the time, I was too upset to realize what he meant.

"Do you think you could talk to him, David?" I asked, looking up at him. Once again, he hadn't turned on any lights in the room. The only light there was to see by spilled in from the windows, the bluish light coming in from the Rotunda. In its glow, David's green eyes were hard to read. Still, I plunged on. "Your dad, I mean. He might listen to you."

But David said, "Sam, I hate to disappoint you, but the one thing I make it a point never to discuss with my dad is politics."

Even though David said he hated to disappoint me, that's exactly what he ended up doing. Disappointing me, I mean.

"But it's not fair!" I cried. "I mean, that painting is the best one! It deserves to be in the show! Just try, David, okay? Promise me you'll *try* to talk to him. You're his kid. He'll listen to you."

"He won't," David said. "Believe me."

"Of course he won't, if you don't even *try*."

But David wouldn't say he'd try. It was like he didn't even want to get involved. Which only made me more peeved. Because he was acting like it didn't matter. He obviously didn't understand how important it was. I thought he would, being an artist, and all. But he didn't. He really didn't.

I was so frustrated that I couldn't help saying, "*Jack* would try."

And even though I'd been saying it mostly to myself, David overheard.

"Oh, sure," he said in a mean way. "Jack's perfect."

"At least Jack is willing to take a stand," I said hotly. "You know, Jack shot out the windows of his own father's medical practice with

205

a BB gun in protest of Dr. Ryder's using medications that had been tested on animals."

David looked unimpressed. "Yeah?" he said. "Well, that was a pretty stupid thing to do."

I couldn't understand how David could say such a thing. How he could even *think* such a thing.

"Oh, right," I said with a bitter laugh. "Pretty stupid of him to take a stand against cruelty to animals."

"No," David said coolly. "Pretty stupid of him to protest against something that saves lives. If scientists don't test medications on animals, Sam, before they use them on humans, they might make people sicker, or even kill them. Is that what Jack wants?"

I blinked at him. I hadn't actually thought of it that way before.

"But hey," David went on with a shrug, "Jack's a—what was it you called him? Oh, yeah. A radical. Maybe that's what the radicals of today are rebelling against. Making sick people better. I wouldn't know. I'm obviously too lacking in moral rectitude."

And then David, like he couldn't stand to be around me a second longer—like I was one of those gross hors d'oeuvres—turned around and left me sitting there. In the dark. Like the blind person Rebecca had accused me of being.

And the really sad part was, I was beginning to think she might be right. Because despite what Susan Boone had said, I had a feeling I wasn't seeing anything. Anything at all.

★ 22 ★

$\mathcal{W}$hen $\mathcal{I}$ got home from the White House that night, I was shocked to find Lucy in the living room, thumbing through a copy of *Elle*.

"What are *you* doing here?" I blurted out before I was able to restrain myself. I couldn't help it. I hadn't seen Lucy home on a Saturday night since her twelfth birthday. "Where's Jack?"

Had they, I thought, broken up at last? Had seeing me with another guy at Kris Parks's party finally made Jack realize his true feelings for me?

But the bigger question was, if it had, why didn't I feel happier about it? I mean, why would it actually make me feel sick to my stomach? Unless that was the result of that one hors d'oeuvre I accidentally scarfed before I realized how gross they were. . . .

"Oh, Jack's in the TV room," Lucy said in a bored voice. She was, I saw, doing her numerology chart. "He has to read some book for English class . . . *Wuthering Heights*. The report's due Monday, but of course he never read it. And they told him if he flunks English, they won't let him graduate in May."

I took off my coat and the lace sling and flopped onto the couch beside her. "So he's reading it now? At our house?"

"God, no," Lucy said. "It's on A and E. He's upstairs watching it. I tried, and even though it's got Ralph Fiennes, I just couldn't take it. What do you think of this skirt?" She flipped to a page in the center of the magazine.

"It's nice, I guess." My mind seemed to be working at a very sluggish pace, even though all I'd had to drink at the International Festival of the Child was 7-Up. "Where're Mom and Dad?"

"They're at that thing," Lucy said, turning back to her magazine. "You know. Some benefit for North African orphans, or whatever. I don't know. All I know is, Theresa cancelled because Tito broke his foot moving a refrigerator, so I'm stuck here making sure Miss ET-Phone-Home doesn't blow up the house. Oh, my God." Lucy lowered the magazine. "You should see it. Rebecca has a little friend over, spending the night. Remember when you used to have Kris Parks spend the night, and you two would play Barbies until the crack of dawn, or whatever? Well, guess what Rebecca and her friend are doing? Oh, just creating a DNA strand out of Tinkertoys. Hey, what about this suit?" Lucy showed me the suit. "I was thinking we could get you one like it for your medal cere-mony," Lucy said. "You know, we've only got about two weeks left to get you a really hot outfit. I told Mom we should have hit the outlets on the way home from Grandma's—"

"Luce," I said.

I don't know what made me do it. Talk to my sister Lucy, of all people, about my problems.

But there it was, all coming out. It was like lava, or something, pouring out of a volcano. And there was absolutely no way I could stuff it all back in once it came oozing out.

The weirdest part of it was, Lucy put the magazine down and actually listened. She looked me right in the eye and listened, and didn't say a word for, like, five minutes.

Normally, of course, I don't share details about my personal life with my big sister. But since Lucy is an expert on all things social, I thought she might be able to shed some light on David's weird behavior—and possibly my own. I didn't mention anything about Jack, you know, being my soul mate, and all. Just the stuff about the party, and how mean David had been to me at the International Festival of the Child, and the weird frisson, and stuff like that.

When I was through, Lucy just rolled her eyes.

"God," she said. "Come to me with a hard one next time, okay?"

I stared at her. "What?" I mean, I had just revealed my soul to her—well, most of my soul, anyway—and she seemed disappointed that my problems weren't juicier. "What do you mean?"

"I mean, it's totally obvious what's going on with you and David." She swung her slippered feet up onto the coffee table.

"It is?" Strangely, my heart had started speeding up again. "What, then? What's going on between us?"

"Duh," Lucy said. "I mean, even Rebecca figured it out. And her own school admits she has, like, zero people skills."

"Lucy." I was trying very hard not to scream in frustration. "Tell me. Tell me what is going on between David and me, or I swear to God, I'll—"

"God, chill," Lucy said. "I'll tell you. But you have to promise not to get mad."

"I won't," I said. "I swear."

"Fine." Lucy looked down at her fingernails. I could see that she'd just gotten a new manicure. Each nail was a perfect oval with a clean white tip. My own nails, of course, had never looked that clean, being almost constantly embedded with pencil dust from drawing.

Lucy took a deep breath. Then she let it out and said, "You love him."

I blinked at her. "*What? I what?*"

"You promised not to get mad," Lucy said warningly.

"I'm not mad," I said. Though of course I was. I had poured my heart out to her, and this is what she came up with? That I was in love with David? Could there be anything further from the truth?

"But I don't love David."

"God, Sam," she said, rolling her head against the back of the couch with a groan. "Of course you do. You say when he smiles at you your heart feels like it's flipping over. And that when you're around him your face always feels hot. And that since he's been so mad at you for parading him around Kris's party like a prize trout you'd caught in some dating fishing stream you've felt miserable. What do you think all of that is, Sam, if not love?"

"Frisson?" I suggested hopefully.

Lucy picked up one of the satin sofa pillows and hurled it at me. "That's what love is, you idiot!" she yelled. "All that stuff you feel when you look at David? That's what I feel when I look at Jack. Don't you get it? You love David. And if I am not mistaking the signs, I think it's a pretty safe bet to say he feels the same way about you. Or at least he used to, before you, you know, screwed it all up."

I couldn't tell her that she was wrong, of course. I couldn't tell her that it was impossible for me to be in love with David; since I'd been in love with her boyfriend from almost the first time she'd brought him home.

But I had to admit, it did sound a little . . . possible. I mean, given the whole frisson thing. Much as I loved Jack, I had to admit, my heart didn't start beating faster when I saw him. Not like it did with David. And I never had trouble meeting Jack's gaze—even though his pale blue eyes were every bit as beautiful as David's green ones. And while I blushed around Jack, well, the truth is, I'm a redhead; I blush around everybody.

But the person I blush around most is David.

And what about that thing David had pointed out? I mean about Jack's urban rebellion being kind of . . . well, bogus? Because it *was* bogus, now that I thought of it, for him to shoot out the windows of his dad's medical practice in protest of something that, .yeah, might hurt animals but helped sick people.

And the time he'd skinny-dipped at the Chevy Chase Country Club? What had he been protesting then? The country club's restrictive bathing suit rule? You know, I bet there are a lot of people at the Chevy Chase Country Club you wouldn't want to see swimming nude. So wasn't a bathing suit policy a good thing, then?

So what did it all mean? Was it possible Lucy was right? Was such a thing even remotely likely? That I had somehow fallen out of love with Jack, and into love with David, without even being aware of it myself . . . until now?

And how could I, Samantha Madison, who for so long had thought she'd known everything, have turned out to know so very, very little?

I was still trying to figure it out when, five minutes later, I left Lucy (feeling satisfied that she had solved all of my problems) in the living room and went into the kitchen for a snack, since the food at the party had hardly been satisfying.

You can imagine my discomfort when, as I was biting into a turkey sandwich I'd just made (with mayo, nothing else, on white bread), Jack came in.

"Oh, hey, Sam," he said, wandering over to the refrigerator. "I didn't know you'd gotten home. How was the party?"

I swallowed the hunk of sandwich I'd been jamming into my mouth just as he'd walked in. "Um," I said. "Fine. *Wuthering Heights* over?"

"Huh?" He was busy peering into the fridge. "No, not yet. Commercial. Hey, so what's the deal, Sam?" He took a carrot out of the vegetable crisper and bit into it noisily. "Is my painting going to New York or what?"

I had known I was going to be having this conversation sooner or later. I'd just hoped it would be later.

But I might as well, I figured, get it over with.

"Jack," I said, putting down my sandwich. "Listen."

Before I could get the words out of my mouth, however, Jack was going, with a look of total disbelief, "Wait a minute. Wait. Don't say it. I can tell by the look on your face. I didn't win, did I?"

I took a deep, steadying breath, preparing myself for the pain I knew was going to come flooding in when I said the word that would hurt him so much.

"No," I said.

Jack, who had left the refrigerator door hanging wide open, took a single step backward. Clearly, I had hurt him. And for that, I would be eternally sorry.

But incredibly, no hurt came. Really. I'd been ready for it. I'd been totally prepared for it to come pouring over me, this intense sorrow for having hurt him.

But it didn't come. Nothing. Nada. Zip. I was sorry to have hurt his feelings, but doing so caused *me* no hurt whatsoever.

Which was weird. Very weird. Because how could I hurt the man I loved—my soul mate, the man I was destined to be with forever— and not feel his pain throbbing along my every nerve ending?

"I can't believe it," Jack said, finding his voice at last. "I cannot freaking believe this. I didn't win? You're seriously telling me I didn't win?"

"Jack," I said, still stunned by the fact that I didn't feel even a tremor of his pain. "I'm really sorry. It's just that there were so many great entries, and—"

"This is unbelievable," Jack said. He didn't say it, exactly. He sort of yelled it. Manet, who had come into the kitchen as soon as he'd heard the fridge open, as was his custom, lifted both ears upon hearing Jack's raised voice. "Un-freaking-believable!"

"Jack," I said. "If there's any way I can make it up to you—"

"Why?" Jack demanded, his bright blue eyes very wide and very indignant. "Just tell me why, Sam. Can you do that? Can you tell me why my painting didn't get chosen?"

I said, slowly, "Well, Jack. We got a lot of entries. I mean, a *whole* lot of them."

Jack, so far as I could tell, wasn't even listening. He went, "My painting was too controversial. That's it. It has to be. Tell the truth, Samantha. The reason it didn't win was because everyone thought it was too controversial, didn't they? They don't want other countries to see how apathetic the youth of America are today, is that it?"

I said, shaking my head, "No, not exactly . . ."

But of course I should have been just, like, Yes, that was it. Because that would have been more acceptable to Jack than the real reason, which I lamely revealed a second later, when he demanded, "Well, why, then?"

"It's just," I said, wanting to make him feel better, but at the same time wanting him to understand, "that you didn't paint what you saw."

Jack didn't say anything at first. He just stared down at me. It was like he couldn't quite process what he'd heard.

"What?" he said finally, in a tone of utter disbelief.

I should have known. I should have gotten the hint. But I didn't, of course.

"Well," I said. "I mean, Jack, come on. You have to admit. You didn't paint what you see. You go around making these paintings of these disenfranchised kids—and they are really great, don't get me wrong. But they aren't real, Jack. The people you paint aren't real. You don't even know people like that. It's like . . . well, it's like me sticking that pineapple in. It's nice, and everything, but it isn't honest. It isn't real. I mean, you can't see a Seven-Eleven parking lot from your bedroom window. I doubt you can even see a garbage can." I did not, of course, know for a fact what Jack could see from his bedroom window. I was only guessing about the garbage can.

Still, I must have hit pretty close to the truth, since I managed to thoroughly enrage him.

"Didn't paint what I see?" he bellowed. *"Didn't paint what I see?* What are you *talking* about?"

"W-well," I stammered, taken aback by his reaction. "You know. What Susan Boone said. About painting what you see, not what you know——"

"Sam!" Jack yelled. "This isn't a damned art lesson! It's my chance for my artwork to make it to New York! And you ruled my painting out because I didn't paint what I *see*? What is *wrong* with you?"

"Hey." A familiar voice broke the tense silence between Jack and me. I looked over and saw Lucy standing in the doorway, looking annoyed.

"What's going on?" she wanted to know. "I could hear you yelling all the way across the house. What is with you?"

Jack pointed at me. Apparently, he was so upset he couldn't even find the words to explain to his own girlfriend what I'd done.

"Sh-she . . ." he sputtered. "Sh-she says I d-didn't paint what I see."

Lucy looked from Jack to me and then back again. Then she rolled her eyes and went, "Oh, God, Jack, would you get over yourself, please?"

Then she stomped up, took him by the arm, and started steering him from the kitchen. He let her, like a man in a daze.

But Jack wasn't the only one who felt dazed. I did, too.

And not because of the way he'd yelled at me. Not even because, soul mates though we might be, I did not, even for a second, feel

Jack's pain as he heard the bad news.

No. The reason I felt dazed was because of what happened when Jack first came sauntering into the kitchen, when I'd been cramming that sandwich into my mouth, totally not expecting to see him. He'd come into the room, filling the doorway with his big shoulders . . .

And my heart hadn't flipped over.

My pulse hadn't gotten any quicker.

I had no trouble at all breathing, and not even a hint of a blush crept over my cheeks.

None of the things that happened when I saw David happened when Jack came strolling into the kitchen. There was no frisson. There was not the slightest hint of frisson.

Which could mean only one thing:

Lucy was right. I was in love with David.

David, whose dad even couldn't stand me, on account of the way I didn't agree with him over the whole painting thing.

David, who got me the daisy helmet and said he liked my boots and carved my name in a White House windowsill.

David, who I'm pretty sure never wants to see me again on account of how I used him to try to make Jack jealous.

David, who all along had been the perfect guy for me, and I was too stupid—too blind—to see it.

Suddenly the turkey sandwich I'd been chowing down on didn't taste all that good. In fact, it tasted wretched. And the bits I'd swallowed felt like they might come right back up.

What had I done?

What had I done?

More important . . . *what was I going to do?*

Top ten reasons I am most likely to die young (not that that would be such a tragedy, under the circumstances):

10. I am left-handed. Studies show that left-handed people die ten to fifteen years sooner than right-handers, due to the fact that the entire world, from automobiles to those desks you take the SATs at to cash machines at the bank, is slanted toward the right-handed. Finally, after a while, we lefties just give up the struggle and croak rather than try one last time to write something in a spiral-bound notebook with all those wires poking into our wrist.

9. I am redheaded. Redheads are eighty-five percent more likely to develop terminal skin cancer than anyone else on the planet.

8. I am short. Short people die sooner than tall people. This is a known fact. No one knows why, but I assume it has something to do with the fact that short people like me are unable to reach bottles of vital antioxidants at the General Nutrition Center because they always put them on the highest shelves.

7. I have no significant other. Seriously. People in romantic relationships just plain live longer than people who are single.

6. I live in an urban area. Studies show that people who live in areas of dense population, such as Washington, D.C., tend to perish sooner than people who live out in the country, like in Nebraska, thanks to higher emissions of carcinogens like bus exhaust and random gunfire from urban gang warfare.

5. I eat a lot of red meat. You know what group of people lives the longest of anyone? Yeah, that would be this tribe of people who hang out in, like, Siberia somewhere, and all they eat is yogurt and wheat germ. Seriously. I don't think they are vegetarians; I think they just can't find any meat because the cows all froze to death. Anyway, they all live to be, like, a hundred and twenty years old.

I can't stand yogurt, let alone wheat germ, and I eat hamburgers at least once a day. I would eat them more often if I could get someone to make them for me. I am so dead.

4. I am a middle child. Middle children die sooner than their older and younger siblings due to being routinely ignored. I have never seen documented proof of this, but I am sure it is true. It is a story just waiting to be busted wide open by *60 Minutes*, or whatever.

3. I have no religious affiliation. My parents have completely ignored our religious upbringing, thanks to their own selfish agnosticism. Like, just because they aren't sure of the existence of God, we aren't allowed to go to church. When, meanwhile, there is statistical evidence that churchgoers live longer and have happier lives than nonchurchgoers.

And just where is my memorial service going to be performed when I die? I wish my parents had thought about these things before they went with this whole "Let the kids decide for themselves what they want to believe" thing. I could very well be dead before I ever even get to explore all my religious options. Though at the moment I am leaning strongly toward Hinduism because I am totally into reincarnation. On the other hand, I doubt I could give up beef, so this might be a problem.

2. I am a dog owner. While pet owners in general live longer than non-pet owners, cat owners live the longest. It is entirely likely that thanks to Manet's being a dog, I could perish five to ten years sooner than if he were a cat.

And the number-one reason I am likely to die young:

1. My heart is broken.

It really is. All the signs are there. I can't sleep, I can't eat—not even burgers. Every time the phone rings, my pulse leaps . . . but it's never for me. It's never *him*.

I realize it is my own fault—I messed everything up myself. But that doesn't make it feel any better. Self-inflicted wound or not, it's still there.

And the fact is, human beings can't really function with a broken heart. I mean, sure, I could live without David. But what kind of life would it be? An empty-shell sort of a life. I mean, I had a perfect chance at love, and I blew it. BLEW IT! Due to the fact that even though my eyes were open, I was not seeing. I wasn't seeing anything at all.

I give myself two weeks before I croak.

★ 23 ★

I stood on Susan Boone's front porch, feeling lame. But then, since I've pretty much felt lame my entire life, this was no big surprise.

On the other hand, usually I feel lame for no particular reason. This time I really had a reason to feel lame.

And the reason had to do with the fact that I was standing on Susan Boone's front porch, uninvited, and probably unwanted, on a Sunday afternoon, waiting for someone to answer the door, only no one was coming.

And it seemed to me like if someone did come, they would be all, "Um, don't you know better than to come over to someone's house without calling first?"

And they would be perfectly within their rights to say this, since I hadn't, of course, called first. But I'd been afraid if I called first, Susan would have been like, "Can't we just talk in class on Tuesday, Sam?"

But I couldn't wait until Tuesday. I had to talk to Susan today. Because my heart was breaking, and I needed someone to tell me what I should do about it. My mom and dad were no use. The whole thing just seemed to confuse them. And Lucy was no good. She just went, "Put on a tight little skirt and go over there and say you're sorry. God, what are you, retarded?" Rebecca just pressed her lips together and said, "I told you so," and Theresa was still over at Tito's. There was no point in even asking Catherine. Her head was filled with nothing but Paul.

So I was standing on Susan Boone's front porch without having called first. It is much harder to not see someone when that person is already standing on your front porch than when that person calls on the phone. I know this thanks to all the reporters who have been trying to talk to me.

There really is no worse feeling than standing around, waiting for someone to answer the door, when you know he or she is probably just going to slam it in your face . . .

. . . with the possible exception of standing around waiting for this person with five loaves of French bread in your backpack. I would have felt bad enough without the French bread, but the bread helped.

It was just that I had to bring something. I mean, you can't just show up at someone's house uninvited and not even bring a present. And yeah, I had to admit, the bread was kind of a bribe. Because I have never heard of anyone turning down a piece of the Bread Lady's bread. I was hoping that whoever answered the door would get a whiff of it and be all, "Oh, come right on in."

And it wasn't like I hadn't gone through hell, practically, to get my hands on these loaves. I'd had to get up extra early in order to drag Manet out for his morning walk in the opposite direction that we normally go in, something he really did not appreciate. He kept trying to drag me toward the park, while I was trying to drag him toward the Bread Lady's house. My arms were sore all the rest of the day. Manet weighs almost as much as I do, I think.

Also it turns out the Bread Lady doesn't get up before eight on Sunday mornings. She answered the door in this very fancy negligee (for a married lady).

But she didn't seem to think it was strange, me pounding on the door and commissioning French bread for later that afternoon. In fact, she seemed kind of pleased that someone liked her bread that much.

And she delivered on time, thank God. Five loaves of golden steaming French bread, the kind you can't find anywhere in D.C. The smell of them almost made *me* hungry. But only almost. People with broken hearts, it turns out, really have no appetite.

Then, of course, there was the whole riding-the-Metro-with-five-loaves-of-hot-out-of-the-oven-French-bread-sticking-out-your-backpack thing. Not an experience I cared to repeat. Especially since the Junior National Geographic Society was in town, and the Metro cars were jammed with all these Midwestern families with, like, ten kids each, all wearing these bright yellow T-shirts that said, "Ask me about my Junior National Geographic Champ," which I so thoroughly did not.

But all these blond kids kept going to their parents, "Mommy, why is that girl carrying all that bread?"

To which their parents responded by telling them to "Hush up, ya'll." Fortunately, no one recognized me as the girl who saved the president because I was wearing one of Lucy's Adams Prep baseball caps with my hair tucked all inside.

Still, one tiny Junior National Geographic Champion looked at me very suspiciously for a long time before leaning over to whisper to her friend, who also looked at me, then said something to her mom.

Fortunately, by that time the train had pulled into Adams Morgan, where Susan Boone lived, so I got off fast, leaving the Junior National Geographic Society members to their fate, whatever it was.

It was a long walk from the Metro stop to Susan Boone's house, but I used the time to reflect upon my misfortunes, which were many. By the time I got to the large blue house with the whitewashed porch railings with all the wind chimes hanging from them, I was practically crying.

Well, and why not? Nothing but sheer desperation would have forced me to ask Susan Boone's advice about anything. I mean, up until a couple of weeks ago I had totally hated her. Or at least strongly disliked her.

Now, I had this weird feeling she was the only person I knew who could tell me what I'd done to mess up my life so thoroughly and how I could make it right again. I mean, she had taught me how to see: maybe she could teach me how to cope with everything I was seeing, now that she'd opened up my eyes.

But I have to admit that in spite of this conviction, when I finally heard footsteps—and Joe's familiar squawking—coming toward me from inside the house, I felt a little like running.

Before I could run away, however, I saw the lace curtain in the window by the front door jerk back a little, and one of Susan Boone's blue eyes looked out. Then I heard the locks on the door being undone. The next thing I knew, Susan Boone, in a pair of paint-spattered overalls, and with her long white hair done up in braids on either side of her head, was standing in her doorway, staring at me.

"Samantha?" she said in an astonished voice. "What are you doing here?"

Shrugging off my backpack and quickly showing her the bread, I said, "I was just in the neighborhood, and I thought I'd say hi. Would you like some of this bread? It's really good bread. A lady on my street makes it."

Okay, I'll admit it: I was babbling. I just didn't know what to do. I mean, I shouldn't have come. I knew the minute I saw her that I shouldn't have come. It was insane that I had come. Stupid and insane. I mean, what did Susan Boone care about my problems? She was just my drawing teacher, for crying out loud. What was I doing, going to my drawing teacher for advice about life?

On Susan's shoulder, Joe screeched his usual greeting of "Hello, Joe! Hello, Joe!" at me. I don't think he recognized me with my hair hidden under the baseball cap.

Susan Boone, smiling a little, stepped back and said, "Well, come in, then, Sam. It's very nice of you to, um, stop by with bread."

I went into Susan's house, and wasn't surprised, as I crossed the threshold, to see that it was furnished in a manner very similar to the studio. I mean, there was a lot of old, comfortable-looking furniture, but mostly there were canvases stacked everywhere against the wall, and more than a hint of turpentine in the air.

"Thanks," I said, coming inside and taking off my hat. As soon as I did so, Joe launched himself from Susan's shoulder to mine with a happy cry of "Pretty bird! Pretty bird!"

"Joseph," Susan Boone said warningly. Then she invited me into the kitchen for a cup of tea.

I pretended like I didn't want to put her out or anything, and said I was sorry for bothering her and really, I was only going to stay a minute. But Susan just looked at me with a smile, and I had no choice but to follow her into her bright, sunshiny kitchen, the walls of which were painted blue—the same blue as her eyes. She insisted on making tea, and not in a mug in the microwave, either, but the old-fashioned way, with a kettle on the stove. As the water was boiling, she examined the baguettes I had brought and seemed pretty pleased by them. She got out some butter and a little jar of homemade jam and put them on the butcher-block table in the center of her big, old-fashioned kitchen. Then she broke off one end of a loaf, just to taste it, and looked very surprised as the crust, which was already pretty buttery without anything spread on it, melted on her tongue.

"Well," Susan said. "It's very good bread. I haven't had French bread like this, as a matter of fact, since the last time I was in Paris."

I was pleased to hear this. I watched as she broke off yet another piece, then ate it.

"So," I said. "How was your Thanksgiving?" It seemed like a stupid thing to ask, something only, you know, boring people, not artists, talked about. But what else was I supposed to say? And fortunately, she didn't seem to take offense.

"It was fine, thanks," she said. "How was yours?"

"Oh," I said. "Good."

There was this silence. Not really an awkward one, but you know. Still a silence. It was filled only with the sound of the kettle starting to boil, and Joseph muttering to himself as he ran his beak through his feathers, preening a little.

Then Susan said, "I came up with a big plan for what to do with the studio this summer."

"Really?" I said, relieved someone, at least, was talking.

"Really. I am thinking of keeping the studio open every day, from ten until five, for people like you and David to come in and sketch all day, if you want to. Like art camp, or something." I didn't say anything about how I doubted David would be showing up—not if he knew I was going to be there. Instead, I went, "Great!"

Right then the kettle started to whistle. Susan got up and made the tea. Then she handed me a dark blue mug that said "Matisse" on it, and kept a yellow mug that said "van Gogh" on it for herself. After she'd sat back down at the butcher-block table, she said, holding the mug in both hands so the steam came up and framed her face in smoky tendrils, "Now. Why don't you tell me what you're really doing all the way out here on a Sunday afternoon, Samantha."

I thought, you know, about not telling her. I thought about being like, "Really, I'm on my way to my grandma's," or some other lie like that.

But something about the way she was looking at me made me be honest. I don't know what it was, but suddenly, as I sat there messing with the little tag to my tea bag, the whole story poured out. Just poured out of me, all over that butcher block, while Joe sat on my shoulder and, from somewhere in the house, I could hear the faint strains of some classical music.

And when I had gotten it all out—everything, about David, and about Jack, and about the From My Window contest and Maria Sanchez and David's dad—I finished with, "And to top it all off, I found out last night that Dolley Madison's only kid who lived past infancy was from her first husband. She didn't even have any kids with James Madison. So I'm not related to her. Not even one tiny bit."

Finished with my long speech, I sat there and stared down into my tea. I couldn't see it all that well, since my eyes were sort of moist. But I was determined not to cry. To do so would have been perfectly ridiculous, even more ridiculous than riding the Metro with five loaves of French bread sticking out of my backpack.

Susan, who'd listened to my entire recitation of my many problems in silence, now took a sip of her tea and said, in a very calm voice, "But, Samantha. Don't you see? You know what it is you have to do. David already told you."

I lifted my gaze from my cup of tea and stared at her from across the table. On my shoulder, Joe picked up a strand of my hair, pretending just to be casually holding on to it, though we both knew that when he thought I wasn't paying attention, he would try to yank it out and make his escape.

"What are you talking about?" I said. "All David said was that he wouldn't talk to his dad about Maria Sanchez."

"He said that, yes," Susan said. "But you didn't really listen to him, Sam. You heard him, but you didn't listen. There is a difference between listening and hearing, just as there is a difference between seeing and knowing."

You see? This is why I knew I'd had to come. I didn't know this. The difference between hearing and listening, I mean. Any more than I'd known the difference between seeing and knowing.

"David," Susan said, "told you that you have the right to free speech, just as much as any other American."

"Yeah," I said, nodding. "So?"

"So," Susan said with an emphasis I didn't understand. "*You have the right to free speech*, Samantha. Just as much as any other American."

"Yeah," I said. "I got that part. But I don't see what that has to do with—"

And then, suddenly, I did. I don't know how or why. But suddenly, Susan's—and David's—meaning sank in.

And when it did, I couldn't believe it.

"Oh, no," I said with a gasp—and not just because Joe had finally made his move, yanked out a strand of my hair, then taken off in triumphant flight for the top of the refrigerator. "Ow. You don't think he really meant *that*, do you?"

Susan said, breaking off another piece of bread, "David tends to mean what he says, Sam. He's no politician. He isn't a bit likely to follow in his father's footsteps. He wants to be an architect."

"He does?" This was news to me. I was beginning to realize I really knew nothing about David at all. I mean, I knew he liked to draw, and that he was good at it. And I knew about the giant serving fork and spoon, of course. But there seemed to be a lot I didn't know, as well.

And that made me feel worse. Because I had this very bad feeling that it was too late for me to find out about them. The things I didn't know about David, I mean.

"Yes," Susan Boone said. "I think it's easy to understand why he wouldn't necessarily want to get involved in his father's business. He certainly wouldn't want his father involved in his."

"Wow," I said, because I was still reeling from her earlier revelation. "I mean . . . wow."

"Yes," Susan Boone said, leaning back in her chair. "Wow. So you see, Sam. It's been there all along."

I frowned. "What has?"

"What you wanted," she said. "You just had to open your eyes a little to see it. And there it was."

And there it was.

And there I still was ten minutes later—not quite believing that I was there at all—chatting with Susan Boone, a woman who'd once accused me of knowing but not seeing, when the back door to the kitchen banged open. A large man with his long hair pulled back into a ponytail and his arms filled with grocery bags came in. He looked at us with surprise on his handlebar-mustached face.

"Well," he said, looking at me with friendly, but curious, light blue eyes. "Hey."

"Hey," I said, wondering if this was Susan Boone's son. He seemed to be about twenty years younger than she was. She had never mentioned kids or a husband before. I had always thought it was just her and Joe.

But then maybe I had only been hearing, and not really listening.

"Pete," Susan Boone said, "this is Samantha Madison, one of my students. Samantha, this is Pete."

Pete put down the grocery bags. He was wearing jeans, over which were fastened a pair of leather chaps, like cowboys and Hell's Angels wear. When he reached out to shake my hand, I saw that his arm had the Harley-Davidson logo tattooed on it.

"Nice to meet you," he said, pumping my left hand, on account of the cast still being on my right. Then his gaze fell on the French bread. "Hey," he said, "that looks good."

Pete pulled up a chair and joined us. And it turned out he wasn't Susan's son at all. He was her boyfriend.

Which just goes to show that Susan was right about one thing, anyway: Sometimes what you want is right in front of you. All you have to do is open your eyes and see it.

★ 24 ★

I chose Candace Wu.

Lucy thought I should have gone with someone more famous, like Barbara Walters or Katie Couric. But I liked Candace, because she'd been so nice that time I'd fallen off the podium into her lap during my press conference at the hospital.

And Candace turned out to be pretty tough. She didn't take any guff from anyone. When Andy, the White House press secretary, said under no circumstances could she bring her film crew into his office to shoot footage of Maria Sanchez's painting, she said that the White House wasn't private property. It belonged to the people of the United States of America, and that as American citizens, she and the film crew had just as much right to be there as he did.

Unless, of course, he had something to hide.

Finally, Mr. White gave up, and I showed Candace all the paintings, including Angie Tucker's. I said Angie's painting was very nice and all, but that my choice had been Maria Sanchez's.

"And is it true, Samantha," Candace asked me on camera, just as we'd rehearsed earlier that day, when she'd met with me after I'd called her station, "that the president told you that you were going to have to choose another painting, one with a less political angle?"

I said the line I had been practicing all morning. "The truth is, Miss Wu, that I think the president may not be aware that American teens aren't only interested in what the number-one video in the country is right now. We have concerns. We want our voices to be heard. The From My Window international art show being sponsored by the United Nations is a perfect forum in which teens around the world can express their concerns. It would be wrong, I think, to stifle those voices."

To which Candace replied, just as she'd said she would, in exchange for my giving her network exclusive world rights to my one and only televised interview, "You mean, the man whose life you so heroically saved will not even allow you to make your own decisions in your capacity as the U.S. teen ambassador?"

I replied, tactfully, "Well, maybe there are national concerns we aren't privy to, or something."

After which Candace made a slashing motion beneath her chin and then went, "Well, boys, that's a wrap. Let's pack up and get over to the hospital," which was where we were all going next, on account of my cast coming off that day.

"Wait a minute," the White House press secretary said, hurrying up to us. "Wait just a minute here. I am sure there is no need for you to show that segment. I am sure we can work something out with the president. . . ."

But Candace hadn't gotten to where she had in the cutthroat news anchorwoman business by waiting around for things to be worked out. She had Marty and the other camera guys pack up, and then she was hustling all of us out of there before you could say "We'll be right back after this message."

It wasn't until we'd come back to my house after getting my cast off, and Candace was filming what she called some "filler" shots of me and Manet romping on my bed, that the phone rang and Theresa came in looking excited and whispered, "Samantha. It is the president."

Everyone froze—Candace, who'd been sharing beauty tips with Lucy, who seemed way fascinated by the whole news anchorwoman thing, a job where you had to look good and got to express your opinions about things; Rebecca, who'd been taking notes on how to act more like a normal person from one of the lighting guys; the cameramen, who were taking, if you ask me, way too close an interest in my Gwen Stefani poster. Everyone seemed to hold his or her breath as I climbed down off the bed and took the phone from Theresa.

"Hello?" I said.

"Samantha," the president cried, his hearty voice so loud I had to hold the receiver away from my face. "What's this I hear about you thinking I don't back your choice for that UN art show?"

"Well, sir," I said. "The fact is, I think the best painting we've received is the one from Maria Sanchez, of San Diego, but from what I understand, you—"

"That's the one I like," the president said. "The one with the sheets."

"Really, sir?" I said. "Because you said—"

"Never mind that now," the president said. "You like that sheet painting, you have it packed up and sent right along to New York. And next time you've got a problem with anything like this, you come to me first, before you go to the press, all right?"

I didn't mention that I'd already tried to. Instead, I said, "Yes, sir. I will, sir."

"Great. Buh-bye now," the president said. Then he hung up.

And so when my exclusive interview with Candace Wu aired the next night—Wednesday—the whole part about Maria Sanchez's painting not winning wasn't in it. Instead, the San Diego news affiliate filmed a piece where they went to Maria Sanchez's house and told her she was the winner. Maria turned out to be a dark-haired girl about my age who lived in a tiny house with six brothers and sisters. Like me, she was stuck right in the middle of all of them.

230

I should have known there was some reason I liked her painting best.

Anyway, when they told Maria she'd won, she started crying. Then, because they asked, she showed them the view out her window. It was just like in the painting, with the wash hanging from the line and the barbed-wire fence off in the distance. Maria really had painted what she saw, just as I'd thought she had, not just what she knew.

And now she and her family were going to get to go to New York and see her painting on the wall at the UN with all of the other entries from around the world. And it looked like I was going to get to meet her, since Andy said the White House would be flying my whole family to New York for the show's opening. I'd already asked my mom and dad if we could go to the Met while we were there, and see the Impressionists, and they said yes.

I am betting Maria will want to go, too.

The night Candace's interview with me aired, we all sat in the living room and watched it . . . me, Lucy, Rebecca, Theresa, Manet, and my mom and dad. My mom and dad hadn't really known all that much about it, since I'd conducted most of the interview after school, while my mom was in court and my dad was at his office. I'd had to skip Susan Boone's on Tuesday in order to do it. But I'd been going to do that anyway, on account of that's when Theresa had been going to take me to my appointment to get my cast removed.

So Mom and Dad were kind of surprised when they showed the parts filmed in our house—particularly the segment shot in my room, which had been somewhat messy at the time. My mom went, in a horrified voice, as she watched the TV screen like someone transfixed, "Oh, my God, Samantha."

But I explained to her that Candace had asked me to leave my room the way it was, as it added authenticity. Candace was way into authenticity. Her goal in producing the segment had been to show an "authentic American hero." According to Candace, the reasons I was an "authentic American hero" were:

a) I had selflessly risked my life in order to save that of another.
b) That other had happened to be the leader of the free world.
c) I am an American.

Candace's view on the matter was, happily, shared by others. For instance, the doctor who sawed off my cast. He was very careful not to saw through any of the pictures I'd drawn on there. He warned me right before he took the cast off that, without it, my arm was going to feel very light and strange for a while, and it turned out he'd been right. As soon as he peeled off the cast, my arm floated upward about three inches, all on its own. Theresa and Candace and the doctor and the cameraman and I all laughed.

Other people who thought I was an authentic American hero turned out to be the staff at the Smithsonian, where we went after getting my cast off. I'd decided that, instead of selling my cast on eBay, I would donate it to a museum, and the Smithsonian was the biggest museum I could think of. Fortunately, they wanted it. I was worried they would think it was gross, my giving them my old cast with Liberty Bells and Dolley Madison drawn all over it.

But since it was, you know, a relic of sorts, denoting an important piece of American history, they claimed to be happy to have it.

The segment about me closed with a piece Candace and I had discussed very carefully beforehand. One of the conditions of my letting her do the interview was that she had to ask this one particular question. And that was about my love life.

"So, Samantha," Candace said, leaning forward in her chair with a little smile on her face. "There've been some rumors . . ."

The camera showed me looking all innocent, sitting on the very couch I was sitting on as I watched the interview being broadcast.

"Rumors, Ms. Wu?" the TV me asked, with her eyes all wide.

"Yes," Candace said. "About you and a certain person . . ."

Then they started showing all this footage of David—you know, waving from the steps of Air Force One, ducking in and out of Susan Boone's, in a suit at the International Festival of the Child. Then the camera came back on Candace, and she went, "Is it true that you and the first son are an item?"

The TV me, turning red—turning red right there on television, and even though I had known perfectly well the question was coming—went, "Well, Ms. Wu, let's put it this way. I'd like it to be true. But whether or not he feels the same way, I don't know. I think I might have screwed it up."

"Screwed it up?" Candace looked confused (even though she knew exactly what I was going to say to this question, as well). "Screwed it up how, Samantha?"

"I just," the TV me said with a shrug, "didn't see something that was right there in front of my face. And now I think it's probably too late. I hope not . . . but I have a bad feeling it probably is."

That was when the real me—the watching-the-TV me—pulled the sofa cushion Manet had been sitting on out from under him and buried my face into it with a scream. I mean, I'd had to say it—I couldn't think of any other way to say it that would make up for the horrible thing I had done—you know, the whole loving-David-the-whole-time-and-not-realizing-it-until-it-was-too-late thing.

But that didn't mean I wasn't embarrassed about it. Or that I had even the remotest hope of it working.

That's why I was screaming.

My dad, who'd been watching the interview with a kind of stunned expression on his face, went, "Wait a minute. What was that all about? Samantha . . . did you and David have a fight?"

To which Theresa replied, "Oh, she blew it with him but good. But maybe if he sees this, he'll give her another chance. I mean, it isn't every day some girl goes on national television and tells the world that she wants to go out with you."

Even Rebecca looked at me with renewed respect. "That was pretty brave of you, Sam," she said. "Braver even than what you did that day outside the cookie store. Not, of course, that it's going to work."

"Oh, Rebecca," Lucy said, hitting the mute button, since the interview was over. "Shut up."

It isn't often that Lucy comes to my defense in familial battles, so I glanced up from the sofa cushion in amazement. It was only then that I realized what was bothering me about Lucy. What had *been* bothering me about Lucy for the past day or two.

"Hey," I said. "Where's Jack?"

"Oh," Lucy said with a careless shrug. "We broke up."

Everyone in the room—not just me—stared at her in open-mouthed astonishment.

My dad recovered first. He went, "Alleluia," which was a strange sentiment coming from an agnostic, but whatever.

"I knew it," Theresa said, shaking her head. "He went back to that ex-girlfriend of his, didn't he? Men. They are all . . ." And then she said some bad words in Spanish.

"Oh, God," Lucy said, rolling her eyes. "Puhlease. He didn't cheat on me, or anything. He was just such a jerk to Sam."

I would not have thought it possible for my jaw to sag any more than it already had, but somehow, I managed.

"Me?" I squealed. "What are you *talking* about?"

Lucy looked heavenward. "Oh, you know," she said, sounding

impatient. "That whole painting thing. He was being such a tool. I told him to—what's it called again, Rebecca?"

"To never again darken your doorway?" Rebecca offered.

"Yeah," Lucy said. "That's it." Then Lucy, who had been channel surfing the whole time she'd been speaking, went, "Oooh, look. David Boreanaz," and turned the volume up.

I couldn't believe it. *I couldn't believe it.* Lucy and Jack, broken up? Because of *me*? I mean, I will admit, I had been fantasizing about this moment for months. But in my fantasies, Lucy and Jack always broke up because Jack finally came to his senses and realized that I was the girl for him. They never broke up because Lucy happened to spy Jack being a jerk to me.

And they certainly never broke up after I'd realized I didn't love Jack anymore . . . had maybe never really loved him in the first place. Not the way you're *supposed* to love someone.

This was not the way things were supposed to go. This was not the way things were supposed to go *at all*.

"Lucy," I said, leaning forward. "How can you . . . I mean, after all the time you two have spent together, how can you just *dump* Jack like that? I mean, what about the prom? Your senior prom is coming up. Who are you going to go with, if not Jack?"

"Well," Lucy said, her gaze riveted on David Boreanaz's abs, "I have narrowed it down to about five different guys. But I am thinking of asking my chem partner."

"*Greg Gardner?*" I all but shrieked. "You are going to go to the prom with *Greg Gardner*? Lucy, he is, like, the biggest nerd in school!"

Lucy looked annoyed, but only because all my shrieking was drowning out the dulcet tones of Mr. Boreanaz. "Dude," she said, "duh. But nerds are totally in right now. I mean, you should know. You're the one who started the trend."

"Trend? What *trend*?" I demanded.

"You know." A commercial had come on, so Lucy put the TV on mute again, rolled over on her back, and looked at me. "The whole dating-a-nerd thing. You set it off by bringing David to that party. Now everyone is doing it. Kris Parks is going out with Tim Haywood."

"*The national science fair winner?*" I gasped.

"Yeah. And Debbie Kinley dumped Rodd Muckinfuss for some geek from Horizon."

"Really." My mother, who was still in the room, listening to our conversation with growing annoyance, finally couldn't take it anymore. "Listen to you girls! Geeks! Nerds! Don't you realize that you are talking about *people*? People with *feelings*?"

Like my mom, I was getting more and more upset as well. But not for the same reason.

"Wait a minute," I said. "Wait just a minute here. Lucy, you can't break up with Jack. You love him."

"Well, sure," Lucy said simply. "But you're my sister. I can't go out with a guy who's mean to my sister. I mean, what do you think I am?"

I just stared at her. I really couldn't believe it. Lucy—my sister Lucy, the prettiest, most vacuous girl at Adams Prep High School—had dumped her boyfriend, and not because he'd been two-timing her, or because she'd grown tired of him. She'd dumped him for me, her reject little sister. Me, Samantha Madison. Not the Samantha Madison who'd saved the life of the president of the United States. Not Samantha Madison, teen ambassador to the UN.

No. Samantha Madison, Lucy Madison's kid sister.

That's when the guilt came rushing in. I mean, here Lucy had made this enormous sacrifice—okay, maybe not so enormous for her, but whatever, still a sacrifice—and what kind of sister to her had I been? Huh? I mean, for the longest time, all I had done was wish—no, *pray*—for Lucy and Jack to break up so that I could have him. Then it finally happens, and why?

Because, according to Lucy, she loves me more than she could ever love any boy.

I was the worst sister in the world. The lowest of the low. I was scum.

"Lucy," I said. "Really. Jack was just upset the other day. I totally understood. I really don't think you should break up with him just because . . . just because of me."

Lucy looked bored with the conversation. Her show had come back on. "Whatever," she said. "I'll think about it."

"You should, Luce," I said. "You really should. I mean, Jack's a great guy. A really great guy. I mean, for you."

"All right," Lucy said, looking irritated. "I said I'll think about it. Now shut up, my show is on."

My mom, realizing a little belatedly what was going on, went, "Um, Lucy, if you want to date this other boy—your chemistry partner—that's really quite all right with your father and me. Isn't it, Richard?"

My dad hastened to assure Lucy that it was.

"In fact," he said, "why don't you bring him home after school tomorrow? Theresa won't mind, will you, Theresa?"

But the damage was already done. I knew Lucy and Jack would be back together before lunch tomorrow.

And I was glad. Really glad.

Because I didn't love Jack. I had probably never loved Jack. Not really.

The only problem, of course, was that I was pretty sure the person I did love didn't feel the same way about me.

Though I had a good feeling I was going to find out for sure, one way or another, at Susan Boone's tomorrow.

★ 25 ★

"*Do you* see this skull?" Susan Boone held up a cow skull, bleached white by sun and sand. "All the colors of the rainbow are in this skull. And I want to see those colors on the page in front of you."

She put the skull down on the little table in front of us. Then she went to go chastise Joe the crow, who had already successfully stolen a wad of my hair before I'd gotten a chance to don my daisy helmet.

I sat straddling my drawing bench, keeping my gaze carefully averted from the person sitting next to me. I had no idea whether David was happy or sad to see me, or if he simply didn't care either way. I had not spoken to or seen him—except on TV—since the night of the Beaux Arts Trio and our argument about Jack. I had no idea if he'd seen my interview or knew that I had, in fact, exercised my freedom of speech, the way he'd suggested. Or that I'd basically admitted, right there in front of twenty million viewers, that I loved him.

I quizzed Rebecca about it at length, seeing as how she went to his school. But being eleven, Rebecca had no classes with David. She even had a different lunch period. She didn't know if he'd seen it or not.

"Don't worry," Lucy kept saying. "He saw it."

And Lucy, of course, would know. Lucy knew everything there was to know about boys. Hadn't she gotten Jack back, as casually as she'd dumped him? One day they were broken up, and the next day they were sitting in the cafeteria together at school like they'd never been apart.

"Oh, hey, Sam," Jack said when I walked by their table, headed for my own. "Listen, sorry about that art show thing. I hope you aren't, you know, mad at me, or anything. I was just kind of disappointed."

"Um," I said, totally confused. Where was Greg Gardner? But I think I covered pretty well by going, "No problem."

And it wasn't a problem. What did I care about Jack? I had way more important things to think about. Like David. How was I going to get David to believe that it was him I loved, not Jack? I mean, what if he hadn't seen the interview? I couldn't imagine how he could have missed it, since it had been the number-one rated show for its time slot, and besides which, had been extremely heavily advertised, ever since Sunday, when I'd set the whole thing up.

Still, there was a chance he didn't know. A chance I was going to have to tell him to his face.

Which was somehow way worse than saying it in front of twenty million strangers.

And here I was, sitting right next to him, and I couldn't think of a single thing to say to him. I mean, we'd smiled at one another when we'd come in, and David had been like, "Hey," and I'd been like, "Hey," back.

But that was it.

And as if fate hadn't played enough cruel tricks on me lately, David was wearing a No Doubt T-shirt. My favorite band in the whole world, featuring Gwen Stefani, only the best singer in the entire universe, and the guy I had this huge colossal crush on was wearing one of their concert T-shirts.

Life can be so, so unfair.

And now my palms were sweating so badly, I could barely hold on to my colored pencils, and my heart was doing this weird Adrian Young drum solo inside my chest, and my mouth was all dry. *Say something,* I kept telling myself.

Only I couldn't think of what to say.

And then it was time to draw, and the studio fell silent, except for the classical music on the radio, and everyone started working, and it was too late to say anything.

Or so I thought.

I was busy looking for the colors in the white cow skull in front of me, totally absorbed, as usual, in my drawing—because even being as hopelessly in love with David as I happened to be, I could still get caught up in my drawing . . .

. . . so caught up that when he happened to throw a little slip of paper into my lap, I jumped about a mile.

I looked down at the piece of paper. Then I looked over at him.

But he was bent over his own drawing. In fact, if it hadn't been for the barely noticeable smile just tilting up the corners of his mouth, I wouldn't have known the paper had come from him.

At least until I opened it up.

There, written in the tiny, precise handwriting of a would-be architect, was one word:

Friends?

I couldn't believe it. David wanted to be friends. With *me. Me.*

My heart pounding, I bent over and started to write:

Yes, of course.

But something stopped me. I don't know what it was. I don't know if it was just that, because of everything that had happened, I had finally learned a thing or two, or if the invisible hand of my guardian angel, Miss Gwen Stefani, reached out and stopped me.

Whatever it was, I tore a new piece of paper off the edge of my drawing pad. And on it, I wrote, my heart in my throat, but knowing—just knowing—it was now or never, and that I had to tell the truth:

No. I want to be more than friends.

Although I tried to pretend like I was thoroughly engrossed in my drawing, this time I really was watching David out of the corner of my eye. I watched him open the piece of paper I'd tossed to him, and I watched him read what I'd written. Then I watched his eyebrows go up.

Way up.

And when, a few seconds later, a new wad of paper showed up in my lap, I knew he'd tossed it there, because I'd seen him do that, too.

Feeling like I couldn't breathe, I opened the new note. On it, he'd written:

What about Jack?

That was an easy one. In fact, it was practically a relief to write:

Jack who?

Because that was really how I felt.

Still, the last thing I expected was a note back from David saying how *he* really felt.

But that is exactly what I got.

And if I had ever been happy before—if there had ever been any-thing, anything at all that had ever made it feel as if joy was just bub-bling up inside of me—that was nothing compared to how I felt when I opened the next folded slip of paper he threw into my lap, and saw that on it, he had drawn a heart.

That was all. Just a tiny little heart.

For which there was only one explanation. I mean, really. And that was that David loved me. He loved me.

He loved me.

He loved me.

★ 26 ★

$\mathcal{A}$ week later, they had the award ceremony. The one where I got my presidential medal. You know, for valor, and all of that.

I didn't wear black. I didn't even want to wear black. I didn't care what I wore. When you are in love, that's how it is. You don't care about things like clothes, because all you can think about is the object of your affections.

Well, unless you're Lucy.

But even though I didn't care how I looked, my mom and Theresa and Lucy made sure I looked good. They put me in another suit—this one light blue—that later, after the award ceremony, while we were all having cake in the Vermeil Room, David said matched my eyes.

Anyway, the award ceremony, as promised, was in front of the official White House Christmas tree in the Blue Room. It was way beautiful, with all the decorations and lights and everything.

It was also way serious. Everyone who was anyone was there, including all these colonels in fancy uniforms, and senators in suits, and my family, and Theresa, and Catherine and her family, and Candace Wu, and Jack and Pete and Susan Boone, whom I'd invited especially.

The president made a speech about me, and it made me feel way patriotic. It went, "Samantha Madison, I award you this medal for extreme bravery in the face of personal peril . . ." blah blah blah. Actually, it was kind of hard to pay attention, on account of David standing right there next to his dad, looking totally cute.

I can't believe there was a time I used to think David looked geeky in a tie. Now the sight of him in one makes me go frisson all over. Well, the sight of him in anything does, really.

Anyway, after I got my medal—which was pure solid gold, hanging from a red velvet ribbon—everybody applauded, and we had to pose for about a million photos, while everyone else started filing around for cake. David, instead of going for cake, waited for me, and when I got done with the photos he came up and kissed me on the cheek. A photographer took a picture of that, too, but we weren't embarrassed or anything. That's because in that past week we'd been doing a lot of kissing, and not just on the cheek, either.

And let me tell you something: kissing—which, needless to say, isn't something I had really had a whole lot of experience with up until now—is *nice*.

Anyway, after we joined everyone for cake, I went around, trying to make the different clusters of people I'd invited feel comfortable with each other. Like I introduced Susan Boone and her boyfriend to Catherine's parents, and David introduced Jack and Lucy to the attorney general and his wife, and so on.

And then, while everyone was shaking hands with each other and saying what a nice time they were having and all, David came over to me with one of those secretive little smiles of his and whispered to me, *"Come here."*

I whispered back, *"Okay."*

I followed him out of the room and down the hall to where we had first had burgers together, looking out over the White House's back lawn.

And there on the windowsill where David had carved my name, I saw that he had added something.

244

A plus sign.

So now it said:

David

+

Sam

Which, all things considered, is not a bad way to leave your mark on history.

Top ten reasons I'm glad I'm not actually Gwen Stefani:

10. I don't have to go on tour. I can stay home with my dog. Plus see my boyfriend whenever I want to . . . well, until my eleven o'clock curfew on weekends, ten o'clock on weeknights, and only so long as I keep my German grades up.

9. Between school, art lessons, being teen ambassador to the UN, and my social life, I really don't have time to put that much thought into my wardrobe. Dressing whimsically is actually a lot of responsibility.

8. I don't think singing and songwriting could ever be as satisfying creatively as drawing a really excellent egg.

7. Gwen has to give a lot of interviews, which I can completely relate to in my capacity as teen ambassador to the UN. But Gwen gets interviewed by, like, *Teen People*, who totally report on what you are wearing to the interview. I get interviewed by *The New York Times Magazine*, who totally don't.

6. Gwen wears a lot of navel-baring outfits. My navel isn't exactly my best feature. Fortunately, my dad told me if he ever caught me in a navel-baring outfit, he would force me to work as a summer intern in his office, instead of letting me draw eggs and cow skulls all summer at Susan Boone's.

5. According to Theresa, whose sister is a licensed beautician, if I dyed my hair as often as Gwen has, it would all fall out.

4. Gwen has to hang out all day, every day with the rowdy boys in her band. The only boys I ever have to hang out with are my boyfriend, my sister's boyfriend, and my best friend's boyfriend, and none of them, so far, has expressed any interest in playing the drums wearing nothing at all, which, if you ask me, would be totally embarrassing.

   But then again, one must make sacrifices for art, I suppose.

3. Gwen may not be aware of this little known fact: that geeks make the best boyfriends. It sounds surprising, but it is true. You know those smiles of David's, the little secret ones he always seemed to have on his face? Those smiles, he says, are on account of me. Because, he told me, he never thought he'd meet a girl as cool as me.

   Besides, there is something to be said for having your parents actually like the person you are going out with.

2. Gwen's sister, though she's probably nice and all, can't possibly be as cool as Lucy, who, even though she can be a real pain sometimes, is actually pretty righteous the rest of the time. I mean, she was willing to dump her boyfriend for me. Does that *tell* you something?

And the number-one reason I'm glad I'm not Gwen Stefani:

1. Because then I wouldn't be me.

ARE YOU AN
★ **ALL** ★
AMERICAN
GIRL?

If so,
seventeen
wants to know why.

Check out the September issue (on sale August 9, 2002)
or go to **www.seventeen.com** (now until October 31, 2002)
to find out how to enter!

What could you win?
There's a thrilling grand prize and sixteen fabulous
second prizes (for a total of **seventeen**, of course).
Samantha Madison would be all over it.

But you have to check out the magazine
or the website first. So go!

Contest not available outside the U.S.

seventeen is a registered trademark of PRIMEDIA Magazine Finance, Inc.